TEARLESS
AYO DEFORGE

Copyright © 2023 by Ayo Deforge

The moral right of the author has been asserted.

This is a work of fiction. All characters, organisations, and events portrayed in this novel, other than those clearly in the public domain, are either products of the author's imagination or are used factiously.

All rights reserved.

No part of this publication may be reproduced, stored in a retrieval system, or transmitted, in any form, or by any means, without the prior permission in writing of the copyright owner. Nor be otherwise circulated in any form of binding or cover other than that in which it is published and without a similar condition including this condition being imposed on the subsequent purchaser.

Legal Deposit to BnF: December 2023

E-copy ISBN: 9782959075506

Paper copy ISBN: 9782959075513

Hardcopy ISBN: 9782959075520

Dedication

To God who called me an author when all I wanted to be was a reader.

Praise for Tearless

The characters in Ayo Deforge's rich episodic novel bring to life a melting pot of metropolitan cultures as their story travels between Lagos and Paris, past and present, young and old, traditional and trendy.

The author's fresh and lively take on the human condition invites us to plunge into a world that will be new to many, yet, Tearless transcends its unique mise en scene to remind us of the universal joys of friendship, the importance of family and the redemptive power of love.

Geoff Mead, author of Coming Home to Story: Storytelling Beyond Happily Ever After.

With Tearless, Ayo proves she has a full grasp of human experiences. She weaves this story with beautiful and smooth language.

Chukwuemeka Famous, author of We Will Live Again.

In Tearless, Ayo Deforge reveals the sad truth of the *World Health Organization's (WHO) 2022* data on child abuse.

Through Lami Davis' compelling story, the author reveals these startling statistics: *"Nearly 3 in 4 children - or 300 million children - aged 2–4 years regularly suffer physical punishment and/or psychological violence at the hands of parents and caregivers".*

Lami bravely shares her traumatic experience with her abusive father and explores the profound impact it had on her life and the lives of her siblings. This compelling book confronts the quiet echoes of a pervasive problem and challenges readers to confront and address the hidden struggles of so many.

Oyin Olugbile, author of *SANYA*

ONE

2009, Present day

I opened my eyes and saw nothing. My hand shot under my pillow where I always kept my phone but it wasn't there. I fumbled around me on the bed, but still couldn't find it. I flicked the light on, but the room remained pitch-black.

Gripped by an ancient fear, I could feel the hysteria creep into my brain at the thought that I might have gone blind in my sleep. At that point, I remembered the window above my bed and reached out to pull the curtains back. Twinkling stars peeked through the clouds in the night sky and generator sets hummed in the distance. Relief swept through me as the panic that'd seized my heart in its claws loosened its grip.

I can see. I can see. Everything is alright.

My breathing calmed and my heartbeat slowed. I began groping around my night table again to find my phone. Where was it? I had it with me before I fell asleep. I was never far away from my phone or charger. I was always prepared to kill darkness when it crept upon me.

Suddenly, the TV flickered to life, and security lights lit up the compound, flooding my room. In the distance, someone shouted, 'Up

NEPA!' As generators died out one after the other, it began to grow quieter. I turned on the lamp and located my phone on the floor. It was still Thursday; half-past nine. It seemed to me as though I'd slept an entire night. Later, as I stood in front of the mirror on the wardrobe door, wiping my face clean of makeup, I tried to recall the dream that had woken me up.

The day before had been Papa's birthday and Mama's death anniversary. I'd yet to return to Mama's grave since her funeral twelve years earlier. A familiar overwhelming guilt settled over me. It was a guilt I carried every year, around her death anniversary, yet I was unable to gather enough courage to return to the cemetery.

I saw Mama often in my dreams, her eyes boring holes into me. "Lami, where are your brothers and sisters? You don't know? Okay." Her voice always bore a hint of pain and sometimes, accusation as if I was the eldest who should take care of every other person.

I had tried to distance myself from the woman we'd buried by telling myself she looked nothing like Mama. Even though I knew deep down, it was her. Unconsciously, I'd convinced myself that the pain was easier and more tolerable this way. Now, at twenty-four, I knew it was time to do away with all the lies, but I just didn't feel ready for that either.

Every year, in the days leading up to Mama's death and burial anniversaries, I always dreamt about her. The sense of loss had remained deep and raw, unhealed by time. No matter how hard I tried, the pain I felt never diminished; instead, we'd grown together, inseparable like a shadow. It trailed me closely. Sometimes, it caught up with me and walked beside me. Sometimes, it sat upon my shoulders and I carried it around with me. It had followed me from childhood through to adolescence and right into adulthood. Like dirty clothes, I wore it everywhere, a reminder of the misfortunes that had befallen my siblings and me.

***

The flat was cloaked in a graveyard silence. Standing at the tiny counter of the tiny kitchen, I dished myself a plate of leftover jollof rice from the day before.

"Ma copine!" Ada exclaimed, startling me.

Smiling, I turned to see my flatmate enter the kitchen, carrying a tray of used dishes. She had her hair in a messy bun atop her head and was clothed in a black lace nightie and satin slippers.

"How na?" I asked, my gaze returning to the pot.

"Are you just eating?" Ada said.

"I got back from work and fell asleep. Hunger woke me up."

"I thought you'd eaten and cleaned up your dish." She opened the refrigerator and reached inside for a sachet of pure water. "Andrew is here."

"I know," I said, grabbing hold of the door before she could shut it. I returned the pot of rice to the refrigerator and shut the door. Then I placed my dinner in the microwave.

Ada tore open the sachet of pure water with her teeth, then she grabbed one of the glasses from the tray she had brought from her room and poured herself a cup. After downing it in one go, she began to dance for no reason, like she always did. I smiled as I watched her. She reached out and grabbed my hands, trying to get me to dance with her.

"Coupé décalé!" she sang, swaying her hips.

I pulled back until my back was against the sink, but Ada continued to dance wildly as if she didn't have a care in the world. I laughed, but I couldn't bring myself to join her.

I was slightly taller than her, but she was thicker and dark-skinned. She was beautiful in a way that made one think she hadn't grown out of her baby features. The black in her eyes left little space for the white and her small teeth had small gaps between each one. She was the Tutu I imagined my little sister to have grown into and the extroverted Lara I wanted my big sister to have been.

Ada loved my friends and hated my enemies. The weekends she wasn't away from the flat, my demons didn't come out to haunt me. I was simply happy when we were together. She made me laugh until I cried. She made me watch the same films and listen to the same songs over and over again. I consoled her when she cried while watching a sad film and screamed at the top of my lungs along with her when we watched horror movies at night.

We would listen to music on Trace TV and dance crazily the way I could never do in public. We would push each other to take the perfect position in front of the mirror so that we could admire ourselves while shaking our waists and acting silly. We were still best friends after half a dozen years and the bond we shared continued unabated, withstanding every test of time.

The microwave alarm beeped, interrupting Ada's dance steps. I carried my plate to the living room, with Ada trailing behind me, still dancing.

"Andrew is waiting for you," I said, sitting down at the round glass table to devour my food.

She stopped and sat down in one of the chairs, breathless. I took a mouthful of rice and reached for the TV remote. I flipped through the channels, searching for something to watch as I chewed.

"Bébé," Ada said.

I looked away from the TV to meet her gaze. Her tone was serious. "Ca va?"

"You've been very quiet lately," Ada said once I had settled on Trace TV. "Is everything okay at work?"

I nodded again, spooning up a small chunk of meat.

"Or have I done something wrong?"

"You? No. It's nothing. It's just that I haven't been sleeping well lately, that's all."

It was the truth, but not the whole truth. I didn't want to remind her that the day before had been my mother's death anniversary and my father's birth anniversary. My stomach churned with the sense of melancholy these events always evoked in me.

"You know what the problem is? You work too much. One day is not enough to rest."

"It's not like I have a choice. I need to have enough savings to live on when I go back to school."

It wasn't the first time we were talking about why I had to work on Saturdays. We'd been having the same discussion for over a year about my working too many hours a week to fund the cost of doing a master's course in France. We drifted into silence as I carried on eating. Then she asked me what I wanted to do for my birthday. It was in eight days. I told her I would like to keep it simple—a quiet evening at home after work.

Her eyes went to the TV and I followed her gaze. A red car was pulling into a deserted driveway. The driver jumped out and hurried to the front, carrying red roses. Before he reached the door a beautiful woman ran out the door and flung her arms around him kissing him.

"So, what are you planning on wearing for your date?"

"What date?" I said with food in my mouth.

She raised her brows in feigned anger.

"Oh! Tunji. I forgot all about him."

Tunji was Andrew's best friend. Ada and Andrew had been trying for a year to matchmake us because we were both Yoruba and single. Tunji was also as reserved as I was with people he didn't know too well. It was for this reason Ada thought we were compatible.

"Well, what are you wearing?"

"Clothes."

"Ma chérie, you can't wear jeans to that type of restaurant, and please don't wear your teaching clothes."

"I still have two days to decide."

I'd twice refused Tunji's invitation to go on a date with him. Finally accepting was the only way I could get Ada to stop pestering me about giving him a chance. I'd already prepared for him the same words I'd recited to several men to keep them at bay. A colleague at work. Another teacher at the primary school where I'd been posted for NYSC. A Corper at the NYSC camp and many others.

Unfortunately for these men, among other reasons, my first true attempt at love had also failed, confirming my fears that men couldn't be trusted. I'd been so badly bruised by the betrayal and rejection of my ex, that trying again always made me nervous.

"I'll help you choose a dress." Ada yawned and stretched. "Tunji is a good person. I'm sure you'll be happy together."

After she had gone to bed, I stared at my half-eaten dinner. I wished I hadn't agreed to go on a date with Tunji. Despite having turned down many admirers, the task didn't get any easier for me. I still had to hold my breath while they digested my rejection, hoping they would react well to it. I still had to tell them there was nothing wrong with them, and that I found them attractive, but I just wasn't ready for a committed relationship.

My experience with Ben at the university taught me to guard my heart jealously. The pain I experienced had similarities to the one I felt after Mama died and Papa separated me from my siblings. To expect people to stay in my life was asking too much. People stayed for as long as they were getting something out of the relationship. Once, there was nothing left to get, they moved on without looking back. But I didn't blame them for wanting to move on. Even Mama hadn't stayed. I could only be disappointed in someone if I *appointed* them in the first place. I therefore learned that the only way to protect myself was to be emotionally unavailable.

***

Ada and I met in 2002 at a hair salon in Dolphin Estate. I was sixteen, preparing to write the next JAMB exam, although yet to decide which aspects of engineering I wanted to pursue a career in. I'd just started to grow out my hair. During my entire junior and senior secondary school years, I had worn my hair short, like a boy's.

Ada and I began talking after NEPA cut off the power supply and we both had to come out from under the hood of the hairdryer to wait for power to be restored. Sitting together on the terrace, we talked as if we were old friends as our hair air-dried. When she received a call from her aunt in fluent French, I felt something stir in me that I couldn't explain. The language was like music to my soul. I'd learned French in my primary and secondary schools, but I couldn't speak it and had never heard any of my teachers speak it so fluently, so lyrically and so beautifully.

After Ada's phone call, we spent the remainder of the afternoon talking about French and everything French. I learned she was half Igbo and half Togolese and she spoke a little Igbo and French as fluently as she spoke English. We soon discovered we had many other things in common. We both loved reading novels, watching movies, and listening to music on Cool FM. The only thing we didn't have in common was dancing. The last time I danced, my mother was still alive. Nothing had been able to make me happy enough to dance ever since.

The hairstylist grabbed a portable battery radio off her shelf and tuned it until she discovered a channel playing Sisqo's Thong Song. Ada jumped up from her seat and began to dance. She swayed her hips like a Congolese dancer, and the hairstylist soon joined her, both of them dancing without shame or inhibition. They didn't care about the onlookers or passersby.

"Join us!" Ada called out to me. I shook my head with a smile, relieved that she didn't push further. Ada and the hairstylist laughed until they were out of breath. While the hairstylist sat down to catch hers, Ada kept dancing. I had wondered if it was possible to be this happy for no reason.

After waiting for an hour and a half, we left the salon together, with our hair still wound around curlers. She had on big yellow curlers while mine were small blue ones. As we walked to our homes, she told me more about herself. When she lost her Nigerian father to cancer at ten, her paternal uncles took over the house because her Togolese mother didn't have a male child.

Homeless, her mother relocated to Lomé, leaving her under the care of a maternal aunt who lived in Dolphin Estate. When it was my turn to share my story, I did so in a single sentence—after my mother died, my father abandoned us. It summed up why my father, although alive, was not in my life. It wasn't a rare case. With the right voice, over the years, my ready-made well-rehearsed biography has proven effective. It was enough to quench people's curiosity and stop them from wanting to know more than I was willing to reveal.

Before we said our goodbyes, Ada offered to give me free French classes and I was giddy, almost matching her energy. I showed her the flat I lived in and she promised to bring me some French grammar books. This was how she became my French tutor. She was kind and jovial, never missing a class. Over a week, we became best friends and did most things together. We would go shopping together and buy the same things. We would go to the hair salon together and have our hair styled and our nails done the same way.

My elder sister, Lara, hated it when we wore matching clothes. Ada loved it and I didn't mind. I enjoyed doing things with Ada. I let her make up my face and practice cornrows with my hair. Although she was a year older, we acted like twins, pretending to be sisters. I was the sister she never had; she was the sister I wanted to have. She would call me *bébé, ma chérie,* or *ma copine.* We shared secrets and memories; about her father and my mother. I rarely told her about Papa—there weren't many loving memories to share.

I was happy to have found someone who did not prefer silence to being with me. We went around speaking French freely in public places like we were living in a French country. Every last Saturday of the month, we had a ritual of attending Buffet Rencontre—an event where French speakers came together to eat a French petit déjeuner and make new French-speaking friends.

We attended every event organised by French organisations in Lagos—vide-greniers, brocantes, concerts, films, and parties. Ada's playful nature meant she always wanted to laugh, sing and dance. Unlike Lara, she never dragged me down; instead, her lively spirit always pulled me up along with her.

TWO

1997, Twelve years before

When the rain abated, everyone came out to play. The sun and the waves seemed excited to play too. The children stood by the edge of the ocean with their feet covered in white foam, tempting the waves. They waited until the waves rolled out close to meet them before racing towards dry land.

We wanted to play in Eleko Beach, but we were wary of its violent waves. They wielded immense strength, rose high above our heads, and towered over us before crashing down with dreadful force. They kept inviting us closer into their alluring embrace but we were not fooled. We knew they could slide backwards, sweep us off our feet, and then pull us into the depths of the ocean—a nightmare of a watery tomb.

Parents shouted the names of their children when they got too close to the shoreline. The women's voices were loud, the men's were sharp. Papa did not come to the beach with us. He never did anything with us. Mama sat on a wide mat under a palm tree. Sparkling white sand stuck to the soles of her feet. Her eyes were divided between watching all five of us and reading her book with two people kissing on the cover.

Each time she looked up, she either shouted 'Move back' or 'You are getting too close'. Tutu, who was in her arms, kept trying to grab her book or her reading glasses. Wale played football with some boys he had met at the beach, while Fola and some other children teased the restless waves.

Lara and I stayed away from the waves. We sat side by side, our arms touching like Siamese twins. We were wearing the same pink swimsuit and our skin shone with the coconut oil Mama had rubbed on us. We sat with our feet buried deep in the wet sand so that we could feel its coolness against our skins. We sipped coconut water through a straw and watched the people around us.

A man with short dreads strolled by holding the reins of a dark brown horse, "Hey children, come ride my horse. Run to Mama and ask for a hundred Naira."

"We've already gotten a ride. You asked us when you went that way a while ago," I said, pointing towards the direction he was coming from.

A moment later, a large wave rushed toward us and swept away our sandcastles. While I immediately began moulding new ones around my feet, Lara stared intensely ahead. I traced her gaze to where the sky and ocean merged into a symphony of blue, and after a while, I asked, "What do you think is on the other side?"

She turned and looked at me but didn't say anything. No longer expecting an answer, I scooped up a handful of sand and added it to my feet.

"America," she finally replied, rolling her 'r', her voice gliding over the mesmerising melody of another huge wave crashing loudly against the shore.

"Move back Lami, Lara," Mama shouted. "You are too close."

"But we haven't gotten up since we sat down here," I argued.

Tired of rebuilding new sandcastles every time a brave wave reached us, I decided to hunt for pretty shells. I got up and wandered the upper beach, playfully stepping on different footprints across the sand, fitting my feet into the big sizes, and erasing the smaller ones to print mine.

Around me, several scared little crabs scurried in confusion, in different directions, looking for the nearest holes they could find. As I continued my pursuit of seashells, I pictured myself in my new school uniform walking with Lara to school. Mama had given me a leather watch because I had passed the Common Entrance exams in class five and would be skipping the next class to go straight to secondary school. I was happy because she'd also promised to replace my rubber sandals with Bata leather shoes.

After picking as many shells as I could hold with both hands, I knelt on the warm sand and filtered them, selecting those without blemishes and cracks. Then I put them into a transparent plastic bag lying around and went to sit next to Mama on the mat.

"Would you like to carry Tutu?" Mama asked.

I knew that smile, the one she wore when she wanted me to do something I had the right to refuse. I stood and stretched out my hands toward my little sister. Eagerly, she came into my arms and grabbed my neck. I laid back on the mat with my head propped up with towels, and then I sat her on my tummy.

"Fola, what did I tell you?" Mama shouted.

Startled, Tutu jumped and fell on my face. Afterwards, she giggled and tried to suck at my sticky skin. I sucked at her cheek in revenge and tasted the salt from the sea that had clung to her smooth baby skin. Digging my heels into the dry sand, I tried to lift her, but my hands were not strong enough to hold her up for more than a few seconds at a time. Each time I lowered her, she would try to attack my eyes with wet kisses. It was at this point the doorbell rang, thrusting me back into the present.

***

I closed the English textbook before me and rose from my chair to see who was at the door. The bell rang again just as I reached the entry. I opened the door to find Mama's brother standing there.

"Good morning, Uncle," I said with a huge smile.

"Good morning, Lami," he replied in a weak voice.

A faint smile crept to his lips and hung there. It refused to move up to his puffy eyes to lighten them up. For a few seconds, I stood and stared at him wondering why he was still dressed in his pyjamas and indoor slippers. I'd never seen him looking so dishevelled with an unkempt beard and uncombed hair. His light blue shirt which was unevenly buttoned exposed a part of his hairy chest, and the dark blue dressing gown he was wearing on top, was all rumpled on his slender body. He looked as if he'd not slept for two days in a row. Another strange thing I noticed was that he'd come without his distinct smell. Usually, when he came to visit, his perfume would fill the house and everyone could tell who had rung the bell before the door was opened.

"How are you?" he asked, averting his gaze. His voice too was different. It sounded like Mama's, after an eight-hour praise vigil at the Pentecostal church.

"I'm fine, Uncle," I replied, unlocking the big black padlock on the burglar-proof bars. He walked past me without giving me a bear hug as he would normally do.

"Today is Papa's birthday," I whispered.

He nodded and said, "Yes, I know."

But he'd come with nothing—no cake, no gift, not even a birthday card. Nothing for us either. This too was unusual because he never visited without a packet of Choco Milo or Éclairs chocolate candies.

"How is Mama?"

"She is fine," he replied quickly just as a strong breeze forced its way through the door of the front balcony, flinging it wide open and rushing down the corridor. I shuddered as it brushed past me, momentarily leaving goosebumps on my body.

"Is everything all right?" I asked.

He nodded but still wouldn't look me in the eye. Instead, he pulled at the belt of his dressing gown which had been hanging loose, and began to fasten it around his waist.

"Where is your Dad?" he asked without lifting his head.

"In his room," I whispered again, "He is ill. We wanted to come last Saturday like we promised Mama, but he refused to bring us or let us take the bus."

Reaching out a hand, he rubbed my short hair and walked into the living room. His strange attitude baffled me. I'd never seen Uncle Kay looking as serious as a detective at a murder scene. In times past, every time he was at the door and we asked who it was, to make us laugh, he would reply, 'It's Frank Spencer', impersonating the voice of the British actor from the television sitcom *Some Mothers Do 'Ave 'Em*. That afternoon, he wasn't in the mood to play the comedian. As I pushed the heavy padlock into place, I wondered if he was upset because Papa hadn't gone to visit Mama. I also wondered, if perhaps, Papa would allow us to return with Uncle Kay to Dolphin Estate to see Mama.

After shutting the door, I returned to the dining table where I'd been sitting. It was three years since the table was moved out of the dining room to take a temporary place in the corridor. Each time Papa and Mama had a fight and she stood up to him, to punish her, Papa would ban her from going into their room. Mama would then transform the dining room into a temporary abode until they settled their differences and she was allowed to move back into their bedroom. But their last fight lasted longer than all the others, and when they finally made up, Mama didn't want to go back anymore. She was finally tired of moving in and out, preferring to sleep in the dining room permanently.

Eager to tell Lara and Fola that Uncle Kay had come to visit, I packed up my textbooks and ran down the corridor. The last room on the right was the girls', and opposite, Fola's which he shared with Wale, our eldest brother whenever he came visiting. I shared a room with my sisters, Lara and Tutu. It was painted in a glossy light blue like the rest of the flat. A brown wooden bunk bed was on the left. Pictures of Michael Jackson in different sizes—cut out from magazines and newspapers—were pasted on the wall of the lower bed.

There was a brown cot by the wall opposite the door and a dark brown reading table on the right by the entrance. Just above the table was a corner shelf with two picture frames. One was of an unsmiling Lara and a smiling me standing right next to her. The other had been taken to our old apartment. It was a picture of my siblings and me sitting side by side on a sofa. Lara was the only one who was not smiling. Tutu was not in this picture as she'd not yet been born when it'd been taken.

"Uncle Kay is here!" I cried, bursting into the girls' room.

Lara was sitting at the desk with a textbook open before her, however, she wasn't studying. Instead, she was playing a brick game on her game set. As I'd hoped, my news pleased her. She turned to look at me and a small smile appeared on her lips. Her eyes sparkled like newly-cut diamonds behind her reading glasses. Although the smile swiftly passed, I was grateful for the opportunity to witness its brief appearance. Without saying a word, she slipped her hand into the top drawer of the desk and brought out her writing pad and her new fountain pen. I could tell she was about to write Mama a long letter.

Lara loved to keep to herself. She spent her free time writing long letters which she kept locked away on her side of the wardrobe. No one knew where she hid the key. She was always scribbling things in her diary that no other eyes except hers had ever seen. When she was upset with me, she would write me a letter. The same thing happened when she was upset with her seatmate at school, Chichi. She wrote Papa letters too, but she never gave them to him. She also wrote long letters to her imaginary friends, amongst whom was Michael Jackson.

Many times, she wouldn't have lunch at school so that she could save up some money to buy stamps. On several occasions, I walked with her to the post office at Sabo to send letters to the Neverland Valley Ranch. Thereafter, she would check the letterbox each time she passed by it as if the mailman didn't come by only once a day. Did the letters ever get to California? Did Michael Jackson ever read them? Did the post office workers throw them out after reading them and laughing their heads off?

I would never know as she never got a reply, nor did she give up writing to him. She was certain that someday, Michael Jackson would reply and agree to adopt her. Then she would change her name from Lara Davies to Pamela Jackson. I had dreams he would adopt me too and I would also change my name from Olamide Davies to Jennifer Jackson.

As Lara scribbled away on her writing pad, I felt proud of myself and gloried in my success at having brought her news that made her face break into its first smile of the day. Each time I made her smile, I felt as though I had hit the jackpot, for her smiles were as rare as her words. Mama always said to her, 'Frowning will make you grow old and ugly, no man will want to marry you.' Other times, Mama would say, 'You are not even fifteen but you look like the old woman who lived in a shoe.' We would all burst out laughing except for Lara who would sulk and keep to herself all day. At school, several of the girls said Lara and I could pass for twins although she was two years older. I was light-skinned like Papa, while Lara was as dark as roasted coffee beans, just like Mama.

To me, Lara was a Yoruba goddess with long dark full hair. Her eyeballs were the colour of white pap and her teeth were whiter than the inside of a coconut. But Lara's beauty was however always hidden behind a scowl. Often, she would drift into frightening moods and I would occupy myself with searching for what to say or do to see her take off her mask and reveal the artwork of God. When I failed to get her spirits up, something which happened often, I would leave the room and let her be. Most times, I would pick a book and go to the dining table to read. At other times, I would go into Fola's room to chat with him. After Mama moved out of the master bedroom into the dining room, she would let me come into her room to read or just sit and watch her sew.

As I was about to go to Fola's room to continue to spread the good news of Uncle Kay's visit, there was a tap on the door. Fola pushed the door slightly open and popped his head in. His eyes were reddish and he had lines printed on the right side of his face as if he had slept on rumpled clothes.

"Who rang the bell?" His voice was thick with sleep and his full eyebrows were raised curiously.

"Ooooh Betty," I said, mimicking the British accent.

"Uncle Kay is here?" he asked, raising his brows even higher.

I nodded in response and a wide smile pushed up the corners of his lips, lightening up his eyes. He opened the door and stepped inside the room. Fola was two years younger than me and too tall for a ten-year-old. He had short curly hair, and like Wale, his skin was the same tone as caramel cookies.

"Did he come alone?" Fola asked.

I was about to respond when a long loud cry came from the direction of the living room. It was Papa. His scream pierced through me as if a sharp object had been plunged into my chest. For several seconds, we all remained transfixed until Lara dropped her pen and reading glasses on her writing pad and rushed to the living room. Fola and I ran after her.

***

Papa who had stayed in bed all morning was now sitting on a sofa. Before that day, I'd never heard nor seen him cry. I stood at the entrance of the living room, in case he looked up and found us watching him. If he got enraged and shouted '*gerrout*', I'd be the first to scurry down the corridor, as fast as my legs would permit me. But Papa didn't seem to care if we saw him in such an unmanly state. He held his head in his hands and his body shook as he wept.

"What happened to Mama?" Lara, who was standing in front of Papa, asked.

When Papa didn't raise his head nor reply to her question, she turned to Uncle Kay. He was standing in front of the television, his lips pulled into a thin line. His eyes were closed, yet tears streamed down his face. Lara fell to her knees at his feet as if in worship. She covered her face with her hands and moaned, *'no no no no no'*, while shaking her head as if it would make the tragic news go away.

As I watched her, my heart began to pulsate in an unfamiliar rhythm. It sounded like a strange passage played on a talking drum, incomprehensible to the listeners. All the tears in the room made me understand why Uncle Kay had red puffy eyes and why he'd come in pyjamas from Dolphin Estate on Lagos Island.

Fola who was now sitting on the sofa next to Papa sobbed quietly. He stared at the empty three-seater opposite him. Mama often lay there when she wasn't in her room. Some afternoons, when we returned from school, she would be lying on the blue leopard-patterned three-seater sofa because the living room had better ventilation. I remembered her frail body in an oversized Bubu gown, her dried thin lips, her eyeballs that had taken refuge inside their sockets, and her scalp that looked as if it had never been graced with long hair.

I also remembered the first time she died on that sofa. Lara had shaken her back to life while screaming 'Mama, wake up! I beg of you! Please, wake up!' Mama's face was pale and distressed when she was resurrected.

I could still hear her saying, 'I was almost gone but I fought hard because I don't want to leave my children. If I die, your father won't take care of you.' Lara and I had held her hands and tried to comfort her, and at the same time, we'd struggled not to break down. As Mama's breathing became easier, I heard her muttering, 'If I die, my children will suffer.' She kept repeating this in a low voice until she fell asleep again.

Uncle Kay didn't need to tell us what had happened to Mama. We knew she'd been battling for her life and that death had won. We knew God had refused to grant our prayers as we'd been told He would. We also knew Papa had robbed us of our chance to say goodbye to Mama.

Mama had been ill for about two years. Grandma moved in with us in February to take care of her. Mama had stopped having house help. She never told me why, but Lara told me it was because Papa always slept with them. Two months after Grandma arrived, she returned to Dolphin Estate taking Mama with her. She needed assistance to take care of her daughter and Papa wasn't giving her a helping hand. Mama also needed a change of environment. Papa must have been glad about the decision because he started to come home early every night after they moved out. He'd also been glad when Grandma first arrived because he no longer had to give Mama her bath or disinfect the big lumps that had grown on her left thigh.

The last time we'd seen Mama had been two weeks before. Papa didn't drop us off in front of the block of flats where Mama was living with her parents. Instead, he stopped us on Osborne Road's expressway bridge which passed by Dolphin Estate. He and his elder sister, Mama Ola, were going to see the piece of land he owned in Agbara Estate. Papa had said he wanted to start building his own house because he paid too much rent where we lived. Mama Ola sat in the passenger seat, with Tutu on her lap who was fast asleep. Mama Ola talked non-stop. She pulled down the visor so she could do her makeup. She rubbed some talc powder on her dark face and then applied her green lipstick over and over again until it turned red on her lips. From time to time, she would scratch her palms and interrupt her monologue to say, 'Oh money is coming. Somebody is bringing me money.'

When we arrived at Mc Gregory Canal, Lara, Fola and I jumped from the bridge and landed on a heap of refuse the residents had dumped on Corporation Drive. After we watched Papa drive off, we didn't go straight to see Mama. Instead, we went to Isolo Street to visit an old baboon locked up in a cage.

We'd not eaten our bananas at breakfast but hidden them in our backpacks because we wanted to give them to the baboon that had no hair on its buttocks. After feeding the poor animal, we said our goodbyes to it many times before heading for our destination. While Lara walked ahead of us, Fola and I held Tutu's hands and pulled her up every four steps so her feet didn't touch the ground. Excited, she laughed loudly and kept repeating, 'Again, again.'

Tutu refused to go into Mama's room all through our visit. She would stand by the door and peep in, then she would give Mama a shy smile and call her, 'Baba.' Each time Mama invited her to come in, she would run away only to come back a while later to repeat the process. This made Mama cry. She had faded away before her eyes until becoming unrecognisable to Tutu, for she looked skeletal and all her hair had fallen out during chemotherapy.

When Aunty Jire, Mama's only sister, returned from choir rehearsal, she stood at the window so she could alert us when Papa drove up the street. We watched movie after movie, ate non-stop, and had catnaps. The sun had already set when Papa returned to pick us up. He and Mama Ola still wouldn't come up to see Mama. Papa was vexed with Mama and her parents for not allowing him to see her the last time he'd visited. He said he'd been told she was asleep but he'd heard her coughing loudly for a couple of minutes.

"She can't fall asleep when she coughs like that," he'd said. "She didn't want to see me. They didn't want me to see her and I'll never set foot in that place again!"

When Papa honked the first time, Tutu was sleeping on the three-seater sofa in the living room. Fola, Uncle Kay, and I were playing Scrabble at the dining table while Lara was listening to Michael Jackson's songs in Uncle Kay's room. We all rushed to Mama's room to say goodbye. When Papa honked a second time, I was kissing Mama's wet face. The strong smell of antiseptic and Robb ointment filled my lungs. I placed another light kiss on her thin hand. It was nothing like the hand I used to know. Her nails were clubbed and her skin was as thin as cellophane film.

"Don't cry Mama," I said, resisting the urge not to break down too. "Saturday will soon be here again."

For several hours that day, she'd sat up in bed with her back against the wall, braced by pillows. When she told us she would be returning home anytime soon, her eyes were no longer those that had been dimmed by cancer. They were like those of a survivor—they beamed with hope. When she'd said that God had healed her, I believed her. Not because the lumps that had sprung up in every part of her body had now disappeared but because of the dream she'd had.

In that dream, a huge being, radiating white light and peace who was dressed up like a Yoruba king in Aso Oke agbada had sat beside her on the bed and had pulled out a pin from each lump. After she woke up from the dream, her body no longer burned with pain. She'd said she felt better and stronger every day since then. I didn't doubt her for a second. I believed she was returning home soon and that everything would be back to normal.

"I can't wait for you to be back home so we can dance to *You Gotta Be Stronger*," I'd said to her. She smiled and curled her hand around mine, threading her fingers in between mine and tightening them briefly.

When Papa honked the third time, my siblings and I ran out of the apartment and down the stairs. We looked forward to the following Saturday when we would return to Dolphin Estate to see Mama and everyone else. But when Saturday finally arrived, Papa refused to take us to see Mama. He also refused to allow us to go by bus even though we'd behaved well all week. We'd given him no grounds to prevent us from going. So as Papa cried that morning, hiding his face in his hands, I couldn't tell if the tears came from his soul. Was it shame, grief or relief?

"Did it happen today?" I asked Uncle Kay.

My voice didn't let me down. It remained the same. It didn't tremble. It hadn't thinned with anguish nor had it been burdened with unshed tears. Uncle Kay nodded in response. A sudden rush of anxiety overwhelmed me and my heart felt as though it weighed five times its normal size.

Could Mama be gone? Didn't she say she wouldn't die and leave us? Didn't she say as children, God didn't count our sins and He would hear us and save her if we prayed? I looked up at the picture of the Virgin Mary carrying baby Jesus in an ornate gold Florentine-style wood frame, hanging on the wall at the end of the room. Why didn't God hear our prayers? Why would He let Mama die but let Papa live? Was it not injustice? All these questions without answers left me very confused. How could Mama just die away like that? Could it be possible I would never see her again?

I longed to look into her eyes while she told us stories about her past. I loved to watch them soften with cherished memories, harden with pain, brighten with hope, or become distant with regrets. I have the same eyes as hers, almond-shaped tell-tale eyes, set deep in the head, and yet, wide apart from each other. Each one was upturned, slightly lifted at the outer corner. They told our personal stories. They denuded our hearts and shamelessly bared all to those looking into them.

Tutu who had been sleeping in Papa's room, walked into the living room, holding a pink stuffed bunny rabbit. She stood still in the doorway, holding her favourite pink blanket in one hand and looking frightened as she watched the faces of everyone in silence. When she walked up to Papa and touched his knee, he uncovered his face, looked at her, and burst into fresh tears. Tutu joined him, with robust tears running down her face, even though she didn't know why he was crying.

Uncle Kay picked her up and cuddled her. I squeezed my eyes shut. I wanted to break down and cry too. I wanted to weep like everyone else around me. I wanted to have tears running down my cheeks but I couldn't even cry. Deep down, I felt as though if I let myself be overwhelmed, I would be signing a binding contract with God that Mama could die. I would be releasing her to death and testifying that I could manage without her. To me, grieving her meant I would be giving up on her and agreeing to let her go. Mourning became an irreversible mistake and for the first time, I saw my inability to shed tears as a blessing.

I was going to be twelve in nine days and I wanted Mama to wake me up to the smell of baking cake as she always did on our birthdays. To wake us up, she would either sprinkle cold water on us or tickle under our feet. Then she would begin to sing *Happy Birthday to you* in her beautiful voice.

A pain stabbed my chest as these memories flooded my mind. Then it grew worse when a storm of guilt seized me. I was suddenly convinced God hadn't heard my prayers because I hadn't prayed hard enough. Many times, I had dozed off during prayers for Mama's healing and when I awoke at the end of the prayers, I would ask God to forgive me for my lack of concentration. Didn't He forgive me? I felt anger stir within me, against me. I should have prayed all night and every night until she got healed. Next, I felt my anger steer toward Mama. She too should have kept her part of the promise of not abandoning us. She should have fought harder to stay alive. Next, I rerouted my anger towards God. Couldn't He have overlooked my shortcomings and answered my prayers? Couldn't He have had mercy on Mama and saved her?

Suddenly, the world began to spin fast around me or maybe it was me who was swirling around in my head. I managed to walk to the three-seater sofa where Uncle Kay was sitting and cuddling Tutu who had stopped crying and gone back to sleep. I settled down next to Uncle Kay and looked around the room. Papa too had stopped crying but he still wouldn't keep his head up. Fola sat still and his eyes were fixed on the white ceiling. Lara's cries were soft and weak as she lay on her side, curled up like a cat.

    I knew instinctively I had to get out of there. I'd done it several times before to escape pain, and most of the time, it worked. I pulled my legs up, rested my chin on my knees, and put my arms around them. Then I detached myself and broke away. I became a little cloud up in a dark sky, watching them from above, soaring higher and higher.

THREE

Present day

Friday was hot and humid. Golden light poured through the windows of the air-conditioned language class which smelled like a perfume shop. The first bell to start the school day rang while I was writing out the names of popular French perfumes on the board. I leaned against my table and breathed calmly, waiting for my pulse to return to normal. I knew I might never get used to the sudden sound of bells without being reminded of Papa's bell.

My second class started immediately. The children from primary four raised their noses and sniffed the air as they filed into the classroom and took their seats. They listened bright-eyed as I started the class. It was my second year as a French teacher at a private school on Victoria Island. I hadn't grown up thinking I wanted to become a teacher.

A career in education had been highly respected when my grandparents were teachers, but not now. I'd been a science student in secondary school. So, when I achieved the required grades to be accepted to any university, I decided I would become a petroleum engineer like Wale.

But by the time I was filling out my J.A.M.B. form, I had become a full-fledged Francophile, thanks to Ada.

So instead of engineering, I chose to study the French Language. I knew that becoming a French teacher wasn't a desirable profession like medicine, pharmacy, engineering or programming, but for once, I'd wanted to study something I loved and not what others wanted me to do because they thought it was better for me or because I had the intelligence for it.

"How can you go to the university to study such a stupid course?" Aunty Nike, Mama's first cousin, had asked. "How can a science student study French Language? French can't put food on your table. You want to become a teacher, and worse still, a French teacher. You do know that teaching jobs in Nigeria are not lucrative, right? Can't you see how Grandpa and Grandma weren't paid their pensions for months? Do you know how many pensioners die at Alausa trying to get their pensions? Do you want to be poor?"

Ada was the only one who encouraged me. I knew Mama would have too. In truth, I chose to study at the University of Lagos because Ada was studying Mass Communication there. Unlike my elder ones who had chosen to study outside Lagos, I remained in the city instead of opting out to escape the ugly memories that tied us to it. I wanted to be there when Tutu would return from London in search of us.

After I graduated from university, I was posted to a public primary school in Ogun as a French teacher for the National Youth Service Corps program. Although teaching hadn't been my dream job, I loved it. I enjoyed helping Fola with his homework when we were little and teaching Tutu the alphabet and nursery rhymes.

Unfortunately, at the end of my NYSC program, I couldn't stay on the job. I was unable to make ends meet on the meagre salary. I returned to Lagos and applied to several private schools in Lekki, Victoria Island and Ikoyi before getting an offer from one six months later. The salary provided me with a decent level of financial security—accommodation in Lekki Phase 1, fuel in my generator set and food in my refrigerator. Still, I knew I could do more and mustn't allow myself to feel too comfortable.

To secure my future, I began working toward a master's degree in France which would allow me to apply for a post at one of the international schools that paid in dollars or euros.

***

Saturday morning was bright and clear. After giving two private home classes in Lekki, I returned home to have lunch before heading to Ikoyi for my afternoon class with Camille Leclerc.

Camille was the only student I taught English and the only one who didn't attend my school. She was French and a student at one of the schools where I hoped to apply for a job after I got my Master's Degree. That day, I planned to give Camille an outdoor class. She thought it was a great idea and her father agreed to it. Mr Leclerc worked with Air France and had relocated his wife and daughter to join him a year after he arrived in Lagos.

Camille was nine, brown-haired and plump with chubby dimpled cheeks. She had her mother's eyes and her father's smile. She reminded me so much of Tutu. Not that she looked like Tutu, but she acted like I was her big sister and I felt the sisterly need to protect her.

We were taken in a 4x4 jeep to three different malls around the Island. Camille learnt the English word for all the things she bought. She got herself heart-shaped retro sunglasses, fluffy rainbow slippers, a floppy sun hat, a feather boa and so many other colourful girly accessories. Our day ended at half-past six in a French cake shop where we had cake and ice cream.

We found an empty table next to the windows, beside a woman with two young boys who were gobbling down their chocolate cakes. I permitted Camille to take a break from English. Excited, she chattered away in French. Smiling, I watched her devour her chocolate chip cookie dough ice cream while talking about the different toppings she had with the massive sundae she'd eaten during her last summer holiday in Paris. It was exactly how I'd always envisaged spending time with my little sister, Tutu.

A few minutes later, we left the cake shop and began to walk back to the car. As we reached the pedestrian crossing, Camille stepped out in front of an approaching taxi. I pulled her back and the driver hit the brake, forcing his yellow taxi to come to a screeching halt.

"What is wrong with you?" the driver shouted through his open window.

"I'm sorry," I said. "She's not from here. In France, drivers stop for pedestrians waiting at the zebra crossing."

"Well, this is Nigeria! You need to teach her how to cross the road."

The driver restarted his engine just as the car behind him honked. I held on to her hand, grateful I'd been holding it before the incident and had pulled her back in time.

"Here, drivers don't stop when they see you waiting before a marked crosswalk," I said to her in French after we had crossed. We were strolling down a narrow street, congested with parked cars on both sides and with foreigners walking past us. "You must always look left and right twice before you try to cross."

"Elle a raison," a voice said from behind us. I turned around to find a young man about my height. He smiled and dimples appeared on his cheeks. "I made the same mistake she made back there when I first arrived. I learnt quickly."

I nodded.

"But why mark the zebra crossing if it won't be respected?" Camille asked the man who began walking with us.

I gave Camille's hand two quick squeezes to get her to stop interacting with the man. He was French. I could tell from his accent. It was similar to Camille's and different from mine, Ada's and my French lecturers at the university. I could understand why it was easier for Camille to talk to a French stranger than a Nigerian stranger. But a stranger was still a stranger.

"I think they interpret it differently here," the man said.

"That doesn't make any sense to me," Camille looked up at me. "Lami, what do you think?"

"Well..." I said and glanced at the man who was now walking beside us. He was stifling a laugh. "I guess you're right."

The man raised a brow and twisted his lips to one side as though holding himself from bursting into laughter.

"It makes no sense," Camille repeated.

When we arrived at the SUV, I knocked on the window and the driver unlocked the doors. Camille climbed in and Sherif, the driver, started the engine. I shut the door and found the French man still waiting there. I took a good look at him. He had light brown hair and hazel eyes.

"I swear, I'm not following you," he said, smiling, and then I heard another engine roar to life.

"Yours?"

"Such a coincidence that we are parked next to each other."

I nodded and tried to walk past him.

"Are you Nigerian?" he asked.

I nodded again.

"I don't know many Nigerians who speak French."

"I'm a French teacher. I don't have a choice."

Walking past him, I strolled around the SUV to the opposite side and climbed in, taking a seat next to Camille. On our way back to Ikoyi, Mr Leclerc called my phone, eager to know our whereabouts. It was the third time he had called me to speak to Camille.

"Where is my daughter?" he said as soon as I picked up.

His question touched a sensitive chord inside me and with it came thoughts of Papa.

Did he ever worry about me? Did he ever worry that his children were out in the world by themselves, with no father or mother to protect them from harm and guide them from making wrong decisions? I would do anything to have a father like Mr Leclerc to care for me and worry about me. A father who would call me several times a day when we weren't together. A father who would make it obvious I was important to him, and cross the seas and climb mountains to come to save me when I was in trouble.

I passed the phone to Camille whose lips were covered in the bright, new red gloss I had just bought for Ada as a gift.

"Allo Papa," she said, taking the phone from me.

I feigned a frown, pretending to be displeased with her for rubbing on so much lip gloss, but it only made her giggle.

"Oui, Papounet," she said, before asking him not to worry because we were already on our way back.

When she was done with the call, I began dabbing at her lips with a tissue to wipe off the gloss.

"It's too much," I said to her. "You better clean it off before we get back."

I gave her a small mirror and a fresh Kleenex. When she saw her smudged lips and chin, she burst into laughter. Unable to resist it, I joined in.

I wondered if Tutu laughed the same way—hair in disarray, eyes glittering with amusement. I wondered if we would have been close. Shared secrets. Did she have a joyful spirit like Ada or was she as quiet and moody as Lara? No, she could never be moody. I could still remember the sound of her baby laughter—cheerful and melodious—rippling out from her chest and through the air every time I tickled her.

Unlike Mama's voice, hers had always stayed clear in my memory.

***

I watched Tunji's Toyota Corolla drive out of the hotel's main gates as I walked toward the hotel's cab services, the multi-storey Eko Hotel building behind me. Tunji hadn't offered to take me home or drop me off at the taxi park. It was a quarter to nine. The dinner had been quick and disastrous. I'd known rejecting his advances in a posh penthouse restaurant was a bad idea, but he'd insisted we met for dinner.

The moment his car disappeared from view, I changed directions and headed towards the main gates, to the taxi park.

"Hey!" a voice said. I looked up from my phone and there he was—the French man from the day before. I raised my brows in surprise.

"You?"

"I swear, I'm not following you," he said in French. There was a playful smile on his lips.

I looked around him but he seemed to be alone. We were standing under a streetlamp, close to the entrance gates of the hotel. The security light poured down on us, like a beam of spotlight. For a moment, we stared at each other. I didn't know how to feel about the strange coincidence.

What were the chances we would bump into each other again, in the space of two days, in a city of millions of people?

"How are you?" he asked.

"I'm good, thanks." I wanted to add, "And you?" but it felt like something one said to someone familiar—an acquaintance, a friend, a family member. I didn't even know the guy's name or anything about him other than the fact that he was French and understood the Nigerian traffic rules.

He cleared his throat. "I wasn't expecting to see you here, but I'd sincerely hoped yesterday wouldn't be our last meeting." Then he explained he'd had dinner in a restaurant across the street with colleagues. "I came here to change some money when I saw you."

I raised my brows. "I thought someone like you would change money at the bank."

"The rates here are better," he pointed out.

"The cab services here are expensive," I said with a small smile. "I'm heading to the taxi park by the beach."

"Do you come here often?"

I shook my head. "I didn't come here to change dollars or euros if that's what you are asking."

We both laughed. I told him I'd had dinner with a friend at a restaurant in the hotel's penthouse.

"The Asian-fusion place?"

"Yes."

"I know it," he said. He'd had dinner there many times. He described the African art décor of the spacious restaurant, the waiters who dressed smartly in black waistcoats and trousers, and the view of the sunset and ocean. Then he told me his driver was parked nearby and was waiting for him, so we began walking towards the gates together. Passersby cast glances in our direction, including occupants of passing cars.

"Did you know Victoria Island was named after Queen Victoria in the nineteenth century?" I asked as we neared the taxi park. The words were out of my mouth before I realised I had recently resolved to not always let the teacher in me ask the 'did you know' questions.

"No," he said. "I didn't know that... this is why I need Nigerian friends. I don't learn anything about Nigeria when I hang out with the Total boys."

"Don't you have any Nigerian friends?"

"Of course, I have a few. Mostly males. We play football together every Wednesday evening."

He told me he worked for Total, in rotation for a month between Lagos and Paris. It was his first year in Nigeria. Before he was posted to Lagos, he'd spent three years in Dubai and after three years in Nigeria, he would be sent to Congo or Gabon.

I told him my school was off Akin Adesola Street, not too far away from where we were. We halted when we arrived in front of the taxi park. The street lamps were bright, giving everything a yellow tint and making the yellow taxis glow as they lined up, waiting for passengers.

"This is where we part ways," I said with a smile. I'd enjoyed talking to him, conversing in French with someone other than Ada, and listening to his accent, warm and musical to my ears. "It was nice seeing you again."

"Are you in a hurry?" he asked.

"Why? I'm going home. I have to prepare for work tomorrow."

"Would you like to go for a walk along the beach?"

I glanced in the direction of the beach, and my heart picked up pace. The last time I stepped foot on a beach Mama had still been alive.

"I was wondering if you could spare a few minutes," he continued. "I'd like to see what the beach looks like at night."

I swallowed and shook my head again. "I don't think it's safe."

"What?" He sounded surprised. "For you or me?"

"For both of us,' I said quickly.

I looked towards the beach again. Two white couples were walking out. The men were carrying transparent plastic bags with food wrapped in aluminium foil.

"What about them?" he asked.

I started to shake my head.

"I haven't been there in years... in over a decade."

"C'mon," he said. "Ten minutes."

***

I waited at the taxi park while he went to speak to his driver. I looked around me. The neighbourhood had changed over the years. It bore no resemblance to my childhood memories, and even at night, it had completely transformed into a different entity from its daytime persona, characterised by the hustle and bustle of the metropolis.

I looked towards the beach. It was lit by the streetlamps along Ahmadu Bello Way. I didn't feel ready to return to the beach; I wasn't prepared for how I would feel when I stepped onto the sand. I had passed by the beach in buses, cars, and motorcycles many times, but I had never been compelled to return to one. I'd always refused birthday parties or get-together invitations with a venue at the beach. But here I was, standing on the shifting sand and breathing the sea's salty air because of some stranger.

A cool breeze from the beach brushed past me and howled down the street. I glanced towards the taxi park. I could jump into a taxi and if I was lucky, we would drive away before he stepped out of the compound. I looked towards the restaurant and saw him walking out, smiling at me like we were best friends. My heartbeat accelerated. I stood still, watching him with my hands folded tightly in front of me as he crossed the road.

In silence, we began walking towards the beach. My heartbeats thundered as we drew nearer.

At the entrance, we removed our shoes and carried them in our hands so we could feel the sand between our toes. Entry was free, and the beach was lively with people and different music. With no palm trees to sway, the breeze from the ocean flirted with the paper and plastic litter across the beach. We joined the people wandering along the shore but remained on the dry part of the sand. The bamboo bars and restaurants with different interior coloured lights lined up along the shoreline for a couple of miles. My heartbeat gradually slowed, becoming quieter with each passing moment.

We strolled without talking, but the silence wasn't uncomfortable. I felt calm and peaceful. I began enjoying the ambience and the feel of the breeze on my face and body. I blocked my mind from digging up images of the last time I'd been on a beach with Mama and my brothers and sisters.

"My friends and I prefer Eleko Beach because of the tropical palm trees view and the bamboo huts for rent," he said. "Bar beach looks bare without trees, and the umbrellas they rent don't offer enough protection from the sun or the wind."

I wanted to tell him Eleko Beach was the last beach I'd been to, but I swallowed my words. I feared he would want to know more.

"Did you know Bar Beach was formerly called Victoria Beach in honour of Queen Victoria?" I bit my lower lip. I was doing it again.

"Really?"

I nodded.

"Why was the name of the beach changed but not the name of the Island?"

"Mmm, I don't know, but I'll google it and let you know."

"You would need my number, then." He stopped walking and turned to face me, grinning. He asked for my number, and then he called my phone.

"I still don't know your name," I said. I couldn't believe we'd spent all this while together without knowing each other's names.

"My name is Nicolas."

"I'm Lami—"

"Lami—"

My lips parted, warring with strange emotions. "You heard Camille call my name?"

He smiled. His little dimples twinkled.

We saved each other's numbers and continued walking. A couple wearing the same Ankara patterns smiled at us as they walked past in the opposite direction. He asked me why I thought the beach was unsafe. I told him I never felt safe anywhere in Lagos at night as a woman. He told me he loved the nightlife in Lagos. He mentioned bars, restaurants, and clubs where he often hung out with colleagues after work. He wanted to see more of Lagos, not just the affluent areas like Ikoyi or Victoria Island.

He looked surprised when I said I didn't know Lagos well either, just the more modest areas I'd lived, schooled, and worked in. We talked about how the Lagos State government planned to dredge and sand-fill the beach to reclaim more land to build a modern city. He told me it was why he wanted to see the part of the beach we were walking on before the project swallowed it up. I stopped walking.

"We've had storms... high tides, and enormous waves that have attempted to reclaim what has been stolen from the ocean. That's why they put those huge stones to slow down the waves." I turned and pointed to the other side of the beach along Ahmadu Bello Way. "Every time it happens, people get trapped in their offices and homes by flood. Sometimes, people drown."

"I see," he said.

"You don't have to worry now. Things are better these days, but it may become frequent again or even be worse once the mega-city they're planning to construct is finished."

"That's true.'"

"If ever I can afford to buy a house in the new city, I won't buy one because the ocean may come to reclaim what belongs to it someday," I joked.

"Me too," he said, laughing. "If ever I can afford it."

We started to walk again and then stopped after a few steps. He was thirsty and wanted to get something to drink. While I waited for him, he walked to a makeshift bar. I looked back at our footprints. In my mind's eye, I saw the child prints I'd made over a decade back. I'd come a long way since that day. I'd walked miles alone, since that afternoon with

Mama and my brothers and sister on the beach, yet it seemed like only a short while had passed.

There was no time I had thought about that afternoon that I didn't feel a sharp pain in my heart. A pain similar to what I felt the very first time I realised we would never go to the beach as a family again. But that night, as I stood alone waiting for Nicolas, the pain seemed to fade. I glanced up at the sky. It was a starless and moonless night. I looked towards the ocean, but couldn't see far. I shuddered. The pitch-black waters made me feel uneasy as if I was trapped in a dark wardrobe. I looked down at my scarlet toenails. Small waves attempted to roll up to where I was standing. They lapped the white sandy shore and made white foam and relaxing lullabies.

Nicolas returned with two bottles of La Casera. I thanked him, and we opened our drinks at the same time. The gas eased, spilling the cold drink on my fingers. We both took a sip, our eyes remaining on each other as we drank. The breeze brushed past jealously. I replaced the cap of my drink. He did the same, and we resumed walking down the long stretch of the beach.

He asked me if I knew about the convicted armed robbers and coup plotters who had been executed by firing squad on the beach in front of hundreds of witnesses. He'd heard it from a Nigerian colleague.

"I don't remember that period... I was very young. But I've heard many people talk about it."

When we reached a group of people playing football, we stopped and watched for a while. I glanced at my phone. An hour had flown past. We agreed it was time to leave. He offered to ask his driver to take me home first. I declined, saying it was better if I took a taxi. We started walking back, closer than we had when we walked in. We finished our drinks and disposed of the empty plastic bottles in a trash bin. When we arrived at a fruit vendor, we stopped so he could buy a variety of fruits. They were expensive, but he thought they were very cheap compared to the prices at the Ikoyi supermarket he frequented. He paid the woman and left her some change.

"I've enjoyed talking to you. I've learnt so much in a short while," he said. We'd just finished putting our shoes back on and were exiting the beach.

"I think it's because I'm a teacher. I've learnt to be fascinating to get my students interested in what I teach them," I teased.

"Now I understand..." His dimples winked as he smiled. "Seriously, you're fun to be with. I've only known you for about an hour, and it's like I've known you all my life."

I felt the same way, too, but I had no intention of confessing that to him.

"You're fun to be with, too," I said neutrally.

"Would you like to come and watch me play football?"

"Football?" I asked. I didn't particularly like football and never watched it.

"I can send my driver to come to pick you up and take you back home."

Feigning thoughtfulness, I replied, "I'll let you know."

FOUR

Past

Papa left with Uncle Kay to take Mama's corpse to the mortuary. When he returned, he summoned us all, his voice cracking as he called each of us by our names. Usually, when he needed to call us, he would ring once for Wale when he was visiting, twice for Lara, thrice for me and four times for Fola. But on the day Mama died, it didn't seem appropriate to him to use the bell.

When we were standing before him, in a gentle voice, he asked us to sit and showed us the police report he had collected before depositing Mama's corpse at the mortuary. Afterwards, he began complaining about the stinking police station, the huge sum of money he had to pay to get the report, and the hours he had wasted there. His corpulent body seemed to have shrunk. His protruding belly, which he always blamed on the beers he drank, seemed to have deflated. He looked like a sick child with his pale lips and tired eyes.

Because I had yet to cry since the tragic news, I was the one he chose to go inform neighbours and family friends of our loss. In my mind, I replayed his words, 'You are the strong one. You've been able to control yourself and haven't broken down.' I kept thinking this was a sign that soon he would finally love me and accept me the way I was, despite my *flaws*. Perhaps, he would no longer look at me with contempt and call me names because my eyes never produced tears when I cried.

We didn't go to school that week, even though our exams were close by. At night, in our moonlit room, I would put some saliva on my eyelids and trace the corner of my eyes down to my chin in a futile attempt to fake tears. On Tuesday night, the day before Mama was going to be buried, I still hadn't cried. I knew Mama was dead, but something in me was expecting her to return home. I was waiting to hear her car's horn when she returned from work. Fola and I used to run down the stairs, jumping two, three or even four steps at a time, and sometimes we slid down the bannister. Before the security guard opened the gates, we would scramble into the back seat of Mama's car and smother her with kisses from behind as she drove into the garage. Afterwards, Fola and I would begin to fight over her lunch bag because whoever got it could eat the leftovers.

"It's mine," Fola would say, trying to grab the bag from me.

"Sorry, but I got to it first."

"It's mine! It's mine!"

"No way. I let you have it yesterday."

"Leave it for your little brother," Mama would say to me.

Fola and I continued to argue as we stepped out of her car and climbed the stairs to our flat on the top floor. Sometimes, Mama would blink at me and I would wink back, decoding that there was no leftover in the lunch bag. Then I would burst into a cackle when Fola would open it and find it empty.

***

The funeral took place four days after Mama died. The service was held at a small Catholic Church not far from Dolphin Estate. It was in the same church where she had been baptised, had gone through catechism, had received her first Holy Communion, had been confirmed and had also gotten married. It was in this same church that Grandpa attended the six-thirty Mass every morning.

We arrived early but waited quietly in the car until the Mass was about to start. Papa got a new haircut for the occasion. His full moustache and beard were well-groomed. His eyes, underneath his four millimetres eye-glasses, were big and round. We wore white clothes instead of the usual black. Papa wanted everyone at the burial to wear white. My siblings and I wore the same white damask guinea brocade fabric Papa wore. My sisters and I sewed the traditional Iro and Buba while the men wore Buba and Sokoto.

It was a sunny day, but a mist clouded my eyes and fogged up my mind. My face felt as though it had been carved from dry mud. It didn't stretch into a smile, neither did it crack into a cry. At 10:00 am sharp, when the organ started playing, we walked into the church behind a tall priest and two altar boys.

One of the boys carried a big Bible, while the other swung a thurible with burning incense back and forth. The white smoke from the incense suffused the church quickly, ascending in the air, toward the high ceiling and gathering like a dense cloud. Wale carried a big white candle in a silver candle holder while Fola held up a large wooden cross.

Lara and I walked side by side with our heads slightly bowed and our hands clasped together in front of us. Papa carried Tutu who was holding her old and dirty stuffed bunny rabbit. She waved and smiled at everyone as I tried to remember what we were doing in the church, walking behind the priest like important personalities.

Halfway down the aisle, I started to feel sick and dizzy from the choking scent of the incense. My heart began to beat in an irregular rhythm. It seemed to sound louder than the organ playing and the choir singing, *Rock of Ages*. Fortunately, I made it to the seats reserved for us on the right side of the front row.

Through the eyes of my fuzzy memories, it seemed as though the guests had been headless. Uncle Kay and Aunty Jire sat in the pew behind us, but I did not see Grandpa and Grandma, even though they lived close by. It was later I would come to understand it was a taboo for one's parents to attend one's burial ceremony.

During the mass, I felt a sharp pain in my ears and something round and heavy in my throat. For minutes, I could hardly breathe. The Holy Communion was dry on my tongue as I knelt at the altar with others. My feet and palms became sweaty and my body was warm, as if I had a fever.

We marched solemnly to the cemetery, singing dirges, crying, wailing, sniffing, whispering and shuffling our feet. The coffin was white, balanced on the shoulders of six hefty pallbearers in white suits. I'd looked into the casket but hadn't recognised the thin woman lying in it. Her eyes were closed, and she was dressed in Mama's wedding dress. I had worn it once. When Mama saw me, she said it was a bad omen to wear a wedding dress before one was ready for marriage. Mama's white Bible had been placed on the chest of the woman. Her head was covered with a white head tie and she looked as though she was just sleeping.

Aunty Stella, Mama's childhood best friend, sang Amazing Grace. It was the most soothing sound I ever heard. It had seemed as though her song would herald the end of the world and angels would come down to take us all to paradise in our white attires. When Aunty Nike, Mama's first cousin, recited Mama's panegyric, every hair on my body bristled.

"Ọmọ́ káṣọ sílẹ̀ ẹ̀rú b'aláfọ̀," her angelic voice pervaded the air.

I knew these particular words; I had heard them many times before. The verse appeared in my oríkì too.

Mama used to say them to me when I fell ill and she wanted me to eat so I could take my medicine afterwards. Tears rolled down some cheeks as the casket was closed for the last time, but I couldn't remember whose cheeks they were. Four shirtless men slowly lowered the casket into the ground with thick blue ropes. Papa, Wale, and Lara threw sand on the lid of the casket. Then Aunty Jire tapped me gently, saying, "It's your turn".

I grasped a fistful of warm sand from a shovel someone put before me and held onto it for a couple of seconds before throwing it in the grave. Afterwards, I stared at the remnants that stuck to my wet palm. Fola took a handful, too. He then held out his hand to let it slowly trickle and spatter on the casket. There are also memories of Mama Ola trying to make Tutu throw some sand, too. Did she throw some?

Several other handfuls of sand landed on the casket, and I heard many people burst into fresh tears. I felt a painful tightness in my chest. Some voices around me shouted, 'Hold her! Hold her! She is going to fall into the grave. She's shaking.' Was I shaking? I felt many hands grip my arms, but what I wanted them to grasp was my spirit, for it felt as though it was going to fly away from my body into the grave and never return to me.

As the crowd dispersed, we stayed behind to watch the four men fill the grave. They shovelled sand over the coffin in fast, intense, vigorous movements, sweat dripping from their faces and upper torsos. When we couldn't see the white wood anymore, we finally turned to leave. It was the last time my whole family gathered in the same place.

***

We sat silently in Papa's car as we headed back home. Not a word was said during the entire journey.

Wale returned home with us. He sat on the passenger side of the front seat and stared ahead. He looked so much like Papa—a younger version. I wanted him to live at home with us now and no longer return to Dolphin Estate. Fola, who sat in the middle back seat, had fallen asleep and Lara, who was sitting behind Papa, pressed her forehead against the glass, looking through the window. While Tutu slept peacefully in my arms, I convinced myself it wasn't Mama we'd left behind in that coffin.

Papa's sisters and some guests also returned with us. Papa's eldest sister, Mama Jide, who had come from London to attend the funeral, said to us, "When people ask you where your mother is, tell them she has gone to America." Consequently, I continued to console myself that Mama wasn't dead. The more I reflected on it, the more I became convinced it wasn't her who had been imprisoned in the pitch darkness beneath the ground. I shivered at the thought of being locked up in total darkness. It was unimaginable.

In the long corridor of the flat, many people gathered around the dining table where three silver trays were piled high with Akara balls. It was the only meal we'd served because Mama had died young. The mourners sipped soft drinks through straws from glass bottles and picked up the oily pastries with their fingertips. My siblings and I stood with Papa around the entrance door area to greet people who were coming in and thank those who were leaving. We saw Papa's pockets grow bigger and bigger with envelopes that contained money for the children of the deceased. Papa had instructed us to hand over the envelopes to him as soon as we received them.

Throughout that day, neighbours who weren't at the funeral came to offer their condolences. Uncle Kay also came home, driving Mama's car. He left about an hour later with Wale but without the car. I wished he wouldn't take Wale with him. I wanted him to live at home and take care of us. Wale had been living with Mama's parents since he was born out of wedlock.

After Papa and Mama finally got married and moved in together, they left Wale with Grandpa and Grandma who had become responsible for his education. For his secondary school education, Wale was sent off to boarding school, but he continued to spend a part of his school breaks at Dolphin Estate and the rest with us at home. At sixteen, he was as tall as Papa and had grown a scanty beard around his chin. I'd thought if he lived with us, somehow, he would be able to shield us from Papa's wrath when it rained down on us like fireballs. Or protect me on the days when Papa directed all his fury at me like a tsunami.

Mama was not dead; she just went to a faraway land, I kept reassuring myself. Did not the Yoruba teacher say that some people who died young often go to another city to start a new life? I forced myself to cry for the woman in the tomb, but there was still a big ball lodged in my throat. I blinked hard; and squeezed harder, hoping tears would run down my cheeks as they easily did on Lara's.

That night, after all the guests had left, I heard Lara crying in her bed. Laying in mine, on the top bunk, I gazed out of the window at the stars in the moonlit sky, wondering when Mama would return home.

FIVE

Present day

After three days of careful deliberations, I went to watch Nicolas play football on Wednesday evening.

The sun had gone down by the time I arrived in a taxi at the venue. Bright white halogen lamps illuminated the five-a-side pitch. The small stadium could take about five hundred people, but only three of us were there watching the match. The other two spectators, both male, sat several seats away, but close enough that I could hear them commenting on the game.

Behind us, Alfred Rewane Road was busy with rush hour traffic—okadas honked rudely, cars halted with sudden squeals of brakes and sirens shrieked as ambulances, cash-carrying bullion vans and convoys zoomed past. The air remained thick with the afternoon heat and from time to time, a pleasant breeze brushed past, bringing a little relief.

As the players ran up and down the field, I thought about Fola and wondered what he was doing. I wondered if he had friends at the university and if he played football with them. I wondered if he ever thought of the times we played together in the corridor of the flat using balloons because Papa forbade Mama from buying us footballs. We would collapse with laughter each time a balloon burst, before blowing air into another one.

I pulled my phone out of my handbag and sent him an SMS. 'Hello from Lagos. I'm thinking about you,' when what I wanted to write was, *Hello from Lagos. I miss you so much. I love you.*

In my family, we had never said or written that we missed each other, let alone that we loved each other. By the time the game was over, I still had not received a response from Fola. I'd dozed off a dozen times and mosquitoes had feasted on my legs.

After Nicolas introduced me to some of his friends who all called him *Nico*, we got into his SUV and headed to a small restaurant in Ikoyi. His car was as shiny on the inside as it was on the outside. It looked and smelled brand new. Riding in a 4X4 on Lagos roads was a luxury. Unlike with smaller cars, you didn't feel violated when you bumped up and down over speed bumps and potholes.

We talked about how our week was going during the short drive. Nicolas offered to compile a list of French Christmas songs I could teach the children to sing at the school's carol concert. When we arrived, he gave his driver, Moses, permission to take the car to get his own dinner.

The restaurant was small with a cosy bar. Sitting on the high bar stools, we both ordered the same thing—a chicken salad and a bottle of Malta Guinness.

"I liked hearing everyone call you Nico," I said, pouring a creamy mustard dressing over my salad.

He grinned. 'That's what I've always been called."

"I like it! Can I call you Nico too?"

His grin grew wider. "If you want."

Nico liked the Malta Guinness. It was his first time trying it. Through our meals, we didn't talk about ourselves. Instead, we talked about drinks, about how Nigerian women preferred Malta Guinness or Guinness Stout to wine and how Nigerians preferred champagne to the same. We chatted like old friends. And we both agreed the food was good. We smiled and laughed a lot. I liked talking to him in French. I loved his French accent. I could listen to him talk non-stop for hours and never get tired.

For dessert, he ordered a chocolate cake while I chose not to have any. We continued talking as he ate about French artists we both knew and French movies we'd both seen and loved. To anyone listening, they wouldn't have believed our friendship wasn't a week old.

"Ada and I get asked about speaking French a lot," I said to Nico after the couple sitting nearby asked if he and I were speaking French. "Many Nigerians love French, you know."

"I've noticed that too. Whenever I meet someone and they learn I'm French, they always ask me to say something in French." His eyes twinkled as he grinned. "I wish they would ask me to say something in Yoruba instead."

"Say something in Yoruba." I couldn't stop myself from grinning too.

"'Ok! Greetings. Ekaaro. Ekaasan. Ekuirole. Ekaale. Odaaro."

"Bravo!" I pretended to clap.

"Se daadaa ni. Salaafia. E se adupe. Alafia ni o."

"Well done!" I said, giving him a mock round of applause.

***

As we exited the restaurant, Nico offered to ask his driver to take me home. I declined, so he suggested dropping me off at the taxi park.

"I've enjoyed spending this evening with you," he said as Moses drove out into the street.

"Yes, me too." I adjusted in my seat, refusing to meet his gaze.

"It's like we've known each other for a very long time. I've never felt this way before with anyone."

I could feel all the blood rush to my face as my heartbeat quickened. I felt the connection, too. I liked the way we were so free with each other, with no off-limits. But I wasn't confessing all that to him.

I looked out of the window. There were only a few cars plying Bourdillon Road, heading towards Falomo. I glanced down at my phone, and my heart sank as I noticed there was still no reply from Fola.

When I sensed the car decelerating, I lifted my gaze. Through the windscreen, I saw oncoming vehicles on our lane, flashing their headlights at us. In the opposite lane, vehicles were speeding down the road.

Suddenly, there was a barrage of loud gunshots, as if multiple guns were being fired at once, though we couldn't see anyone shooting. Moses put the gear in reverse. Then he threw his right arm over the back of his seat and swivelled around to watch behind us as he sped in the direction we'd just come from, away from the spraying rounds of bullets. I was trembling, scared to death, my heart pounding loudly in my ears.

"Everything will be alright, Lami," Nico whispered, but his eyes were bulging and his Adam's apple bobbing.

Moses finally veered into a front gate and rapidly made a U-turn, brushing the curb. Then he flashed his lights, alerting the other drivers as he zoomed down Bourdillon Road.

My stomach churned, and I bit hard on my lips, trying not to throw up my dinner. I could feel the air conditioning drying the beads of sweat across my forehead. I glanced at Nico again. His gaze was fixated ahead. I didn't dare look back either, even though we couldn't hear the gunshots anymore. No one said a word as Moses drove on. I couldn't find my voice or bring myself to ask where we were going.

A few minutes later, we arrived at Banana Island and were let into the gated estate by guards in uniform. By then, my stomach had settled and my heartbeat had calmed. Moses rolled down his window to speak to one guard.

"We've just been radioed," the guard said. "Several armed men have set up a checkpoint at Falomo roundabout and are robbing car occupants and hijacking expensive vehicles at gunpoint"

"Has the police been informed?"

"Yes, but they probably don't have enough fuel in their vans to get there, or they're too scared to confront the robbers until they leave."

Moses thanked the guard for the information and started moving again, slowly cruising through the estate. I had no idea how to get home, how long the robbers would be operating, or whether the police would intervene.

Looking out the window, I processed the information, realising the danger we'd just escaped. I noticed the roads of the estate were perfectly paved—no loose stone, no pothole, not one litter. I'd heard so much about the man-made island but had never seen it for myself.

It had ultra-expensive houses, high-rise residential buildings and glass-facade office towers that were lit up by the big spotlights installed on their fences. Through the tinted glass, I observed the Island—the mansions that stretched for days, the limousines and vintage cars that looked to have been abandoned squatting by the roadside, and cleanly cut green lawns edged along the large sidewalks.

Instead of large *Beware of Dogs* signs, small *No Trespassing* warnings with the image of a security camera hung on their electric gates. Unlike the houses in Lekki Phase One that gave the impression the owners were imprisoned in luxury behind their high fences and fully covered tall gates, the mansions here ostentatiously flaunted their opulence through their low fences and see-through grill gates that made visitors like me green with envy.

When Moses drove up slowly to a compound with a series of tall identical buildings that looked like high-end residential complexes, I could tell we had arrived where Nico lived.

"You can spend the night at my place," Nico said as the wrought-iron gates opened electronically.

I nodded and then whispered my thanks, my first words since hearing the gunshots.

Moses drove down a long line of shiny SUVs in three colours—blacks, whites and greys. At the end of the parking lot, he found an empty spot and pulled into it, parking neatly in the row. I thanked him after he turned off the engine.

Suddenly, he threw his head back and started laughing. He laughed until I snapped out of the shock I'd slipped into. Nico broke into a smile and thanked Moses too, and then he complimented him on his Hollywood moves.

"Oga, I know no say I get them moves o," Moses joked back.

I got out of the vehicle right after Nico, only to realise he'd wanted to open the door for me. I hadn't been patient. Feeling a little silly, I walked by his side as he ambled to the entrance of one complex. Security cameras and movement sensors were installed everywhere. Still, there were security guards in uniforms posted by each entrance.

After I filled out the visitors' book at a desk where two guards sat, I followed Nico down the corridor to the elevators. A comfortable silence filled the elevator as we waited to arrive at the third floor. The inside of the elevator was large, lined with sparkling clean mirrors. Through the mirror on the doors, Nico seemed like we didn't just have a traumatic experience together. In my head, the gunshots continued to echo like the sound of firecrackers.

"Are you okay?" he asked, breaking the silence.

I nodded. "I was scared, but I feel better now."

"Me too," he admitted.

"Thank you for letting me stay at your place."

"It's nothing." He brushed it off as if we'd planned for me to spend the night there.

The elevator doors opened up to reveal two girls in beautiful dresses. They were both pretty in their light makeup, bone-straight hair, and caramel skin that seemed unfamiliar with the Nigerian sun.

"Hiii Nico!" the one wearing a sequined dress exclaimed. Her smile was bright and wide.

Nico exchanged smiles and greetings with her. She batted her eyes and called him Nico like they were more than neighbours. As we walked to his door, he told me she was the daughter of the Deputy Governor of Lagos State and her apartment was furnished with the most luxurious furniture he had seen since arriving in Nigeria. I couldn't tell if he liked her or if it was admiration I heard in his voice. But I understood she was in his league. Men like him dated girls like that, whose parents could afford to buy them luxury apartments in buildings and areas favoured by expatriates.

"She's very attractive," I said as he pushed his key into the lock.

He nodded and opened the door, holding it with one hand so I could go in before him. The fragrance in his apartment was unfamiliar. It smelt new and felt foreign. Since we drove into the compound, I'd been feeling as though I was no longer in Nigeria. The open-plan living room was spacious, with a sitting room corner on the right and a fully equipped kitchen on the left. A pool table lit up by recessed ceiling lights stood in the place where a dining table should be. Although I didn't like the idea of having the kitchen in the living room, I still thought his apartment was glamorous.

When he told me he would sleep on the sofa in the living room, I declined and told him I would prefer to sleep on the sofa. But he refused, saying I was his guest. He led me to his bedroom, that had an adjoining bathroom. It was big, spacious, and tidy. The walls were empty and unadorned, just like the rest of the flat.

There was a double-sized bed, neatly made in all-white beddings, that looked like it'd never been used. Opposite his bedroom was another room which was almost empty except for a big laundry basket, an ironing board and a wooden shelf stacked with Adidas and Nike football shoes. There were about a dozen or more of them in different colours. I'd never seen anyone person own so many football shoes.

***

After a quick shower, I tucked myself in bed, wearing Nico's grey pyjamas and taking in the freshness of the bedsheet.

I liked the large fluffy pillow; soft yet comfortable. Nico entered the room and made his way to the adjoining bathroom. As soon as he shut the door behind him, I checked my phone. Fola had still not replied. If I had died in the gunfire, would it have bothered him that he had missed an opportunity to speak to me for the last time? I'd received a message from Ada, so I immediately dialled her number.

"Bébé, where are you?" she said as soon as she answered the call.

"I can't come home tonight. There's a major robbery operation happening at Falomo roundabout."

"Jesus!"

"I'm safe. I'm with Nico. He says I can spend the night at his place."

"I was worried, wondering why you were yet to return." She yawned and promised to call back in the morning.

Nico came out of the bathroom, wearing light blue pyjamas. His wet hair clung to his head, making him look like a teenager. He sat on the edge of the bed and fell on his back with his hands behind his head. I wondered if he was thinking about how close he'd come to dying just because he'd offered to take me to the taxi park. After a long silence, I said, "One million euros for your thoughts."

He turned his head towards me, and I watched a smile play on his lips.

"I was thinking about when I was a child and my mum had to beg me every night to have my bath."

"Naughty boy," I teased, and his smile transformed into a grin and his dimples dug deeper. For the first time, I realised just how cute his dimples were.

"And you?" he said. "What are you thinking about? A million naira for your thoughts."

"I want euros, not naira." I stuck out the tip of my tongue.

He smiled again.

"I was thinking about my little brother, how close we used to be as children, and how far apart we've grown from each other now."

"I'm sorry to hear that. I'm an only child and I grew up feeling alone in a big house with a sizeable garden. In Brittany, it rains a lot, so I had to learn to play alone indoors. I remember wishing so much that I had a brother or sister."

We settled into another silence. I checked my phone to see if Fola had replied, but there was still no response from him. I noticed my battery was low.

"What's the craziest thing you've ever imagined?" he asked.

I glanced up from my phone and found him watching me with sparkling eyes.

"Let me think," I said, lifting my weight off the bed. I retrieved my phone charger from my handbag and found an electric outlet at his reading table. "There are times I dream about being born earlier." I nestled back into the bed, leaving my phone to charge by his reading table. "Especially during the times of Guy de Maupassant or Charles Aznavour. I'm crazy about French artists."

"Mmm... that is truly crazy,' he teased.

"You asked for crazy." I pulled my legs up underneath the duvet. "It's your turn! What's the craziest thing you've ever imagined?"

"Remaining a child all my life."

"If only." I put a hand over my mouth and murdered a yawn.

"What's your worst memory?"

I paused; the only audible sound was the ticking of the table clock.

"You go first," I finally said.

"But it's your turn." He sat up, turned to face me and folded his legs beneath him.

"I never talk about it," I said in a small voice, easing onto my back.

He crawled over the bed and came to lie on his side next to me. Then he reached out and squeezed my right hand, not letting go afterwards. In between us, there was enough space for a third person. Still, I could smell his natural musk.

"Tell me." His voice was low and soft, yet urging.

My hand remained limp in his as I resisted the urge to return the squeeze or move a finger. I wanted to tell him the story of the dark room, but my mind shut down quickly. I wanted to tell him about how ashamed I felt for not returning to Mama's grave since her funeral, but I couldn't. I feared he would wonder what kind of daughter I was to have abandoned my mother's grave for twelve years.

So instead, I told him about the last time I saw Mama alive. I stared at the white ceiling, fixating on its spotlights. When I started, it felt like it had happened centuries ago, but by the time I was done, it felt like it had happened only the day before. My throat constricted with unshed tears, yet my eyes remained dry.

"I didn't cry that day." My voice was raw with emotion. "I forced myself to, but I couldn't."

"Lami, I'm so sorry you and your family had to go through something so traumatic."

"It's OK," I said, forcing myself to sound normal.

He paused, his gaze not leaving me. I rolled from my back onto my side so we were facing each other.

"My grandmother died miserably," he finally said, and his eyes immediately grew sad.

I could tell that what he was about to tell me was something that made his heart bleed. He, too, had pain that wouldn't go away.

"I spent a lot of time with her at the hospital during her last days," he continued, still holding my gaze. "On the night she died, when we were alone, she shared a big secret with me. She said she didn't love her husband, my grandfather, and that she'd been unhappy her whole married life." He paused and pressed his lips together. His charming dimple deepened.

"When she was twenty-one, two men asked for her hand in marriage. One was French. He wasn't handsome; the other was Italian and charming. She chose the second. After they got married, she realised she'd lost her French nationality and was forced to take up her husband's Italian nationality. She said the day she was told she was no longer French, something died inside her. No one had thought it necessary to inform her. She could never look at her husband the same way again. Everything she once loved about him and found charming became all the things she hated, like his accent and his language. She said she felt like her homeland had disowned her and she regretted all her life not choosing the French suitor. She never forgave my grandfather, who made her a stranger in her own land, in the same village where she was born and raised. She refused to learn Italian because of this event."

"That's horrible," I said in a whisper.

"At that time, divorce was disapproved of, so when she told her parents she didn't love my grandpa anymore and wanted a divorce, she was reproached and forbidden to never speak about it again. Her mother told her no marriage is perfect so she must learn to make it work. But Grandpa loved her."

A gentle softness replaced the sadness in his eyes and voice. "He always showed it. We always knew she was unhappy, but we didn't know its source. Not even Grandpa himself. Grandma had two daughters and Grandpa was content, never for once missing not having a boy. On her hospital bed, Grandma told me she hated that she would die Italian because she had never felt Italian. She said she was French and had always remained French at heart. We wept together as she squeezed my hand. I never realised how deeply unhappy she'd always been. She died two days later." His voice broke with delicate emotions.

"I'm so sorry." I didn't know what more to say or how to console him.

Another silence loomed before he spoke again, saying, "Your turn."

His eyes watched my face as I ransacked my memory. I still wasn't ready to talk about the dark room, and I also didn't want to scare him away. Years had passed by and I'd never spoken about it, not even with Ada. My siblings and I never talked about it either. I didn't know what they thought of me being the black sheep of the family. I wasn't ready to share it with Nico. I wasn't prepared to traverse that valley, to unearth terrifying memories. I thought about telling him about the glowing supernal Yoruba King Mama had dreamt about before she died, but I didn't know if he would believe me or her.

"My grandparents died miserably too," I said, my gaze fixed on the joint where the wall met the ceiling. "My grandmother fell in the bathroom the day after we buried my mother. Neither she nor my grandfather were at the funeral. Had my Grandma been allowed to attend, perhaps she wouldn't have been knocked out by grief. Perhaps she would have been able to mourn her child and say her last goodbyes."

"Why wasn't she allowed?" He raised his upper body and propped himself up on one elbow.

I kept my eyes glued to the seam.

"Because our custom forbids parents to attend the burial of their children. My aunt explained to me that children aren't expected to be buried by their parents. If a child dies and the parents are still alive, they are forbidden to attend the funeral."

"Who then will do it?"

"Extended family members."

"And if they don't have relations?"

"Is that possible?" I met his eyes and our gaze locked. Sometimes his eyes looked golden, other times they looked green.

"Yes, in France it is. For such people, the Local Government takes care of their funeral and their properties go to the government."

"Oh! It's quite different in Africa. Well, I mean Nigeria because I don't know the whole of Africa."

"They must have been miserable not being allowed to go to their daughter's burial," he said, falling back on the pillow.

"It's the tradition and if they've been practising it for years, they probably won't see any reason to question it or look for a better way."

"That's true,' he said, turning to rest the back of his head against the pillow and putting his hands under his head. "I didn't think of it that way."

"I'm not for or against this tradition. I don't know what I would choose if I were in that situation."

"I would choose to go, to say my last goodbye," he said with certainty.

"I might choose to live in denial too," I said, then added in a whisper, "as I always do."

"Running changes nothing; it won't make it go away. Face it, challenge it, change it if you can, accept it if you can't."

I settled my head in the centre of the fluffy pillow. There was silence again, beautiful and peaceful. I welcomed its presence. I let myself think about Grandpa and Grandma. It seemed like centuries ago that Mama last drove us to Dolphin Estate to spend Boxing Day with them. All that was left of those very happy days were aromas—aromas of Grandpa's golden morn and chocolate drink and Grandma's stew. What would I not give to experience those days once again?

Sometime during the companionable silence that fell over Nico and me, I went to sleep. I woke up a couple of hours later and found Nico asleep beside me. Unlike me, he wasn't tucked into the duvet. He must have dozed off, too. The lamp was still on. I switched it off and immediately turned it back on again. The darkness was overwhelming. The thick window curtains prevented outside light from passing through.

I got off the bed quietly, switched on the lights in the bathroom, and left the door ajar. Then I climbed back into bed. Propping myself on my elbow, I watched Nico sleep. His face was peaceful. His long lashes fluttered lightly and his chest underneath his white t-shirt rose and fell. I was starting to like him too much, and it wasn't a good thing.

Although I knew he was nothing like Papa or my ex, I feared he could still hurt me. If he didn't do anything to hurt me, I knew I would get hurt badly when it would be time for him to leave Nigeria.

When my eyes became too heavy to stay open, I switched off the bedside lamp and slipped back into sleep's soothing respite.

***

It was pitch-black when I opened my eyes again. I tried to reach for the curtains above my head, but there was none; no window, just a wall—a very cold wall.

Desperate to see anything at all, I felt underneath my pillow, but couldn't find my phone anywhere. I jumped into a sitting position and tried to remember where I was. My memory was blurry and my eyes ached from straining to find the tiniest ray of light from any source. Hysterically, I screamed, "Oh my God, I'm blind, I'm blind." I pushed away the covers and got out of bed.

"Lami?" It was Nico.

He was standing silhouetted against the dim light in the hall. He switched on the bedroom light and I squinted as he walked over to the bed. We stood in similar pyjamas, staring at each other.

"I'm fine now," I said, unable to meet his eyes.

I felt ashamed for having acted like I was crazy. With my heart still racing, I walked past him into the adjoining bathroom to wash my face. I hoped he would have gone back to sleep by the time I came out, so I didn't have to explain my actions.

As a child, I'd hated the Saturday morning hair-wash sessions Mama set aside for Lara and me. I couldn't keep my eyes closed for more than a few seconds without being overpowered by an impulsive urge to verify that I hadn't lost my sight while they were closed. I would wail all through the ordeal and leave my eyes open as shampoo ran down my face.

"Who are you afraid of?" Mama would ask. "Who is coming to get you while I'm here? Am I not your eyes when yours are closed?" Other times, she would say, "No monsters will come and get you while I'm here. Don't you trust me enough to protect you?" But she never did understand that I wasn't merely afraid of the dark and monsters. I was also afraid of going blind. I was terrified that while my eyes were closed, I could lose my sight without realising it, without knowing the exact moment it happened.

This phobia lived in me and I'd never told anyone about why I became hysteric whenever I found myself in pitch-black darkness or how it all started. There was no one I trusted enough to confide in, not even Mama.

Growing up, she always told me the story of how I caught measles when I was a baby and nearly died. She told me of how doctors had said that I would go blind and that there was nothing that could be done to reverse the damage. Papa went and sought help from traditional healers who treated me with herbs and restored my sight. I've heard Mama tell this story several times. Papa, too, had told it repeatedly. His voice was always loud and boastful; the pride in his tone demanded gratitude for his saving gesture.

"If not for me and Baba, by now, you would have been rendered useless. You would have been of no use to yourself or anyone," Papa would say.

What Mama didn't know was that with each telling of this story, my fears of going blind grew bigger and bigger, and after Papa began locking me up in the darkroom, my fear of pitch-black darkness became worse and worse.

I returned to the bedroom to find that Nico was still there, sitting at the edge of the bed. I couldn't shake off my shame at the state of extreme panic he'd found me in, crying and shouting like I had gone stark, raving mad. Once again, I left the bathroom lights on and the door slightly ajar. Then I disconnected my phone from the electric socket while scolding myself in my head. The screen came on. It was 3:15 am. If I'd had my phone with me, I wouldn't have embarrassed myself.

"Do you feel better?" Nico asked, getting up.

I nodded and climbed back into bed. He stood there, hands in his pyjama pockets, looking down at me as if he had questions he was restraining himself from asking. He turned the lights off when he left the room and I lay there for a long time, staring at the light spilling into the room from the bathroom.

Never in my life had I felt so embarrassed.

I had demons, and I'd done well all these years to hide them from people except for one lone incident while I was at the university that had shocked my roommates out of their sleep. I'd woken up in the middle of the night at the hostel and my hysteria had surpassed my astonishment at the intensity of the darkness in the room.

"I'm blind. I'm blind. Help me, please," I'd shouted that night at the hostel, waking up the seven other girls in the room.

I apologised and blamed it on hallucination from the malaria drugs the university doctor had given me for the fever that had kept me in bed for days. I remember one girl saying, "For a moment, I thought you were possessed."

I'd been extremely careful since then to avoid a repeat in public. I always tried to be prepared and never allowed myself to be caught when I would find myself in complete darkness. I'd told myself that I had to learn to manage it. It was my cross, a curse Papa had left me with. Still, I had the best set of eyes in the family. I didn't need glasses like my parents, Wale and Lara, and I was the one Mama called on every time she needed to thread a needle.

Trying to rock myself to sleep, I banned every memory of how the fear first came and settled before it began feeding on other fears and growing into a monster that I could no longer dislodge.

In the morning, as I prepared to leave Nico's apartment, he asked me to have lunch with him on Saturday before his flight to Paris later in the evening. I agreed, knowing very well that once I walked out of his front door, he would never see me again.

I couldn't look him in the eyes as I thanked him for allowing me to spend the night at his apartment. My gaze was fleeting. My smile forced. In my mind, I wondered why he wanted to see me again after the madness I'd displayed.

I was glad he was going to spend December in Paris. It would be easy to cut him off. I would stop picking up his calls and replying to his text messages. By the time he would return to Lagos in January, I would be nothing but a distant memory, I hoped.

SIX

Past

The first Christmas after Mama died was different from all the others.

Mama always wanted to make Christmas memorable and comparable with those our friends had. Papa didn't care for memories.

Normally, after the 20th of December every year, Mama would put up the Christmas tree and then set up the Christmas crèche scene with Mary and Joseph. She always lets us help her decorate the tree with colourful ornaments and lights. Wale would have arrived to spend the holiday with us, bringing with him presents from Mama's family. We would spread them out at the foot of the tree with those Mama got us.

On the 24th of December, we would attend the Christmas Eve Midnight Mass at Saint Dominic and still return there on Christmas morning. But the second time, we would be wearing new clothes and shoes. Papa would be home sleeping when we left for morning Mass and would be gone by the time we returned.

After church, Mama would add baby Jesus to the manger and then spend the afternoon cooking different types of rice—jollof, fried and coconut. She would fry beef and chicken, make fish stew and vegetable soup, fry chin-chins and puff-puffs, and bake a big cake with red, white and green dressing. When she was done, she would send Lara and me with plates of food and drinks in baskets to our neighbours.

After making the rounds, Lara and I would sit and count our tips. I always got more tips and Mama would say to Lara, "Can you see why you should stop frowning and learn to smile like Lami? With her smile, she can sell ice to the Eskimos, but you, with your unsmiling face, you can't sell drugs to a dying man."

On Boxing Day, we would open our presents first thing in the morning. Breakfast would come from the goodies in the hampers that Mama and Papa had received as gifts. In the afternoons, we would leave for Dolphin Estate and spend the rest of the day there. We would cram ourselves into Mama's small Toyota Starlet car and the journey would start. There was always something about leaving the mainland to cross over to the island.

As Mama sped across the long bridge, I felt as though I was leaving the past and heading into the future. When I smelt the odour of Makoko, it meant that we were halfway to our destination. From a distance, the floating village smelt of freshly cut wood, burning sawdust, and smoked fish. The mélange of odours would permeate the breeze that blasted into our car, filling up my nostrils and whipping my hair in my face. As Please Don't Go by KC and the Sunshine Band blared out of the car stereo, I would sing at the top of my lungs alongside Mama, and my mind would become a camera, capturing the beautiful moment and saving it up for gloomy days.

For us, going to Dolphin Estate was like going on holiday. It meant that we would watch the same old movies we saw every time we visited: Home Alone, Annie and Monkey Trouble. It didn't matter how many times we had seen them; they always felt special on Boxing Day.

Grandpa would make us hot chocolate drinks with Golden Morn cereal, and the smell of Grandma's delicious stew would fill our noses and make our tummy growl like hungry little monsters. Aunty Jire would take us to see the baboon on Isolo Street so that we could feed it, and Uncle Kay would fill our pockets with Choco Milo cubes and Éclairs chocolate candies when it was time for us to head back home.

***

The first Christmas without Mama, Wale didn't come home for the holiday and we didn't attend Christmas Eve Midnight Mass or Christmas Morning Mass.

Papa returned the night before Christmas. He was sober, and he didn't leave the house on Christmas morning. He'd bought a redhead cock two weeks earlier because it was cheaper. Fola and I fed it several times daily. We named it Billy and spent a lot of time with it on the balcony behind the flat.

On Christmas morning, Papa decided that it was time for Fola to become a man by killing the cock. Lara washed some rice in a bowl and put it in a sieve. Then she waited for the tomato broth to boil so she could pour the rice in. I'd just finished slicing onions and tomatoes for the jollof rice when I approached the sink to watch Fola struggling to pin the cock down.

"Cut the neck," Papa ordered Fola as he helped to hold the cock's legs down against the sink.

I moved closer to see Billy one more time before he ended up in the pot. To my surprise, Fola didn't seem to tremble at the thought of killing Billy. He held the cock's neck in one hand and a knife in the other hand. Then he used the sharp edge of the knife to part the feathers around the neck so that he could see the skin. Billy had stopped fighting; it was a sign of powerlessness, of acceptance of the inevitable and defeat. I saw myself lying on that zinc in the place of Billy, helpless—recognising that there had been injustice, accepting what life had dealt me and knowing that there was nothing I could do to make Mama return home.

"Ó mà se ò," I said sadly, shaking my head.

A loud deafening slap landed hard across my face before I comprehended that I'd thought aloud. The force sent my head to one side and my ears rang. I lifted my hand to my burning cheek and wailed.

"Ó mà se ò? You idiot," Papa thundered. "As if you will not eat it when it is ready. Get out of my sight, my friend."

Although I was dazed by the slap, I could see the dangerous rage in his eyes that made them red.

"Just look at her? Tearless girl!" I heard him say as I hurried out of the kitchen and down the corridor before he could decide to pounce on me.

As I sat on the edge of Lara's bed, watching sleeping Tutu through her cot's bars, I touched my burning cheek. The skin felt raw. A lump formed in my throat as I wondered when exactly Mama would return home. I squeezed my eyes and put spittle on my lids, tracing lines down my cheeks. I could hear Papa growling and barking orders at Lara and Fola.

When Tutu awoke, I was happy to bathe and dress her. This took me out of Papa's presence and offered me fragile moments of solace and tenderness. I didn't want to be in the kitchen with him, where he was prowling around like a giant looking for someone to trample upon.

By the time lunch was ready at 3:00 pm, I was trembling from not having had breakfast. Papa decided we would all eat at the table as a family. But how could we be a family when Mama was missing and so was Wale? Papa said nothing when Lara placed a piece of chicken on my rice. I stole a glance at him and saw that he was watching me.

"Thank you, Papa," I said. Then I saw his chest and shoulders deflate as though someone had punctured them to let go of budding anger.

We ate in silence, our eyes fixed on the plates of jollof rice before us. When Papa drank, the sound of water running down his throat went gluck gluck gluck. Even the sound Tutu made as she sucked the stew from the chicken seemed too loud.

"I want some more rice," Fola announced suddenly.

I wondered if he was talking to Lara or Papa. Lara looked up at Papa, who then said, "My child, the question I have for you is, have you eaten and not are you full?"—and that settled everything. Lara's eyes returned to her plate. Fola stared at the rest of the rice in the big pot. I looked down at my plate and pretended to chew on my rice. Fear still wouldn't let me touch my chicken.

After what seemed like forever, Papa belched loudly and left the table. We heaved a sigh of relief. Only Tutu was herself before and behind Papa; she seemed immune to his wrath. I gave Fola some of my rice and could finally eat my chicken.

After lunch, Lara and I cleared the table. While she hand-washed the dishes, I rinsed them. We didn't say a word to each other. She hadn't said more than ten sentences to me all day. As usual, she was stuck in her world. I was lost in mine too, but unlike her, I wanted to get out. I didn't want to be there, lonely in a world filled with people.

***

Papa was in a better mood on Boxing Day. Christmas had come and gone. We filled the refrigerator and the kitchen with food, drinks and gifts from neighbours and family friends.

We received more food than all the other years. Pity must have triggered it—sympathy for children who had recently lost their mother. We gave nothing out that year. They must have understood that we couldn't return their gesture.

Papa decided we would have breakfast, but first, we had to brush our teeth the traditional way—by chewing pákò, even though we had toothpaste. He said that Fola's teeth were yellowing and that chewing-stick sessions would make them white again.

"Your mother has spoilt you children with toothpaste," he'd said with utter disgust as he gripped Fola's jaw and forced his chin up to observe his teeth.

Afterwards, he gave us each a chewing stick and asked us to brush our teeth before him. Fola contorted his face at the bitter taste of the stick when it touched his tongue. Standing beside him, I shut my eyes as I chewed one end of the pákò to make it soft before brushing with it. Papa stood at the basin in front of the mirror. The flab of his upper arm dangled with his quick movements as he brushed his teeth. Lara was in a rebellious mood that morning. She left the bathroom where we were all brushing and didn't return in time.

"Where are you, Omolara?" Papa shouted after several minutes had passed.

"Sir," she answered from the kitchen. She arrived a little while later, wearing one of her scariest scowls.

"I'm here," she said grumpily.

The sickly smell of trouble was by now thick in the air. I felt my heart tremble in my chest. I gripped my cup tighter so that I wouldn't spill any water because this could make Papa's anger shift from Lara's lane to mine.

"Where were you?" Papa asked.

"In the kitchen," Lara replied.

"In the kitchen doing what?" Papa shouted.

I turned to look at Fola, who continued to brush and act like his life depended on it. Then I turned again to Lara and found her pouting—her lips were protruding exaggeratedly in defiance. Since when did we get mad at Papa and show it so fearlessly?

"What were you doing?" Papa's voice was louder, her silence igniting his anger.

She took a few steps forward and took her position again in front of the bathtub beside me. With the stick in her mouth, she said, "I went to scrape off the back of my—"

Papa stretched out his arm and slapped her on the back before she finished talking. The scraped stick flew out of her hand and landed in the tub. She held on to the edge so that she didn't fall in. Fola and I shifted quickly to the other end of the bathroom.

"Pick up that pákò now and start brushing. God has saved you this morning that you did not scrape all the skin out. I would have pounced on you," he said, before storming out of the bathroom.

Afterwards, Fola and I spat simultaneously into the bathtub. Lara moved to the basin and rinsed her pákò before putting it back in her mouth. While Fola rinsed off the tub using the hand-held shower, he poured some water on my soiled hands so I could rinse them, too. Some of the water splashed on my feet, so I sprinkled water on his face in revenge. We burst out laughing and then turned to look at Lara. She was brushing in fast and furious movements. Her eyebrows were pressed together and in between, deep creases appeared. I feared that her gums would bleed.

Lara and I made eggs for breakfast. Papa decided we would say a prayer before eating. He shut his eyes and prayed in Yoruba. His voice was calm and tinctured with the utmost respect—a rare variant he used when speaking to elders. There was no trace of anger or infusion of pride, only genuine humility.

From time to time; I cracked my eyes open and stole glances at him. The prayer was long. My stomach gurgled. I heard Fola's too. I shut my eyes when the prayers seemed to approach the end. It wasn't a good day to make Papa remember things about me he couldn't stand. When he finished praying and we all opened our eyes, Tutu had already finished her egg. Papa was miffed. He slapped her oily fingers.

"No one will make you another egg," he roared. "You will eat your bread with tea only."

Tutu began to cry. Papa asked her to hold her lips, as he didn't want to hear a single sound. My heart yearned to hold her, clean her tears and runny nose, and give her a part of my egg, but I didn't dare move.

The rest of the morning was extremely quiet; Lara and I exchanged a few words. In the afternoon, Lara made jollof spaghetti. Papa didn't have lunch with us. He had to be somewhere and had said he'd eat when he returned. He came back some three hours later and asked Lara to serve him his late lunch in front of the TV in the living room.

We were all in the girl's room when the sound of Papa's bell started, causing my heartbeat to accelerate. After the second ring, I prayed harder that it stopped there. When the next one didn't come, Lara got up. I was about to say a thank you prayer when I remembered that God doesn't answer my prayers and that it was nothing but a mere coincidence. Fola and I decided to follow Lara, but we stopped at the door so that we could hear what Papa had to say.

"Did you put bouillon cubes in the food?" Papa shouted.

I didn't hear Lara's response.

"Did I or did I not tell you that you shouldn't cook with them in this house? Where did you get the money from?"

"It's my money," Lara replied, her voice slightly raised.

"How many times have I told you not to cook with bouillon cubes in my house?"

"Plenty times, Papa," she replied, but she didn't sound sorry. She sounded like she didn't care and had had enough of him.

"Yet you defied me? Have I not told you that it is all these artificial seasonings and spices your mother cooked with that killed her? Do you want me to get cancer, too?"

"Bouillon cubes didn't kill Mama. She died from your cigarette fumes," Lara retorted, her voice thick with disdain. Her chest rose and fell rapidly with words that wanted to burst out. Her breasts poked through the top she wore and I wondered if this was what made her bold to defy Papa.

A frightening silence followed. It lasted many seconds. Papa must have been dazed like I was. Had Lara gone nuts? Had she said that or was it the rebellious spirit that had inhabited her since that morning? I trembled as though it was I that trouble had located and not Lara.

"What do you mean by that?" I heard Papa finally say. He seemed to have got to his feet. "Are you saying I killed your mother? Are you calling me a murderer? If my cigarette fumes killed her, why am I still alive?"

"I don't know o," Lara replied rudely.

She took some steps back until we could see her through the door. She looked like she was going to run down the corridor if Papa came close and tried to hit her. Fola and I took refuge in the kitchen, peeping and ducking behind the wall.

"You will not talk to me in that tone in my house," Papa said in a loud voice filled with anger. 'You will leave my house if you do not want to respect me.'

"And I will leave," Lara replied, her angry tone matching Papa's and sounding like Mama's.

At this stage, Fola and I decided that we'd heard enough. We made for the corridor and dashed into our separate rooms. I was clambering up the little wooden ladder into the upper bunk bed where I slept when Lara opened the door with so much force that it hit the chest of drawers.

Tutu, who had been sleeping in her cot, woke up with a fright. Lara walked to the centre of the room and turned around swiftly to face the door. Her hand was on her waist as she tapped her foot against the floor, waiting. She was like a warrior who had just struck her enemy down; now she was watching to see if he would get up.

She looked different—older and taller than usual as she held her back straight and her shoulders high. I feared her; I feared for her; I admired her. I would never have had the courage to face Papa. Soon the half-open door was flung wide again. Once more, it hit the chest of drawers. This time, bottles of lotions, oils, and perfumes fell over. Tutu began to cry.

"Did you walk out on me?" Papa asked. Breathless with fury, his chest, shoulders and belly heaved up and down as if he had just carried something heavy up the stairs. "I will send you out of my house if you will not respect me. This is my house. I pay the bills," he shouted.

I saw the fire in his eyes burn, but that which I saw in Lara's burned brighter. They glared at each other. Papa looked like he was struggling for control while Lara looked like she was ready for him, for anything he would bring on. I feared that if Papa hit her, she would hit him back, and then he would beat her and break every bone in her body. But that day, Papa wasn't Papa. His nose flared; his jaw clenched but his hands were slow to violence. It was strange. I cringed in my bed, afraid that he would notice me, and that somehow, the raging fire Lara had started would burn me as well.

Papa walked over to Lara's bed. She stepped back towards Tutu's cot. Papa pulled off her bedsheet angrily and threw it on the floor. When he pulled the door on Lara's side of the wardrobe, it was locked. So, he threw his shoulder against it and kicked it hard several times until the door finally gave way. Then he began to pack the clothes in each drawer and dump them on the bedsheet.

"I'm taking you to Dolphin Estate this afternoon," he said, panting. "You and I cannot stay under the same roof."

When he'd finished, he tied the bed sheet using its corners. He looked up at Lara, pushed his glasses into place, and said, "Pack your books and other things. If I come out of my room and you're not ready, I'll drag you to the car." Then he stormed out of our room with her clothes. Tutu was no longer crying. I couldn't tell when she stopped. She sat on her cot, her bright eyes shining as she sucked on her thumb.

Lara picked up her school bag and emptied the study desk. She uncovered her pillow and put her books into the pillowcase. I wondered if she'd planned it all; if she'd woken up that morning and decided to provoke Papa as an excuse to move to Dolphin Estate. She picked up the brick game and then put it back in the drawer.

"You can take it with you," I said softly from where I was hiding in my bed. "I hardly play with it and if I want to, I'll play with Fola's."

Lara didn't say a word to me. She threw the brick game and her Michael Jackson cassette tapes into the pillowcase, and then she sat at the desk and emptied the drawers. It was the last time she sat at the desk and it was that last memory of her in our room that stayed with me the longest.

Every time I thought of her, I'd see her at the desk, back hunched over, head dropped as if remorseful. I wondered if she didn't plan it after all. Tutu started crying again. I climbed down from the bunk bed and reached into her cot to pick her up. I rubbed her back until she was calm and sucking on her thumb again. Fola was sitting on his bed; the door of his room was wide open. He had his elbows on his thighs and his hands clasped together. He looked helpless, almost as if he was about to cry.

"Do you want to go?" I asked Lara in a tiny voice. I wasn't sure if she'd heard me until after she stopped packing.

"He hates me because I was always defending Mama while she was sick and unable to defend herself," she finally said.

I nodded in agreement. "But do you want to go?"

"I can't stay here anymore. He can't stand the fact that I look like Mama."

"But I look like Mama too," I protested weakly.

I was feeling sorry for myself, sorry that if Lara left, I would be the oldest, with more responsibility than I wasn't ready for. I was sorry that I would be more exposed to Papa's anger. I was sorry that there would be no one to protect me and I couldn't protect myself.

"I look more like her," Lara challenged. "I have her nose, her hair and her skin colour."

I didn't say anything further. I didn't want to argue with her; I didn't want to get her more upset. I didn't want her to go; I didn't want to say goodbye. Although she often kept to herself and said very little; although we didn't have much in common, I knew that I would miss her silence.

Fola walked quietly into our room, his hands in the pocket of his shorts. He stood by Tutu's cot and stood beside it. After a while, he moved to the window that overlooked the neighbour's compound. He had his back to Lara as she removed all her stuff from the chest of drawers.

"Omolara, get out here," Papa yelled.

"If there's anything I've forgotten, bring it to school," Lara said to me.

I put Tutu back in her cot and walked towards Lara, wondering if I could hug her. She took a moment to get a last glimpse of Tutu before heading towards the door. She didn't hug any of us and no one cried.

"Kiss grandma, grandpa, Uncle Kay and Aunty Jire for me," I said as she stepped out of the room.

I wanted to say, "Lara, I love you," but a big lump had formed in my throat, trapping the words in. I looked at Fola; his eyes had turned very red. I could tell that he, too, was resisting the urge to cry.

We both stepped out of the room so that we could watch Lara leave. We found Papa was standing in front of the bathroom door. Lara walked past him and down the corridor with her schoolbag on her back. She had her pillowcase in one hand and a plastic bag in the other. Her back was straight again—stiff and proud; her shoulders were high and her head was up. She didn't turn to look in our direction for a last glance before stepping out of the flat.

After they left, Fola and I sat on Lara's bare mattress. We were both in shock and still couldn't believe that Lara would now live far away in Dolphin Estate. I stared at Tutu's cot. What would I tell her about Lara when she asked? What would everyone in Dolphin say when they saw Lara arrive with all her belongings? I thought about Wale and wondered if he still wanted to come live at home. I wondered also if Fola too wanted to go to live in Dolphin, but I didn't dare ask him. I was afraid that he, too, would try to rebel so that Papa would send him away. Rebellion to leave... It was something I would never have had the courage to do.

That night, lying on my bed, knowing that Lara wasn't on hers, I put a hand over my mouth and sobbed silently. Tutu, who was in her cot, playing with her bunny rabbit. It was the first time I had cried since Uncle Kay came to announce to us that Mama had died.

Moonlight spilt into the room between the louvres of the two windows. Mama had tied the curtains in knots to keep them off the floor and the room illuminated during the night so that it was never too dark for me. I missed Mama so much. I wanted to feel her hands around me. I missed Lara too—the silence of her presence, the quietness of her actions, and the beauty of her calmness.

Mucus ran down my upper lip and saliva down my chin, but my eyes were dry; as dry as the red sand of Igando under the blazing Lagos sun.

My throat ached. My heart felt heavy with pain I couldn't dissolve into tears. To console myself, I repeated over and over that I would see Lara again once school resumed.

SEVEN

Present day

December passed quickly, and schools soon closed. A few days before Christmas, Lagos emptied as people travelled for the holidays. With each day that passed, the ever-so-noisy city grew quieter. Ada left Lagos for Lome on the 23rd to stay with her mother. She wanted me to come with her, but I had too much to do here: I wanted to work on my Master's degree applications.

Christmas day was as lonely as the previous one. I'd hardly slept the night before. I had a nightmare. Over Christmas, my nightmares had always been the most persistent.

I would dream about Papa and Mama Jide pulling Tutu away from me while I held on to her wrist as tightly as I could. I also dreamt of Papa ringing his bell and stopping on the third peal, of him walking down the long corridor with a bamboo cane in his hand and his slippers making loud scuffling noises.

I had multiple nightmares about the dark room. The darkness would be so thick and palpable that it seemed to envelop me. When I awoke, screaming, gasping for breath and covered in sweat, my palms would be so swollen and painful that I could not fold my fingers. A sickening feeling always followed me into reality from those nightmares—a horrible feeling of having one's heart snatched out.

Sunlight pouring through the window woke me up around noon, warming me up in my cotton pyjamas. I listened to the dogs in the next compound, scraping the ground with their claws as they paced impatiently. I liked it when they weren't barking loudly to greet their owners, or at the sight of visitors. I reached for my phone and read through the Christmas greetings that were flooding in. Then I sent Wale, Lara and Fola Christmas and New Year good wishes, even though I always got the same kind of responses each year.

"Same to you," Lara replied some minutes later.

"Thanks!" Fola simply wrote a few hours later.

When Wale's message remained unread by the day's end, I understood that he was offshore, working through the holiday.

The rest of the holiday passed slowly for me. Every day, I worked on my Master's degree applications. Bordeaux, Strasbourg and Grenoble were my three top choices. I also spent time preparing interesting study plans for French Culture classes. The Culture class on Fridays was less serious and more fun than the Reading, comprehension, composition or grammar classes. For companionship, I had the voices from the TV in the background and the German Shepherds next door who sometimes sniffed the ground loudly. Sometimes, the dogs panted heavily; other times, they growled menacingly.

Although Ada and I texted back and forth throughout the day, I still longed for her company. I could have had a life with many friends if I had wanted to. Back at the university, many of my classmates had tried to get close to me. Many of the other teachers at the school where I worked had also tried to become more than colleagues, but I'd been unable to socialise with them outside the school premises. Tutoring on Saturdays, as well as giving extra classes during the long holiday, didn't allow me to commit to more than one friendship. Ada was three-in-one, a flatmate, a friend and a sister, and even that relationship had begun to seem like it was suffering from a lack of attention.

On New Year's Eve, I spent the entire day in bed, drifting in and out of sleep. The night before, I'd had another recurring nightmare. I couldn't go back to sleep for hours. Gazing at the light from the security lamp reflecting on the wardrobe opposite the window, I plunged into the past, digging through my memories, replaying active ones and struggling to revive dormant ones until the sunup.

One of the called-up childhood memories that'd stayed with me the longest was of me and Mama dancing to Des'ree's, *You Gotta Be*. There was me, jumping up and down holding hands with Mama while Tutu swayed on the bed, wearing just a t-shirt and diaper, her hands up in the air, begging to be carried. Mama picked her up, swung her around, and threw her onto the bed. Then I grabbed her, placed my mouth over her navel and blew some air on it, making loud farting sounds. She laughed aloud until tears ran down the sides of her face. The sound of her cute baby laughs made even Lara smile.

New Year was as quiet as every other day since the holiday started. I slept in and lazed around in bed, enjoying my last free weekend before life returned to normal. Daylight flooded the room in abundance, lighting the colours in the room cheerfully—colourful curtains, carpet, and bedsheet. Whenever I awoke to colours and sunshine, all layers of gloom in my heart would fade away.

Lying there, I listened to Lekki in its temporary silence. It was as though life was on pause. Just as the city awaited the return of its holidaymakers, I looked forward to Ada's return from Lomé.

On Sunday evening, Ada returned to Lagos, looking refreshed and sporting a new hairstyle called *One Million Braids*, which she pulled into a ponytail at the back of her head.

"Ma copine!" she cried as she burst into my room. "I've missed you so much!"

I smiled, dropping the novel I was reading on the bed as she rushed to my bedside. She covered my face with kisses and I giggled as I tried to dodge her. I'd missed her craziness.

"How long did that take?" I asked, referring to her tiny braids. I was still in my pyjamas and the dish I'd eaten my lunch from was still on my bedside table.

"They started at 9:00 am and finished at 4:00 pm. Three people." She raised three fingers.

I picked up the remote and muted the TV. *Gamin* was playing on a French channel on DStv and I'd seen it half a dozen times.

Ada sat down next to me on the bed and handed me a wrapped aluminium foil. I knew what it was before I un-foiled it. She always returned from Lome with raw, unadulterated shea butter for me, handmade by one of her aunts who exported it to Belgium.

"My scalp is thanking you for this." I sat up and kissed her on the cheek.

Her eyes moved to my hair. "They aren't looking bad. You've improved."

She was referring to my self-made braids. The big box braids had taken me two days to finish. She grabbed the butter off my hand and motioned me to come to sit on the floor between her legs. Then she slathers my scalp with Shea butter while telling me all about her holiday. Her mother and aunt had harassed her daily, asking her to bring a man home. They'd constantly reminded her of her unmarried state, of girls her age who were married, the actual year each one got married, and the number of children they already had.

"Why didn't you just tell them about Andrew?" I asked.

"It's too early, ma Cherie. What if it doesn't work out between us in the end?" She worried that Andrew's parents may not want him to marry her because she was only half-Igbo and couldn't speak the language very well. "They'll want him to marry a full Igbo girl. There's no point presenting him and getting my mother's hopes high."

I nodded in understanding, but in my mind, I was wishing Mama was alive and pestering me to bring a man home. We talked about my MA applications and then about what to cook for dinner.

"Merci, babe," I said, looking in the mirror at the shiny butter on my scalp.

She rose and came to stand beside me, checking out her butt. She was wearing a grey tank top and dark blue fitted jeans. Then she suddenly started swaying her hips sensually from side to side, her reflection in the mirror capturing her movements as she sang D'banj's *Scapegoat*.

"You're feeling your new jeans," I said.

"Shey, my bum is not too flat in this skirt?" She ceased her dance and arched her head backwards to glimpse her buttocks.

"No, but I can tell that you're wearing something to pad it up."

"It's not so obvious." She patted her butt as if to pump up her confidence.

"Babe, you're beautiful, bum or not."

"You're pretty too." She smiled and flashed me a smile in the mirror. "Come, let's go to Shoprite for groceries."

"No, no." I shook my head and hurried to the bed, hiding under the bedcovers.

"Aren't you happy that I'm back, bébé?"

"Of course I am."

"I doubt it." She threw the sheets back.

I curled up.

"You've been strange lately. You don't want to go out and meet people. You stay home all the time watching the same old movie. I know you well enough to know something is wrong."

I stared at her. "It's nothing important."

She climbed into my bed and nestled down next to me. I observed the ceiling light like it was my first time seeing it.

"Tell me," she said gently.

I could feel her staring at me. I turned to face her. Our gaze met. Her shaped brows were raised high, urging me to confide in her.

"It's just that since we buried my mother, I've still not returned to her grave. I don't even know the colour of its headstone."

"I'll go with you if you want to visit her grave."

"We buried her at the Ikoyi Cemetery." I held her gaze. "I remember the entrance to her gravesite is on the same side as Dodan Barracks, but I have no idea where exactly her tomb is."

"Wait," she said, pausing as if in thought. "I know a colleague who pays a security guard at this same cemetery to weed his father's tomb. I can ask him to check with the guard if he can find your mother's tomb."

I nodded, even though I didn't feel ready to return to the cemetery. I felt myself beginning to unfurl as memories of the last time I was at the cemetery surfaced in my mind.

***

January passed quickly. Long days wore into short nights that gave way to humid dawns, only to resume the circle at sunrise. My weeks resembled each other like a recurrent dream. Daily, I looked forward to finding university correspondence in the letterbox while dreading having to return to Mama's grave. I didn't know how to tell Ada that I wasn't ready to return to the cemetery just yet. I needed more time. I had until July when I would be going to France for my studies to go and see her. There was no need to rush the visit. I needed to first think about what I wanted to say to Mama when I did finally visit her.

One evening as I was heading home, I saw Nico's black SUV through the vertical bar steel of the gate as it pulled up in front of the school. I spun around and went to hide behind the auditorium, from where I watched Nico speak to the guards sitting at the security post.

One of them rose and went in. He put the phone to his ear and stared up at the TV screen hanging from the low ceiling. I could tell that he was calling the language class. I watched him hang up the phone and return to speak to Nico. I imagined him telling Nico to call my mobile phone, but I'd been ignoring his calls and messages since December. Ten minutes after the SUV had left, I finally stepped out from my hiding place. The two men at the gate immediately began arguing when they saw me.

"You see, I tell you say I never see her waka pass," one of them said.

"Please always tell him I've already left the school whenever he comes looking for me," I said after they'd given me Nico's message. I sincerely hoped that he would forget me.

A few buildings away from the school, I flagged down an okada rider, gave him my address and fastened the helmet he gave me. Akin Adesola Street was congested with after-work traffic. I bumped up and down at the back of the driver who manoeuvred between pedestrians crossing, weaving in and out between cars, swerving at the sound of sirens from police escort vans and going over speed bumps. In front of my building, I paid him, giving him extra for his mad skills and for getting me home safely.

Ada was watching TV when I entered the flat. The room was lit only by the flickering light of the screen. The aroma of the food caused my stomach to rumble, and my mouth to salivate.

"Bébé, I've got good news," she said after I'd locked the door.

"Yes?" I stepped closer to where she was sitting.

"My colleague gave me the security guard's number, so I went straight to the cemetery from the office to talk to him."

I dropped next to her on the sofa and remained speechless for many seconds as the image of the woman in the coffin appeared before my eyes. I shook my head in an attempt to make the image disappear, but it persisted with vicious clarity.

"You already went there?" I finally managed.

"Yes, I gave him your mother's name and my number. He'll call me when he finds it."

"I thought you would let me know first before…"

"Have I done wrong?" Her eyes searched mine.

I opened my mouth but closed it without saying anything.

"I thought you were ready when you gave me her name."

"I'm ready," I said unconvincingly and thanked her.

The news should have made me happy, but I carried it like a heavy burden upon my heart. By the time I sat down to eat, I was no longer hungry. After a few swallows of the yellow garri and oha soup, I started to feel nauseous. I cleared up my unfinished dinner and went into my room, where I crawled and curled up under the covers. My stomach fluttered with anxiety as I lay thinking about returning to Mama's grave. I didn't feel ready to go and see the woman that I'd rejected, the one who I'd begun having difficulty remembering what she looked like when she was healthy.

I hadn't stepped into any cemetery since Mama was buried. I never attended burial ceremonies, not even grandma's or grandpa's. I didn't like hospitals either, or anything that reminded me of death. Still, when I walked past obituary posts of women pasted on walls and lamp poles in the streets, I always stopped to find out their ages. I always wanted to know if they were young and if they left behind children. I would then walk away worrying about their young ones, sincerely hoping that their fathers would not abandon them and that life would not be too harsh on them.

Over the years, despite frequent replays of many events from my past, my memories of Mama continued to fade away. Sometimes, her smiling face appeared to me, like flashes of lightning, blinding and fleeting, gone before I could capture it for keeps. The only images that my mind had protected from deterioration were those of the thin woman in the coffin. How could I have allowed the withering away of memories of Mama? It had taken twelve years to make these memories of my mother and another twelve to lose them.

I missed her so much that thinking about her always made me feel sick to my heart. I thought about our short life together and wondered what I would have done differently had I known that our time together was limited. Had I known that, I would call her name more times in her absence than in her presence. Had I known that life would teach me more about being motherless than about being a daughter?

Unable to fall asleep, I tossed and turned in bed, thinking about the questions that I was still looking for answers to. Questions that riddled me every brand new day. Questions I couldn't answer or get anyone else to. I didn't understand why Mama had died so young or why God hadn't saved her for our sake. Why spare Papa and take Mama? It didn't make any sense to me.

Mama had been asthmatic and had always had a cough. Each time she made the coarse whistling sounds, my siblings and I would rush to get her one of the inhalers lying around the house. We would gather around her, pat her on the back, hand her a tissue paper and offer her a glass of water. Thereafter, she would be breathless for a while, her flat breasts heaving up and down as she tried to regain herself.

After Tutu's birth, it seemed to get worse. She went from 'I have a slight tightness in my chest' to 'I feel severe chest pain'. She changed her church from Catholic to Pentecostal. She began fasting every Friday of the week. She would sing praises to God in the mornings and play Don Moen and Ron Kenoly songs throughout the day.

In the evenings, she would sit before the TV to watch a Christian program by a Nigerian pastor who shouted 'the Lord that answereth by fire' every two minutes. All through the night, Mama would pray without ceasing. Despite all this, there was no improvement. Instead, things got worse.

At one point, she started to cough up blood. Soon after that, she began losing weight and suffering intense pain in her bones. Then came the prescription drugs, the injections, the surgeries, the radiographs and the chemotherapies. And finally, one ordinary day in November 1997, death came calling.

***

Ada returned early from Andrew's place on Sunday morning to take me to the cemetery. The man who would take us to Mama's gravesite was nowhere to be found when we arrived there. Ada called him as we stood by the entrance in the gentle morning sun. While we waited for him, I pretended to watch the cars that sped down Keffi Road. My mind raced faster than those cars as I desperately tried to figure out what I would say to Mama when I got to her tomb. After I returned home from tutoring the day before, I'd sat for hours in front of a blank A4 page with a pen in hand, trying to write a speech that I could say to Mama. No words came.

An approaching siren intruded upon my thoughts. As the sound grew louder and louder, a police van with its red and blue lights flashing appeared, with a string of flashy cars trailing behind. Ada and I covered our ears and watched them drive past.

"When it's not that we have traffic! Argh, I don't see any reason for them to blast the siren so. Noise pollution everywhere." Ada complained, and I smiled at her absentmindedly.

Just then, I saw a small thin man come out of the other entrance to the cemetery, on the other side of the road. He was wearing dark blue trousers which he had cut just above the ankle and his shirt was hanging off his shoulder, a few buttons left undone.

"That's him," Ada said as the man ran across the road and walked towards us.

He had a missing upper front tooth and there wasn't a single hair on his head, face, or chest. When he stopped, he dropped his cigarette in the space between us and trampled on it. He brought out a Tom-Tom candy from his pocket and unrolled it. Then he cleared his throat and spat on the ground before putting the candy in his mouth. Afterwards, he responded to our greetings. He complained in Yoruba about how he'd spent long hours searching for the grave under the blistering sun; how dirty it was when he found it; and how weeds had sprouted all around the tombstone. He went on about how it'd taken him long hours to weed and then ended with how the money agreed on was far too small for all the work he had done.

"Don't worry," Ada said to him in Yoruba. "We'll sort you out."

Looking Ada over, he said, "Follow me!"

He led the way through the rusty gate. Ada followed him while I walked behind them. We stepped in single file through the maze of headstones. The further we ventured, the quieter it became. Although the pebbles grumbled as we trod on them, the silence was heavy and haunting.

I looked ahead, scared that if I read the inscriptions on the stones I walked past, I would be entangled with the stories they told. I was afraid that I might feel their regrets—the things they'd wanted to do but were unable to, the things they did but wished they hadn't. I didn't want to know who they left behind. I didn't want to sense the emptiness; pain and loss of their loved ones might be dealing with. I didn't want to know if they were as young as Mama when they died or if they'd left young children behind.

So, I stared straight ahead, fixing my eyes on the back of the head of the man who was walking before Ada. I hoped he would keep walking because I wasn't ready for him to stop and say, here we are.

"It's here!" the man announced, suddenly stopping in his tracks.

I stared at the white tomb with the words, *In memory of Iyabo Anastasia Davies* engraved on it. A powerful gust of wind brushed past me. The air was chilly and its whispers were harsh. I stood still, as though I was in a trance. The man rambled on again about the troubles he'd had trying to find the plot and the state he found it in. I heard his voice faintly, but his words stayed out of my head.

I struggled to do the same to the guilt that clung to my heart but to no avail. After a while, Ada and the man walked away so that I could have some time alone. I wanted to leave too, to keep running until I got to Ada's car. I wanted to run away from the strange silence, which had created a solemn and weird world, different from the one on the outside.

Unable to remember her face before cancer or erase the images of her face after the disease, I forced myself to remember her alive and well. I imagined her sitting before her sewing machine with pins sticking out of her lips. She had her side turned to me, so I couldn't see her face. Her palms were placed flat on the Ankara fabric as she pushed it under the needle while pedalling with her bare feet at the same time.

I never minded when she made me wear and pull off a dress several times while she sewed it, and neither did I ever mind that her pins pricked me when she removed the cloth from my body. I loved to watch her sew because it always made her happy and relaxed. Just then, a motion picture of her appeared in my mind and I saw her smiling, healthy face with perfect clarity.

I knelt at her tomb and sobbed into my hands. Like twelve years before, my eyes were as dry as the Sahara.

EIGHT

Past

A few days after Lara left for Dolphin Estate, it was mid-morning when Papa rang his bell summoning Fola and me. As I stood before him, tremors from the fear that always seized my heart whenever I heard the peal of his bell still rocked my body.

He ordered us to sit across from him on the sofa, cleared his throat, and said that he had something important to say that required our full attention. I could tell right away that it wasn't good news. It was in his unusually calm voice and the insincere sympathetic look on his face.

He looked straight at us, his eyes moving from my face to Fola's and then back. He was like the CEO of a company who employed a compassionate and respectful voice to inform his employees that the business had been sold and they wouldn't be transferred with the sale, not because he didn't care about them, but because the new owner didn't need them.

Without delay, Papa told us that the landlord had increased the rent and he would rather invest the money in building his own house than pay the high rent. After that, he told us what had happened when he drove Lara to Dolphin Estate. Apparently, on arriving in front of the building where our grandparents lived, he'd left her at the entrance by the roadside with all her things and driven off. Just like that. He claimed it was Mama's family who had told Lara that he was responsible for Mama's death.

"Did they tell you that too?" he asked. He had long since abandoned the subtle voice he'd adopted in the beginning.

"No Papa," Fola and I chorused.

When he said the words, "All these latest developments have required me to take drastic decisions," I assumed that he was going to send us all to live in Dolphin Estate. Instead, he dropped the first bombshell—Tutu would be going to live in the UK with his elder sister, Mama Jide. I couldn't believe my ears. I felt faint and confused at the same time. He explained that with Lara away, it would be too much work for me.

I shook my head and said, "I can handle it, sir."

He exploded in anger. "Will you shut up there and not interrupt me when I'm talking? What do you know about taking care of a child? Can you already take care of yourself? You must be silly for what you have just said. Do you think that bathing her and preparing her food means that you can take care of a three-year-old? I am sending her to London so that she can get proper training from a woman who took care of me while I was growing up. A woman who is raising three children of her own."

After that, he told us that Fola and I would not return to our schools for the next term. I'd thought that despite Lara moving to Dolphin Estate, we would still get to see each other at school. This second bombshell dropped my heart into my stomach.

Papa said that Fola would resume at a boarding school in Ikorodu where a friend of his was the PTA chairman. He would send me off to live with Papa's immediate elder sister, Mama Ola, in Onipanu, where I would attend a school nearby.

I couldn't believe it. I was going to live with Mama Ola again. Mama must have turned in her grave. Lara and I had once lived with Mama Ola for about half a year when we were both toddlers. Papa and Mama had separated after a big fight. Mama had left Lara and me behind because Papa had refused that we go with her. As soon as Mama had gone, he went and dumped us with Mama Ola. Although I can't remember that period, I'd seen photos, and they said a lot about what had happened. It was why Mama always knew that if she died, Papa wouldn't take care of us.

After Papa dismissed us, I ran to the bathroom. The shocking news upset my stomach, causing me to throw up and giving me diarrhoea. Still, in my heart, I found it hard to believe that everything Papa had said would happen. It felt like a dream. A prank. A joke. I believed my imagination was playing tricks on me. He couldn't truly mean to separate us like that. Why not just send us all to Dolphin so that we could all stay together? I couldn't understand it.

Later that same day, Mama Jide came to take Tutu away. Papa had it all planned out, and we didn't get enough time to digest the information before he executed his plans. We had no say. We were pawns, helpless in the hands of the chess master.

Before Mama Jide arrived, Papa ordered me to put all Tutu's belongings in one of Mama's old luggage—the largest of a set of three brown leather portmanteau luggage that Mama always used to pack our belongings whenever Papa sent her packing.

I felt lightheaded and numb as I arranged her things neatly in the box. I folded her best clothes, wrapped up her best shoes in an old newspaper, and added her favourite books and toys. I had consoled myself that perhaps it wasn't so bad after all, since Tutu was only moving to the UK and not dying. I'd see her again when she visited Nigeria on holiday. Looking at things from this angle was supposed to help, but the pain in my heart wouldn't go away.

While Papa wasn't looking, I added all the Tom and Jerry video cassettes we had. Fola and I wouldn't need them. Tutu loved cartoons. I thought it would help her not miss home too much.

For lunch, I made noodles for Tutu and then made Adalu with mashed mackerel for the rest of us. Only Papa had the appetite to eat the soft cooked beans porridge. The smell of the food nauseated me; Fola too said he wasn't hungry. He'd been so calm since Papa turned our world upside down with his plans. It was as though Fola had known that it would happen, as though he'd been expecting it to happen.

I dressed Tutu up in a white dress with dark brown motifs and long white socks. I parted her hair into six, plaited the ponytails and decorated them with colourful elastic bands and beads. When she asked me for the umpteenth time about Lara, I lied again that she would soon be back from the market. I couldn't bring myself to tell her that she wouldn't see Lara for a long time, let alone me, Fola, or our folks at Dolphin Estate.

How could she understand any of these when she still thought that Mama would come back home? When she was yet to understand that it was Mama's burial, we'd been at barely a month earlier.

I wanted to go into Papa's room, kneel before him, and beg him to rethink his decision. I wanted to promise and swear that if he kept us, we would never give him any stress or a single reason for him to regret his change of mind. I even thought about being as strong as Lara and standing before him to demand that he take us all to Dolphin Estate so that we could all be together if he didn't want to *father us*. But I asked none of these questions. Instead, I asked him when we would see Tutu again, to which he replied, "When I can afford a return ticket for her to come for the holidays? For now, I need all the money I can get for the construction of my house."

Mama Jide arrived soon after 4:00 pm. The strong scent of her cologne travelled through the house as she stepped inside. She still wore her dark glasses several minutes after she arrived. She talked incessantly and loudly as if everyone around her were deaf. She complained about the heat. She also complained about the refuse dumps she'd seen along the roadside when she passed through Oyingbo and how she'd almost thrown up in her car.

Tutu, who was more interested in the cartoon she was watching, had no idea she was spending her very last minutes in the flat. I wanted to pick her up and bury my nose in her neck, as I often did. I wanted her to put her chubby little arms around my neck and cover my face with kisses. Her hugs were always comforting. I loved her smell; the smell of baby powder and oil. But I was afraid Papa would be upset at any show of affection and emotions.

When Mama Jide was ready to leave, Papa turned to Tutu with a wide grin: "Do you want to go to Mr Biggs? Yes? Big Mummy will take you there now."

"Lami, follow me," Tutu said, meeting my gaze.

"No, she can't go with you," Papa answered in a firm voice. "She has things to do at home."

Tutu's eyes were glued to the TV as I knelt before her to buckle her shoes. She didn't see my face crumple into a sob or notice my trembling hands. She placed her little hand on my head so she wouldn't wobble or fall as I lifted one of her legs to push her foot into the shoe. It wasn't strange to her that Mama Jide would take her to Mr Biggs when she hadn't even finished her noodles. She didn't notice that my lips quivered when I gave her a goodbye kiss. She didn't ask why my hug was too tight. When I rose to my feet, neither Papa nor Mama Jide noticed that I'd been crying, as no tears were running down my face.

"Please don't take my little sister away from me, please," I was begging inside, screaming at the top of my lungs, but they could neither hear me nor read me.

"I'll buy meat pie for you. You hear? You hear?" Tutu said to me as she stepped out of the flat with Mama Jide and Papa, who had her luggage in one hand.

She didn't see Fola cry because he did so only after she'd left. She didn't notice his clenched fists as we stood on the landing at the top of the stairs, watching her descend. She took each step slowly, holding the rails with both hands. A few times, she looked back at us with the smile she always wore every time she was going out.

Impatiently, Papa picked her up so that they could descend faster. I ran to the balcony at the front of the flat so that I could see her for the last time. Mama Jide had come in a shiny blue Mercedes Benz. The driver quickly got out of the car and ran to take the luggage from Papa. Then he put it in the boot as Papa and Mama Jide said goodbye to each other.

When the car finally drove off, it seemed as though a part of my soul tore itself away from me and flew after the car. Fola and I fled to our rooms before Papa returned upstairs. The house was quiet and lonely for the rest of the day. It felt lifeless. I felt just the same way. I stared at Tutu's cot for a long time before falling into Lara's bed and crying myself to exhaustion. I knew Fola was crying in his room, too. I wondered if Papa cried also; if it hurt him to give his daughter away like a cheap piece of cloth. I wondered why he couldn't take care of us.

All our lives, he'd always treated us like we meant nothing to him. And now, he seemed to be finding opportunities to get rid of us one after the other.

***

Before noon the following day, three men came to pay for Mama's car, driving it away that same day. When I asked Papa if I could keep the white fuzzy dice hanging from the rearview mirror, he asked in a stern voice, "What do you want to use it for?"

On that same day, one of Papa's friends came with his wife to buy Mama's sewing machines. They hurt my head—these sales. I tried to protect the memories I had of Mama driving her car and sewing at her machines. She'd been happy when she bought that car—her first. It was a small green Toyota Starter, and oh, how she loved it. She'd bought it with her savings from her job as a secretary. Same with the machines, which she'd bought because sewing made her happy. She'd said that it helped her de-stress over the weekend before another week started all over again. She had plans to resign from her job someday and start a sewing school.

Fola and I spent the rest of the day in our rooms, packing up our belongings. Papa spent his in Mama's room, which used to be the dining room, discarding Mama's belongings that he couldn't sell. When I finally gathered the courage to go speak to him. I begged him to let me go to the same boarding school as Fola so that we could be together.

"Are you a boy? Immaculate High is a boys' only school," he snapped, folding clothes into a big box.

I stared at his back, wanting to ask him to take me to Dolphin Estate, but too afraid to voice it. I just knew that the mention of Mama's family would make him flare up.

About an hour later, I stood at the door of the girls' room and watched Fola leave the boy's room, carrying his schoolbag on his back and a hand suitcase—the medium size of the set of three portmanteau luggage belonging to Mama. He opened his mouth as if to say something, but no words came out. I too had no voice for words, and as always, no tears for my weeping. I raised a hand to wave him goodbye and heard him gasp a sob that had been caught in his throat. Papa was waiting in front of the bathroom door, just like he had two days before when he took Lara to Dolphin Estate. My throat spasmed and my eyes ached with years of unshed tears as the two of them left the flat.

It felt like I was all alone in the world. I returned to the girls' room and looked at the surrounding emptiness. Three days before, I was sharing it with my sisters. Now stripped of their existence, it was unrecognisable. I climbed into Lara's bed and lay sprawled out, suddenly feeble.

Each breath was a laboured effort. I had barely eaten in two days. With no strength to get up to go find me something to eat, I began to cry. My throat hurt and my eyes burned, but remained dry. I wished I could taste my tears. I wished it would run down my face, dissolving and washing out all the pain I'd suspended for many years. I wished they would flow like lava from a volcano, melting hardened emotions and releasing all the stress and pressure I'd bottled up since Mama died.

***

Papa didn't appreciate having conversations while driving. He always drove as though he feared the brakes would fail as they did in many of the Nigerian movies where the head of the family was killed off in a car accident. He would pay full attention to where he was going and would be focused on traffic signals, road signs, police cars, dance buses, and other motorists. On the eve of New Year's Eve, as I sat in the passenger seat of his car, I stared straight ahead while gathering my thoughts and the courage to speak.

The night before, I'd slept very little and was already awake when Papa banged on the door at 6:00 am. I sat in my pyjamas on one of the dining chairs while Papa shaved my short hair closer to my scalp. Afterwards, he ordered me to have my bath and a breakfast of bread, butter, and tea. I tiptoed between the girls' room, the bathroom and the kitchen, trying not to be heard, afraid to blow up one of his flimsy fuses with my clumsiness.

There was a heaviness in my heart as the countdown to my last minute in the flat grew closer and closer. Suddenly, I didn't want to leave. I wished so hard that time would freeze. I didn't want to stop using the bathroom Mama used or the kitchen she cooked in. I didn't want new neighbours or new friends or a new school. I didn't want to leave the girls' room—my sanctuary.

From the window opposite my bed, while lying down at night, I could watch the moon and the stars. I didn't want to live with Mama Ola. I wanted to continue to see the security man, Baba Dele. I wanted to see his kind eyes and his assuring smile. I wanted his sympathy each time I passed by him. I wanted to always remember that someone else knew that life was unjust and unkind to us.

The entire journey to Mama Ola's went by in silence—a silence that made my thoughts resound loudly in my head. When Papa stopped in front of her building, he kept the engine running. I got out of the car at the same time as him, joining him by the trunk. I straddled my schoolbag on my back and received the hand luggage from him. It was the smallest size of Mama's set of luggage.

"Go up to Mama Ola's place," he said. For once, he didn't order or bark his words as he would normally do.

"You're not going to come in?" My voice was small, begging him to not get upset by asking him a question.

"I don't have time to waste. I have very important things to take care of."

I imagined that was how he'd dropped Lara off like a bag of beans at Dolphin Estate without going up with her to the apartment. It was also how he had dropped us off on the Osborne Road Bridge the last time he took us to see Mama. It was in the same carefree manner he'd given Tutu away and sent Fola off to boarding school. Still, I mustered the courage to ask another question.

"When will you come back?" I asked.

"Come back for what?" My question seemed to surprise him, as though it was obscene of me to expect him to come back. I blinked, swallowed and rephrased.

"When will I see you again?"

Inside, I willed my eyes to indulge me and allow tears to stream down my cheeks for the first time. It would have gotten Papa's attention. It would, perhaps, have led him to change his mind about me. It might have softened his feelings of animosity towards me. Stubbornly, both eyes remained as dry as dust.

"I don't know yet. I'll be busy moving out of the house."

In a trance-like state, I positioned myself before the gate and watched him enter his car without glancing back. I got no kiss, no hug, no goodbye, or even a wave. As he drove away, my gaze followed his black VW Passat until it was out of sight. During the following years, whenever I thought back to that morning, I always wondered if he ever glanced in the rearview mirror at me; if he'd known that day that he'd never come back to see me.

Long after he'd left, I stood motionless in the same spot, thinking of ways that I could escape from this cruel reality. I wished I could run away, never to be seen again. I wished I could melt into liquid and flow into the drain to be lost forever with the wastewater. I wished the ground would open up and swallow me whole, leaving behind no traces that I ever existed.

NINE

Present day

My visit to the cemetery made me feel a lot better than I'd been in a long time. The guilt that had eaten at me for years for not visiting Mama's grave disappeared. I was glad that I'd finally done it.

Just like returning to the beach hadn't been as bad as I thought it would be, seeing Mama's name engraved on the white marble tomb had helped my mind accept reality. Mama was dead and I would never see her again in this lifetime.

Back home, I went into my room to nap. As I lay there waiting for sleep to come, I ruminated on the promises I'd made to Mama. As if to atone for abandoning her, I'd vowed that I wouldn't wait long before returning to her tomb, and also that I would find Tutu and reunite my siblings. I'd come away from the visit to the cemetery with promises I didn't know how to fulfil. I had no idea how to get Wale, Lara, Fola, and me to bond after all these years. Neither did I know how to trace Tutu.

While I was living with Mama Ola, many times, I'd asked her to give me Mama Jide's number in London so that I could call her and speak to Tutu. Her response each time was that she didn't have it. A lie she couldn't convincingly tell.

As the eldest sibling, Wale was expected to step into our parents' shoes and fill the role of the guardian, the *Olori Ebi*. He was supposed to be responsible for finding Tutu and keeping us all together. He could have pulled the seniority card and obliged us to stick together. Instead, he had been the first to leave Lagos and move far away to the South, never calling or worrying about us. Having set an example, Lara too had fled Lagos, but not too far away, as she remained in the West. Upon graduation from secondary school, Fola followed suit. He headed down South, even further than Wale. At the university, I'd known people who had siblings who lived in different states or even countries but were still close. They talked over the phone, remembered birthdays, and spent the end-of-the-year holidays together. Why couldn't Wale, Lara, Fola, and I be close like most families were? I had hoped we'd always care for and protect one another.

Having promised Mama that I would reunite us, I couldn't go back on my word. I would return to Onipanu, to the area where I had lived with Mama Ola, and try to find someone who may know of her whereabouts. After locating her, I'd then locate Papa and, subsequently, Tutu. Although there were no mobile telephones back when Mama Ola lived in Onipanu, I thought that perhaps there would be someone who had stayed in contact with her and now had her mobile number.

Restless and unable to sleep, I rose from my bed to attend to some chores. I set up the ironing board in front of the TV and called my siblings while I pressed my work clothes. Wale's number didn't go through. He'd yet to respond to my Christmas greetings. Fola didn't answer his phone either. Lara picked up on the third ring and sounded like I'd woken her up from a nap.

She was silent as I told her about my visit to Mama's tomb. I informed her that I'd employed the man who'd traced the burial plot to weed and to clean the marble marker regularly. I also told her about the concrete slab that was fractured at the ends.

"It needs some urgent renovations," I said, hanging a freshly pressed white shirt in the wardrobe. "I have to find someone who can repair it ASAP."

"Ok," she said.

Like me, I knew she hadn't returned to the cemetery. None of us had. It was easy to identify tombs that still received visitors when you walked through a graveyard. I wanted to share with Lara the relief and lightness I'd felt when I stepped out of the cemetery, but I hesitated. I didn't want to guilt-trip her into going to visit Mama's tomb or make her feel any worse than she already did. I wanted her to be emotionally ready when she returned there.

Before hanging up, I gathered enough courage to tell her that I thought Mama would be disappointed to see how we had all grown apart, how we were almost strangers now. I told her that if Tutu came looking for us, she would also be surprised to find we'd all moved on to new lives that didn't include each other. I heard her sigh on the other end.

"Lami, the problem is that you have refused to live in the present," she said in a firm voice. "Things will never be as they were when we were children."

A pulsing in my throat darkened my view as she talked about learning to live my life and not disrupting Tutu's life in the name of a reunion. I reached for my phone from between my ear and shoulder and transferred it to the other ear. I walked over to the window and stood staring at one of the identical security lamps on the fence that surrounded the compound. She wasn't going to help me find Tutu, was all I could think.

"Everyone has moved on except you. Can't you see it?" she said.

"I'm not living in the past." I defended myself. She'd made it seem like finding Tutu was something bad. "I just know that Mama would want us all to be closer. She'd be sad to see how we've all grown apart."

"I'm sure that if she could speak to you right now, she'd ask you to move on and stop living in the past."

Her voice was so distant. It sounded as though we hadn't grown up together in the same house and shared the same room until I was twelve and she, was fourteen. I walked back to the ironing board and settled the phone between my ear and shoulder again.

Although I'd known from the start that Lara would be the most difficult to form an intimate relationship with, even as an adult, I felt deeply hurt by her rejection. I'd never understand why she was always so cold towards me.

"Mama would never say that." I picked up the iron. "She always wanted us to be together."

Lara said nothing at first. A burning smell reached my nose. I lifted the iron and the fabric of my favourite blouse remained stuck to it.

"I have to go," Lara said as I pulled the fabric to separate it from the hot iron surface.

She hung up the phone just as she said bye, so I didn't get a chance to reply. I pulled the plug from the socket and sat on the bed, holding my ruined blouse. I sat still for a long time, staring at the shape of the iron on the fabric. I felt the urge to cry, but not for the blouse.

The closer I attempted to get to Lara, the farther she always seemed to get away from me.

***

Despite Lara's rejection, I clung to hope for a reunion with my siblings. Wale's number remained inaccessible, a sign that he was still working offshore. Fola sent me an SMS, apologising and promising to return my call after missing it on Sunday. However, three days passed, and I still hadn't heard from him.

On Thursday during my lunch hour, I sent Fola another SMS, asking him if he could call me or tell me when I could call him. When I stepped out of the language room hours later, the children had long closed for the day. The sun had set and someone had turned the security lights inside the school on. I looked through the notifications on my phone as I walked to the gate, expecting to find a reply from Fola. But what I discovered instead was a long-awaited email, confirming an interview date with a representative from Campus France.

I was elated, but my joy was short-lived as it dawned on me the limited time I had left to bring my siblings back together. I needed to achieve this before my departure to France for the next two years. It would become even more challenging afterwards.

At the school gate, I looked up from my phone and waved good night to the guards. As I exited the premises, I found Nico standing next to his SUV, parked a distance from the gate. It was already too late to hide. My heart fluttered against my rib cage when our eyes met. He and Moses were standing side by side, leaning on the vehicle. Nico was dressed in a blue trouser suit and white shirt. He had a fresh haircut and his skin had taken a lighter shade. I stood still, watching him as he approached me.

"Coucou miss," he said.

"Coucou." I couldn't meet his gaze. I felt guilty and ashamed. How could I explain why I had ignored his calls and messages for so long?

"Happy New Year."

"Thank you. Happy New Year to you too."

He nodded. "How are you?"

"I'm well, and you?"

"I'm fine." His expression was unreadable.

I couldn't tell if he was pleased to see me or not, but I realised that I'd missed him. I wondered if my sudden silence had damaged too much between us. If we could ever go back to being as free as we'd been with each other. He was a good person, and I liked him very much. I wished that I'd had the respect and courage to reply to his messages or pick up his calls.

"I wasn't expecting to see you here," I said to murder the silence.

"I came to see you. I've been wondering why you suddenly stopped talking to me. Did I do or say something wrong?"

"How did you find me?"

"You told me you work off Akin Adesola, so I checked the map and contacted all the schools until I found you here. It's the fourth time I've come here to see you. Did they leave you a message?"

"I'm sorry, Nico. You didn't do anything wrong. It's me. I've had so many things on my mind lately." I told him about how I'd been busy with my university plans and other personal matters. "My life is way too complicated right now to leave time for anything else."

"Is that why you've been avoiding me?"

"See, I like you a lot." I forced myself to meet his gaze. "I like spending time with you and all, but work keeps me so busy, I barely have enough time for myself as it is."

He stared at me. I looked away and towards Moses, who was still leaning against the vehicle, watching us.

"Does this mean we can't be friends at all?"

I paused. Ada had asked me the same question when she noticed I'd stopped picking up his call. I held his gaze again and adopted my firm teacher's voice. "Can a man and a woman ever really be just friends? Without strings? Without it turning into…"

"If we like each other's company, why can't we just be friends?"

I raised my brows.

"Honestly, genuinely, just friends. We'll hang out together only when you want. We'll get to know each other better… I'd like to know you better, to know Nigeria better, I mean Lagos."

I liked the way our conversation was going. The guilt on my shoulders lifted. I agreed to be just friends. We went to have drinks to celebrate our newly negotiated friendship. Moses remained by the car while we walked, searching for the nearest bar. The street lamps had come on and the weekend had already begun. Luxury cars flashing red lights and thumping loud music through the speakers zoomed past us. The interior lights of the glass office towers were off and their gates, which were usually wide open during the day, were closed. The streets were bustling with pedestrians making their way to bus stops or various bars.

We found a bar that wasn't too crowded and noisy and got a table in a corner. We talked about the football match Nico had played the day before and the trip he and his colleagues were planning to take to the Epe fish market. He'd heard that it was one of the largest fish markets in Lagos.

"My mother's side is from Epe, but I haven't visited there since my childhood."

"Then you should come with us."

"Are you from Paris?" I asked, quickly changing the topic.

"Rennes." Then he told me about his hometown, the capital of Brittany in northwest France. He studied there and then was employed by Total after he graduated.

A couple arrived and took the table next to us as the waiter who had taken our order returned, carrying cold bottles with beads of condensation. After he served us and left, Nico asked me about my brothers and sisters. I told him about them, as though Lara hadn't rejected me four days earlier and Fola wasn't avoiding talking to me. I caressed the Sprite bottle as I shared with him fond memories of our childhood, those we made before Mama fell ill. I didn't mention Tutu at once. In my description of our last beach outing, Tutu didn't exist.

"What happened at my place?" Nico asked suddenly, breaking my line of thought and snatching my gaze.

I opened my mouth and then closed it without saying a word.

"Was it why you didn't want to see me again?"

I shook my head slowly, but he continued to hold my gaze like he wanted more than a head shake. So, I gave two slow nods.

"I didn't know about your phobia of darkness," he said gently.

I reached out and touched the empty Sprite bottle again. The droplets of condensation had almost all dripped onto the table.

"I've been unable to sleep in the dark since I was a child." I didn't look away from his eyes or blink. "I can't stay in a pitch-black room and I can't keep my eyes shut for longer than thirty seconds unless I'm asleep."

He leaned forward in his chair, resting his forearms on the table, but he said nothing.

"When I woke up," I continued, "I believed I was in my room. I began searching for my phone, but it was nowhere to be found. I reached out for the curtain near my bed, hoping to glimpse the sky, but there was none. It didn't occur to me that I was at your place, so I panicked. In that moment, I thought I had lost my sight."

He blinked while nodding as if to say, *Now I understand.*

***

Sunday, as always, was a quiet day—a day God and Lagosians rested. The sun was up by the time I awoke and was already heating the city as though we were already paying for our sins. Still, at noon, I stepped out into the heatwave and headed to Onipanu in search of anyone who could tell me the whereabouts of Mama Ola. I arrived at my destination about an hour after I left home when I hoped most people would have returned from church.

I spent half an hour walking around the area, visiting the streets nearby and reviving memories I wished would stay dormant. When I was finally standing in front of the building where I had once lived, a rush of memory left me feeling sick to my stomach. I was thrust back to that day when Papa had left me standing there with Mama's portmanteau on the ground in front of me. Twelve years later I still felt overwhelmed by the same distress the twelve-year-old me had struggled with as I watched Papa's car disappear from view.

"Good afternoon, sir," I said to a middle-aged man dressed in a blue suit and white shirt, leaving the compound.

I asked him about the families I'd known when I'd lived there, too. I learnt that everyone had relocated, except for the family on the ground floor of the building at the rear, who used to have a petty provisions shop near the entrance. The wooden kiosk was no longer there, making the compound look larger than I remembered it.

I walked along the side of the building, and more memories came rushing into my mind. I hated to find myself back in the compound. There were memories of the weekends when I dreamed that Papa would come to visit me, bringing Tutu. There were memories of the nights when my stomach churned acid and I couldn't sleep because I was too hungry. There were memories of the long Saturdays I spent tackling a massive heap of laundry. I hated remembering those lonely days when I wished desperately that I could turn the hands of time back to the last afternoon spent on the beach with Mama and my brother and sisters.

I walked to the ground-floor apartment and knocked. After a few minutes, I knocked again. I was about to leave when I heard a key turn in the lock and a bolt being drawn back.

The door opened, and I saw Mrs Banjo. I introduced myself, fearing that she might not recognise me after all this time since my last visit while I was at the university. She'd gained much more grey hair than I'd imagined. She'd cut her hair short and was now wearing glasses.

"Come on in," she said, smiling as she stepped aside.

It was dark inside and it grew darker after she shut the door. She turned on the yellow ceiling lights instead of pulling back the curtains to let in the daylight. The apartment still looked the same. It was right under the one I'd lived in with Mama Ola—the same layout and dimensions. There were only two rooms. Mama Ola and her husband slept in one. I shared the other with my little cousins—two girls and a boy.

I was still standing by the entrance when I asked Mrs Banjo if she had heard any news about Mama Ola and her children since my last visit. Back then, she'd told me that Mama Ola had moved to Ibadan after her husband left her for another woman. She'd said that Mama Ola had promised to leave her new address but had left without saying goodbye. She believed that Mama Ola had had no intention of leaving her address.

"I haven't heard any news about her since she left," Mrs Banjo said after asking me to take a seat. "What would you like to drink? I have Sprite, Fanta and Coca-Cola."

I opted for water and after I'd taken a sip; I asked her why she closed up her provisions shop. She told me it was a decision she'd had to make after her last child got married and left home.

"Are you sure you don't want something to eat? We still have yam porridge left from lunch."

"I had lunch before I left home, ma," I said and thanked her again.

I sat there, regretting that I hadn't come with anything — some apples or a bunch of plantains. I gulped the rest of the water in the cup as though it would wash down the shame I was feeling. She asked after my siblings, and in return, I asked about her children. She was happy to tell me that her daughter, Yemisi, had gotten married and moved to the US to join her husband.

"I'm going to Maryland next week to help her take care of her baby. I've been a new grandmother since yesterday. The baby came early."

I congratulated her and asked that she send my greetings to her daughter. I liked Yemisi a lot. I had seen her the last time I came. She was studying at the University of Ibadan then. I had thanked her profusely for being kind to me when I was living with Mama Ola. Twice, she had given me food to eat from her mother's pot. I sat on the floor of the shop to eat as fast as I could while she shielded me from view with her body.

"Is there anyone at all you think may know the whereabouts of Mama Ola in Ibadan?" I asked.

Mrs Banjo shook her head but advised me to speak to a woman down the road. I remembered the woman whom everyone called Iya Ibeji. Mama Ola had once sent me to her on a Saturday morning to help her with a complete housecleaning. I'd spent the entire day spring-cleaning her apartment until it was sparkling. It was the weekend before Mama Ola asked me to leave her house.

A moment later, I was ringing at Mama Ibeji's door. She opened it a crack, peering out at me. She didn't remember me or that I'd scrubbed her apartment clean from sunup to sundown for two days. She believed me only after I mentioned that we'd found a dead cat under her bed that day when Mama Ola had lent me to her one weekend to help her with a thorough cleaning. That she remembered.

She continued to speak to me from the door, telling me she'd not heard from Mama Ola since she moved to Ibadan. She suggested that I go to the church where she used to worship and speak to the Pastor. She was right. Mama Ola could be in touch with her pastor, as he was someone she held in lofty esteem.

As I tried to locate the church, I discovered that it had changed streets. A young girl directed me to its new location. The service had already started when I arrived at the church. To my surprise, the Pastor had changed. It wasn't the same one who had laid his hand on my head to cast out so-called demons after Mama Ola had told him that I didn't cry tears.

After the service, I waited to speak to the new pastor. He told me that his predecessor had been transferred to South Africa, where he was pastoring a Nigerian Pentecostal church. Unfortunately, he didn't have the name of the church or his contact information. He spoke to a few women from the Women's prayer meeting, but none of them remembered Mama Ola or knew anyone who could help me locate her.

TEN

Past, After the separation

A day before the beginning of my WAEC exams started, Mama Ola woke me up at 5:00 am.

It was a Sunday and an hour earlier than I was allowed to sleep in during the weekend. She asked me to have my bath and head to Dolphin Estate from where I would write my final exams. According to her, she had no idea about Papa's whereabouts, and he hadn't been sending money for my upkeep.

Without the money, she couldn't afford to feed me. Her place was only a fifteen-minute walk from my school, but she wanted me to live on the Island and travel to and from the Mainland every day for the last two weeks of my SSS years.

As early as 7:00 am, she sent me out of her home with just enough money to get to Dolphin Estate. Her three children were as dazed as I was because everything had seemed so normal the night before. No one could've imagined she would want me gone in the morning.

I arrived in Dolphin Estate carrying the books I needed for my final exams in my schoolbag and another bag containing a few clothes, which included my school uniform. It surprised everyone to see me after almost half a decade. Uncle Kay was still in bed, but he came out of his room when he heard the unusual noises. He was wearing the same pyjamas as on the morning he came to announce to us that Mama had died. I learnt that Wale and Lara were away, studying at the university and that Grandma had died.

Grandpa had changed so much; there was no single trace of black hair on his head. His pace around the apartment was much like that of a baby just learning to walk. I wanted Uncle Kay to drive me back to Onipanu so that I could go retrieve all my belongings, but he asked me not to worry about them and just concentrate on my final exams.

It wasn't until after my exams that Uncle Kay took me to Mama Ola's place, but she wouldn't let me in or even speak to me. She informed me from behind her front door that my belongings were under the stairs. I found the luggage right there, covered in dirt and cat scratches. The sight hurt my heart. I didn't understand why she left it there. It was under these same stairs all the stray cats in the area found shelter.

On our way back home, Uncle Kay tried to cheer me up, but I was distracted. My mind burdened itself with queries of why this woman hated me so much that she didn't think my belongings deserved a place in her home until I returned, like under a bed or in the store where there surely was plenty of space.

She knew that the luggage belonged to Mama and she couldn't have been dumb enough to not know that it must have sentimental value. Every woman knew it as bridal luggage—a part of the wedding preparations, one of the wedding gifts a groom offered to his bride, inside which were filled with wrappers, jewellery, shoes and bags. But Mama hadn't received the set of leather portmanteau luggage from Papa since she'd had their first child, Wale, out of wedlock. She'd gifted it to herself from her first salary after she got her first job. Only Wale was older than the luggage.

Wale and Lara came home to Dolphin Estate during the long holiday. Wale was at this time studying Structural Engineering at the University of Port Harcourt. He had dreams of working with Shell or Chevron. Lara, on the other hand, was at the University of Ilorin studying Business Administration. They were both surprised to find that I'd also relocated to Dolphin Estate. I'd thought that reuniting with my elder siblings would be an opportunity for us to get close and make up for the lost years, but apparently, they'd moved on with their lives and wanted me to do the same.

***

Before the end of the summer holiday, Fola arrived at Dolphin Estate one afternoon looking haggard. It wasn't a surprise to anyone to hear that Papa had abandoned and forgotten him at the boarding school. Usually, Papa sent word to Fola through his tutor, the PTA chairman, just like he'd done with me, through Mama Ola, but he suddenly went quiet many months back.

With his tuition and board fees still owed, the housemaster had asked him to go home at once and collect the fees, but he had no home and had no idea where Papa was. He turned to his tutor, who refused to pay, citing that Papa still owed him some of the fees he had advanced for his last term, including sports fees.

Having no one else to turn to, Fola had borrowed some money from a classmate, but it hadn't been enough to get him to Dolphin Estate. So, he'd trekked for over five hours from Ijanikin to Mile 2, where he caught a bus to Obalende, before finishing the rest of the journey on foot again. He couldn't remember the location of the flat when he arrived at the estate, so he'd asked for directions to the baboon's cage and then, from there, traced his way to the street and the building.

I remember being so happy to see Fola after almost half a decade. He'd grown taller, darker, and had a thicker voice. His change was so sporadic, that I almost couldn't recognise him. Pimples and dark spots were scattered around his face and hair had grown on his upper lip and chin. If he was happy to be reconnected with everyone at Dolphin Estate, he didn't show it.

As the day wore on, it became clearer that Fola was indeed no longer Fola. Boarding school had changed him in so many ways. It seemed to have robbed him of all the beautiful memories we had made together: the pillow fights; the racing down the stairs or sliding down the stair rails; the times we spent on the balcony at the back of the house washing our school uniforms while watching children in tattered clothes rolling old rubber tyres in the street; and the many times he taught me how to whistle. Most of all, I missed the long nights we spent talking and sharing secrets in his room as he lay on his bed and I on Wale's.

After Uncle Kay and Aunt Jire returned from work, we gathered together for a family meeting. Fola said very little while his matter was being discussed. His eyes roamed restlessly, unable to meet anyone's gaze, and he only spoke to answer questions directed at him.

When Uncle Kay began to explain the financial difficulty Papa had put on him, Aunty Jire and Grandpa since Lara and I relocated to Dolphin Estate, Fola couldn't hide how uncomfortable he was. He knew he, too, had become a burden to Mama's family. In the following weeks, I tried everything to get close to him, to make him pull down the walls he had built around himself or let me in, but it was of no use.

He slept till very late and went for long walks in the evenings. Sometimes, I felt as though he was mad at me for something I'd done. Sometimes I wondered if he thought that I'd had an easier life at Mama Ola's because she was family, unlike the PTA chairman who had been his guardian. Since moving to Dolphin Estate myself, I'd come to understand that Wale and Lara didn't have it so easily just because they lived with Mama's parents. They had experienced financial instability, coupled with the burden of Grandma's illness.

The weekend before the new session resumed, Uncle Kay took Fola back to his school and paid all his outstanding fees. When Fola was with the PTA chairman, Papa used to pay extra fees so he would remain at the boarding house during the school holiday. After Uncle Kay declared himself as his new guardian, Fola had to come to Dolphin Estate during the holidays, but he didn't want to come home. Dolphin Estate was no longer the paradise we used to love visiting as children. During all those years, I never forgot Tutu and having no news about her left me with a sore heart.

After Fola joined us in Dolphin Estate, I'd wanted to return to Mama Ola's place to try to convince her to give me Papa's contact details. I just couldn't believe she wouldn't know how to reach him, considering how close they were and how they couldn't stay for long without news from each other. I also considered convincing her to give me Mama Jide's number so that I could speak to Tutu. I wanted to be sure that she wasn't being maltreated, but Wale and Lara were against my plan. Lara said that it should be Papa who should come looking for us because it was he who abandoned us. Wale agreed with her.

Aunty Jire, who was a lawyer, had wanted Papa to be brought to justice for not taking up his responsibilities as a father. Grandpa and Uncle Kay, on the other hand, didn't agree with her. They opined that if we took Papa to court, we could never live together as a family again. They truly believed that someday Papa would return to his senses and come looking for us. They didn't want us to burn bridges that may lead to reconciliation in the future.

As the four of us were already a huge financial burden on Mama's family, in the end, they all agreed that it was better not to go looking for Tutu and that she was better off in the UK with Mama Jide.

"Let him at least take care of one," Uncle Kay had said. "We've already taken four."

***

During my first year at the university, I travelled to Lara's school to see her for a long weekend. I'd not seen her since she came home last Christmas holiday. I'd planned to say to her, 'Lara, I love you,' and 'Lara, I missed you.' I didn't mind if it made her feel uncomfortable. I'd wanted to know if she remembered what Mama looked like without first having to glance at a picture of her. I'd wanted to meet her friends because whenever she came home for the holiday, she was always so eager to go back to school.

I'd wanted to find out if she smiled and laughed with them. I'd imagined the kind of laughter only friendship can cause out of the heart. One that would be so loud it would ripple out.

I'd gone to Ilorin with a mission, not just to watch others make her laugh but to do so too.

Bearing beverages and cereals, I located Lara's address, which she had given to Uncle Kay after he paid her rent. The university was closed for the Id-el-Fitr holiday and almost everyone had gone home. For Lara, she was home.

She lived in a tiny airless room, painted in the same colour as our room back on Lawani Street—a glossy light blue. She didn't have a reading desk and her mattress lay on the blue sheet of vinyl that covered the floor. In one corner, she placed a plastic chair next to her books, neatly arranged on the ground. Just below a small window, there were a few disks and a compact CD player. At the foot of the mattress, she kept her utensils and two buckets filled with water.

After the first day, our conversations were still cold and monotonous. I was no longer the girl Mama had said could sell ice to the Eskimos. On the second day, the lights went off at midnight while we were listening to an album by Lighthouse Family. We were suddenly engulfed in complete darkness. A high fence, which blocked any illumination that could have come from the stars and moon, obstructed the window. I raised my hands in front of my eyes and couldn't see anything.

"Please, light a candle or a lantern," I said to Lara as I felt intense panic preparing to erupt inside me.

"I don't use a lantern and I don't have any candles left. I forgot to buy more."

"Why would you forget when you know that I can't sleep in darkness?"

"I thought you'd got over it."

"How can I ever get over it? How could you think that I got over it? Have you ever asked me if I got over it? Have you ever bothered?" I accused her, shouting at her for the very first time.

"I didn't think it was important," she said in a low voice.

I couldn't even sense her outline in the thick darkness, but I could hear the apology in her voice. It also sounded like guilt.

"You didn't think it was important? Have you ever seen me go to sleep with the curtains pulled close? I chose to cut my hair so I wouldn't have to close my eyes when Mama washed it. I chose karate over swimming so I wouldn't ever have to shut my eyes while under the water. You never cared about me. You never asked me. If you saw tears rolling down my face now, you wouldn't ask me how I made it happen. You wouldn't even ask why I'm crying. You've never asked me what living with Mama Ola was like. You don't care about me. You never cared." I was hysterical. With my hands stretched out to feel the walls, I tried to find my way to the door. I opened it and there was more darkness.

"I want to go outside," I shouted, becoming paranoid. "I must go outside."

"It's too dark. There is no sane person outside at this hour."

"I don't care."

"I don't want trouble o. This is why I discouraged you from coming, but you wouldn't listen."

"Just lead me outside."

"Some cultists would probably be out now, looking for prey, and the landlord will hear us open the bulgar proof. I don't want to have any problem with him. Or do you want him to send me packing? Or maybe you want us to get raped? Or do you want everyone living here to get robbed?"

I fell silent as she found my arm and held on to it. I let her shut the door; together, we felt our way back to the mattress. I sat, staring into the dark. I was petrified of going blind before morning and not realising it until the sun came up.

Shifting close to the wall with the window, I felt the mattress move when she laid down on it. We didn't say a word to each other. Her silence angered me. I stared toward the window, increasing the pressure on my pupils. I could feel my pulse in my eyeballs as I mentally prepared to stay awake until morning when I would be assured that I wasn't already blind.

I strained my eyes for a long time until exhaustion and sleep came to my rescue. I woke up the following morning with burning eyes and the feeling of not having had enough sleep. After having my bath, I packed my bags and returned to Lagos.

***

They sold the flat in Dolphin Estate after Grandpa's death. It was decided that the sale would help sponsor Wale, Lara, Fola and me through our first degrees and a Master's if we wanted to further our education.

The flat had been the only thing holding Wale, Lara, Fola and me together, however loosely. Uncle Kay used to insist that Wale, Lara, and

Fola come home from the university for Christmas. But it was nothing like it used to be when Mama took us to Dolphin Estate on Boxing Day. There was nothing merry about the holiday. We did not set a Christmas tree up. We got gifts of money instead of wrapped presents. And we never sat down to eat together as a family.

After the sale, the fragile bond broke down easily. Mama's share of the inheritance, one-third of the sale of the property, was shared equally between the five of us, making us millionaires. Tutu's share was deposited in a bank account to earn interest.

With the apartment sold, we stopped spending Christmas together. Aunt Jire got married a month later, while Uncle Kay announced his for three months later. They had put their lives on pause so that they could put us through the university. Wale spent all his holidays in Rivers State, where he got a job as an offshore engineer on a fixed platform.

Fola spent his in Calabar, where he was studying Economics at the Federal University there. Lara too spent hers in Ilorin, where she'd settled after she graduated from the university.

In the beginning, I desperately wished that she wouldn't find a job and would be forced to relocate back to Lagos. But she eventually found one at a book publishing company there and stayed. I'd wanted us to share an apartment and catch up on the years apart, but she refused, saying that she no longer liked Lagos and would rather remain in Ilorin. I tried to convince her to return to Lagos, where she would have found a better-paying job than what she got, but she wasn't interested.

The sale of the Dolphin flat was done through an agent, and only Uncle Kay and Aunt Jire had attended the signing. I left the new occupants my phone number and email address, asking them to be given to Papa or

Tutu should they come looking for us. I knew it would be the first place Tutu would try.

I intended to use my inheritance for my studies in France. Although I still didn't want to be far away from Lagos in case Tutu visited, I understood the importance of furthering my education. Deep down, I also believed that in France, I would be closer to Tutu than ever and the chances of finding her would be higher.

Leaving Dolphin Estate meant being far away from Ikoyi cemetery, where Mama was laid to rest. Despite the cemetery being just a kilometre away, I couldn't bring myself to visit her grave. Nonetheless, there was a strange comfort in knowing she was nearby, and a profound melancholy when the flat was sold, forcing me to move further from her last resting place.

I longed to visit Mama, yet the thought of dismantling the protective walls I had built around my emotions terrified me. Returning to the cemetery meant acknowledging that Mama lay there, accepting her absence, and moving forward with my life. But I wasn't ready yet. I wasn't prepared to let go of the pain and sorrow that came with her loss. I dreaded the idea that if I stopped carrying my grief with me everywhere, I would slowly forget Mama, and that thought also terrified me, as if I would lose her forever.

On some days, I got tired of carrying my grief and wanted to end my mourning once and for all. On other days, I clung to it, carrying it like a heavy burden, not wanting to let go because I didn't want Mama to think that I was happy without her. I didn't want her to think that I'd stopped loving her. I wanted her and God to know that when she left the equation, my world didn't continue spinning as if nothing had happened. I needed them both to see the consequences of making me motherless. I needed God to know that His decision was wrong; His calculation was inaccurate; and if His plan was, in any way, meant to result in a positive outcome, it failed miserably.

Mama should not have died; God should have spared her life for our sake. Couldn't He tell that it was Papa who should have been hewn down and not Mama?

ELEVEN

Present day

Nico invited me to a fish dinner at his place. He and his colleagues had planned to visit the Epe fish market that day, and he wanted to prepare a special dish for me using the fresh fish he would buy.

Despite being unfit for company, I took a taxi to Banana Island. I'd wanted to cancel the invitation but had felt bad about standing him up. I recognised the effort that would have come with selecting the fish at the market, cleaning it and making a nice meal out of it. I knew I had made the right choice the moment he welcomed me into his apartment wearing a grin and an apron. I would have regretted dampening his good spirits if I had called to cancel our plans.

"I'm happy to see you," he said, kissing my cheeks.

I caught a whiff of his cologne and felt a rush of excitement.

"Me too." My voice sounded like I had been running as my face heated up.

I trailed behind him to the kitchen area, glancing around. There was no sign that he had already begun cooking, and I couldn't detect the aroma of fish or any other cooking in progress. I took a seat on the island, wondering if he had been waiting for my arrival before beginning.

"There's something I need to tell you," he said, taking a seat on the island chair opposite me. I noticed how he was suddenly looking serious.

"Yes?"

"We didn't go to the fish market this morning. We had to postpone it."

"Oh!"

"I still wanted to cook you dinner though so... do you like crepes?"

"French pancakes?" I gave two quick nods. "I like, I like."

"Then I'll make you some crepes with ham, eggs and cheese." He rose, walked to the sink and washed his hands. When he turned around again, he said, "I've already prepared the batter."

I stepped down from the high island chair and strolled over to the aluminium sliding window.

"I don't have an amazing view." I heard him say. I turned around to face him. "I don't even have a balcony. A friend who lives on the other side has a great view of the lagoon."

"I like the view of the garden. It's beautiful and the way it's lit up reminds me of the way the pitch is lit up in Fantasy Land. You really do play well."

"Osé." He grinned.

I liked how he always made an attempt to infuse the Yoruba words he learned when we talked. I went and stood by him and watched as he gathered ingredients on the counter.

"Is this how you cook for all the Nigerian girls you know?" I teased.

"You're my first attempt." He smiled.

I looked away from his golden-green eyes. I wondered if I had any tell-tale signs of being flushed. Was I falling in love with him? I rejected the thought. I didn't think he was the man for me. After three years, he would be sent to another country. Maybe find another local girl he would ask to show him her country.

The doorbell rang, seeming to catch us both by surprise.

"Did you invite someone else?" I asked.

He shook his head and went to answer the door. I knew who it was as soon as I heard her voice. It was the sequined dress neighbour. I could hear flirtation in her voice as distinctly as the bass in a singing voice. I was a bit surprised when I heard her ask to borrow Nico's charger. I had no idea that wealthy people in Banana Island borrowed chargers from one another.

"I think she likes you," I said to Nico after she'd left.

"We're just friendly neighbours." He shrugged as he washed his hands at the sink.

As I watched him cook, the realisation that I was jealous of the sequined dress girl dawned on me and frightened me. I fell into silence, feeling ashamed that he must have sensed my jealousy. When he added the batter to the hot pan with melted butter, he swirled it around quickly so that it would spread and fill the pan, then some minutes later, he flipped the pancake up in the air. It changed sides mid-air before it landed in the pan.

"Wow! How did you do that," I exclaimed.

"Practice," he said grinning and then he gave me a wink.

He added ham to the crepe, cracked an egg in the middle, sprinkled a little grated cheese, folded the edges of the crepe and covered the pan.

Then he whistled and did a quick tap dance. I laughed. My first laugh that day and, in fact, that weekend. He wore a big grin as he placed the crepe in a dinnerware. He looked extremely happy as he melted some butter in the pan to repeat the process to make another crepe. I realised at that moment how much I liked being around him.

"You cook like a seasoned chef," I said as he poured the batter onto the pan. "I mean a Celebrity Parisian Chef."

"I'm one and I'm cooking for a celebrity. She's Miss Lagos, the most beautiful girl in Lagos."

"Don't flatter me," I said shyly, dropping my gaze.

When dinner was ready, we sat side by side to eat, our backs to the sitting area. Because the only sound in the room was the hum of air conditioning and the refrigerator, the noise of cutlery on plates seemed amplified. During the meal, he joked and touched my hand lightly as though we were old friends. He was gentle in his ways and he kept trying to make me laugh. I hadn't been that genuinely happy in a very long time.

After eating, we moved to the sitting area to watch some TV. While I flipped through the channels looking for something that might interest us both, he sat next to me, picked up his laptop from the coffee table before us and opened it.

"Do you have a Facebook account?" he asked.

"I know it, but I don't know anyone who has an account."

"Well, now you know me."

"I don't think it's essential for me to have one."

"It isn't, but it's great for catching up with friends. I found many old friends there... friends I've been to school with but haven't heard from in years."

"Oh!" I gasped. "Really?"

"Yes, friends from as far back as primary school."

"Can you have an account if you're under eighteen?" I asked, my heart racing.

"It's possible... but many parents don't want their children having accounts because of sexual predators."

When he returned his eyes to the screen, I stared at his fingers as they danced over the keyboard. At the same time, the word *reconnect* was echoing in my head. My mind began to swirl with a mix of emotions. I felt hot and cold at the same time.

"How does it work? Can you show me please?" I asked, shifting closer to him so that I could see the screen.

Nico helped me create a profile. Using his webcam, I sat before his laptop and took my first profile picture. For a long time, the photo would remind me of the renewed hope of finally finding Tutu. I sent Nico my first friend request and wrote my first Facebook message to him, thanking him for opening my account. My heart rate increased, pumping rapidly as I typed *Tutu Davies* in the search bar.

A ton of profiles with similar surnames came up. Davies was such a common name. Most of them were White and none had Tutu as a first name. I couldn't believe that I'd found and lost a means that should have led me to find Tutu so rapidly.

"I'm sorry," I heard Nico say. He must have seen the disappointment on my face. "Facebook is getting more popular each day. Someday soon, the person will create an account."

"It's ok," was all I said.

In the space of a few minutes, my hope had been as tall as the Eiffel Tower until it flicked like a pack of cards. The despair I'd felt as I left Mama Ola's church earlier in the day returned and I retreated into myself. I wanted to climb into my bed and crawl under the covers.

***

Ada and I screamed at the top of our lungs as a man in a boiler suit used a clamp tool to chop off a woman's toes in the horror movie we were watching. It was Monday evening. We'd just finished eating dinner and were sitting in front of the TV.

"Bébé, why did you scream like that now," Ada said, laughing. "You scared me."

"It was you who scared me."

Just then, my phone began to ring. I reached for it on the coffee table and hesitated for a moment.

"It's my little brother, Fola," I said, glancing up at Ada, who also reached for the remote to pause the movie.

Rising to my feet, I walked to my room.

"How are you doing?" I asked.

"Fine," was all he said.

I got the same response when I asked him how school was going and how his friends were doing.

"What did you say you urgently needed to speak to me about?" He sounded impatient like it was I who had called while he'd been in the middle of something very important.

I started by explaining that I had gone to visit Mama's grave and had arranged for someone to regularly tend to it. Next, I told him about my trip to Onipanu in search of Mama Ola.

"What for?" he asked.

"What do you mean, *what for*? To reconnect with Tutu of course."

"But she has her own life now."

"Does that mean she'll have no space in it for her real family?"

"For chrissakes Lami, it's time to move on. You can't force things to happen your way."

I opened my mouth and swallowed the air. I'd thought that he of all people would understand. He and I had spent a lot of time together playing with Tutu when we were little, but he was now acting like Lara, making me feel that I was the one with a problem.

"I'm not forcing anything," I finally said. "I'm just trying to do what Mama would have wanted us to do."

"That's the problem. Mama is dead. She's never coming back. Tutu lives in the UK. She'll never leave a stable country to come and live in an unstable one. We all have our lives now. You need to start looking forward to the future. I've let go of the past and accepted what happened."

"This isn't just about the past. It's also about the future. I've come to accept what has happened. I just don't want to look back someday and regret all this time we're not taking advantage of."

I could still remember Fola's red eyes as he cried when we stood on the balcony to watch Mama Jide take Tutu away. Had he forgotten already? Did he truly not care about seeing Tutu again?

"Have you ever thought about the possibility that Tutu doesn't want to be found?" Fola asked then.

Truly, I hadn't thought about it. She could have made a life for herself in which there was no more space to include four siblings with whom she'd had no contact in over a decade. It was indeed a possibility, but should it deter me from trying to find her? My main goal was to know that she was doing well. If she welcomed me into her life, then that would be the icing on the cake. If I found her and she wasn't interested in a reunion, then I would respect her wish.

Lying in bed after the call, replaying Fola's words, a sudden idea struck me. I sprang out of bed, connected my laptop to a dial-up modem, and accessed the internet. Logging into my new Facebook account, I decided to make another attempt with the search engine. I entered Tutu's full name, Adetutu Davies, and to my astonishment, only one result appeared. My heart skipped a beat when I noticed that the location of the account was set in London.

During the next few minutes, I studied the profile, looking for signs and hints that she was my little sister. The profile picture was of an adorable kitten. I couldn't see what was on her wall or who her friends were. All I had access to was her location and a few pictures of flowers and beautiful Islands. One of them was a shadow over the beach sand at sunset. I stared at it. Could it be Tutu? Could she have visited all these paradise-looking Islands? I sent her a short message that took almost an hour to draft.

Dear Tutu,
It's me, Lami, your big sister. I can't believe I've finally found you after twelve long years. I'm so elated, I'm screaming. After all these years apart, life has finally given me a chance to reconnect with you.

I have so much to tell you that I don't know where to start. I can't wait to hear from you. Please write to me soon.

Lots of love from Lagos,

Olamide Davies.

The following day was the longest day of my life. After a restless night, I remained overly excited and couldn't wait to get home. I spent my entire evening on Facebook, waiting to catch her message the moment it arrived. I sent out friend requests to people I knew; people I'd attended schools with—primary, secondary and university. I marvelled at Facebook and how quickly I'd found people I'd not seen in a decade—old neighbours from Lawani Street and other acquaintances.

I searched for Mama's childhood friend, Aunty Stella, whom I'd not seen since Mama's funeral. My siblings and I had grown up calling her *Aunty Stella* even though there were no blood ties between her and Mama. We'd also considered her children as our cousins and our grandparents as their grandparents. Aunty Stella was mine and Lara's godmother and she'd been like a second mother to us until Mama died and we didn't see her anymore.

The Facebook search pulled up many people with similar names and surnames. Although none of the profiles was Aunty Stella, one of them was her daughter; Vivian. Looking through her pictures reminded me of the good times when our families got together. I sent her a friend request and a message asking for news about her mum and her sister.

After dinner, I recharged my phone with airtime and called Lara to tell her about my discovery. It was the longest minutes we'd spent on the phone since I got her number. She promised to go to the cyber cafe the following day to create a Facebook account and send Tutu a message as well. After the call, for the first time in a long time, I felt some sense of closeness to Lara. It was at that moment that I realised that Tutu might be the glue that would reunite us all. A few days earlier, I'd thought that I would be unable to keep my promises to Mama before leaving for France. And then, a Facebook account later, I'd found Tutu, and Lara was interested in the reunion. I decided that as soon as I received a response from Tutu I would inform Fola and Wale.

In the following days, my excitement was replaced by restlessness. I was greatly perturbed by Tutu's lack of response. During my lunch hour, I would go to the school library to use one of the computers to access my Facebook account. After I returned home, I logged in and refreshed the page every few minutes. I didn't go to watch Nico play football on Wednesday or accept his invitation to attend a parlour party organised by one of his friends on Friday night. He was to return to France that weekend. By the end of the week, I still had no response from Tutu, but I had over fifty friends on Facebook. The bulk of them were students at the school where I was working.

It took four days for Vivian to confirm my friend request and reply to my message. We spent Saturday night sending messages back and forth, catching up on the years we had missed, and sharing childhood memories. After Mama died, her mother remarried and moved to South Africa with her husband. Vivian had also gotten married right after university and moved to Canada with her South African husband. He worked in a large Canadian pharmaceutical company while she was pursuing a Master's degree in Psychology. She sounded happy, as though everything was perfect in her life, and I wished that I had as much good news to share in return.

***

Aunty Stella called the following day. I remembered the last time I saw her, the tears rolling down her cheeks as she sang, *'Amazing Grace'* while we stood around the open grave at the cemetery. Although these memories were difficult to unearth, I was happy to have reconnected with her. She had grown up with Mama in Obalende and they had been very close. Aunty Stella had also been very present in my childhood. Our families had spent many Saturdays together, rotating between spending the day at our place or theirs. Sometimes, we packed up some food and went to one of the many beaches in Lagos or picnicked at a park or the zoo.

Aunty Stella told me stories about Mama that I'd never heard before. Mama had been the fastest runner in primary school and had won many prizes during inter-school competitions. No one had ever mentioned it, not even Mama herself. Aunty Stella wanted to know everything about my life and each one of my brothers and sisters. She'd wanted to come to see us after the funeral, but Papa had asked her to wait until the New Year. In January, she discovered that we'd moved out of Lawani Street. When she tried to find out more from Papa's friends, she'd learnt that Papa had sold his house in Agbara and relocated to Germany. She didn't know if Tutu moved to Germany to live with Papa or if she remained with Mama Jide in the UK. It was no wonder no one knew Papa when I went in search of him in Agbara back while I was at the university. He never lived there.

When I told Aunty Stella about my intention to trace Tutu and the lack of response to my message to her on Facebook, she offered to join me in my search, promising to make calls to people who might have news about Papa. She'd been present the first day Mama met Papa at a party and had been the first to know when Mama got pregnant for him. In those days, having sex and getting pregnant before marriage was frowned upon. Mama's out-of-wedlock pregnancy brought shame to her family, especially to Grandpa who had been a Catholic Knight.

Papa and Grandpa had their initial encounter when Mama invited Papa to her twenty-first birthday party. Grandpa was taken aback to witness Papa smoking stick after stick of cigarettes. By the time the party ended, he and his friends had been so intoxicated they spent the entire night outdoors—none of them had been sober enough to lead the pack home.

This embarrassing incident unfolded before the entire neighbourhood, serving as a clear indication to Grandpa that the man his daughter had brought wasn't a suitable husband. For this reason, he decided to send Mama to the UK in an attempt to break up the relationship. However, Mama and Papa decided to have a baby so Grandpa would have no choice but to accept their love. Their plan initially didn't go as expected as it led to Grandpa disowning Mama for many months. It was only after the birth of the baby that Grandpa forgave her and agreed to organise their marriage, on the condition that she furthered her education.

After Mama gave birth to Wale, Grandpa and Grandma agreed to raise him so that Mama could continue her education. To get an administrative job, she attended a shorthand school. Afterwards, she found a job in an import-export company where she worked for many years until she died. She and Papa married two years after they had Wale and moved in together. Aunty Stella, who had gone to a nursing school, married a doctor some years later. Unfortunately, the two childhood friends both married similar men.

"Macho men," Aunty Stella called them.

They'd fought to marry for love and had both made the same mistake—they'd chosen men whom they loved more than they were loved in return. Both men were heavy drinkers and woman-beaters. Aunty Stella suffered physical and mental abuse from her husband because she had only one boy and he was autistic. One day, when she'd had enough, she escaped her marriage, leaving her children behind. Her husband remarried less than a year later and sent his children to a boarding school. Three years after that, when she was able to afford to care for her children, Aunty Stella went back for them.

Mama, on the other hand, had stayed in her violent marriage because she knew she wouldn't be able to leave with us or without us. She'd once tried to leave when I was three and Lara was five. Papa had refused to let her leave with us and then had gone on to dump us with Mama Ola who at that time wasn't married and didn't have children of her own. Papa had also insisted that his son Wale be returned to him.

Three months after their separation, Papa and Mama reconciled because they were expecting Fola. Mama took pictures of Lara and I when we returned to her. In the photos, we looked unhealthy. Our hair had been shaved because we had lice crawling in it and our scalps were covered with sores from a fungal infection that had not been treated. Mama hid the pictures at Dolphin Estate so that she could use them against Papa in court someday. They coexisted as strangers under the same roof, and Mama no longer paid attention to his infidelity as she bided her time to serve him with divorce papers. Sadly, she became pregnant with Tutu, and shortly afterwards, she became terminally ill.

"I returned for you," Mama had said to Lara and I one day while she was showing us the photos of us looking unhealthy. "I couldn't bear to see you looking like orphans while I'm still alive."

Had we been inconsiderate all the times we'd shown our incomprehension at Mama's decision to remain with Papa? Would she still be alive if she too had left her marriage permanently as Aunty Stella had done?

After the call with Aunty Stella, I tried to remember the different reasons Mama had given for not leaving Papa. Most of them had come from the fear of what people would say or think. If she remarried and had kids with her new husband, people would have looked down on her for having children who had different fathers. She would have also been tagged a divorcee if she remained unmarried.

At that time, when a woman separated from her husband, her parents were blamed for not having prepared her for marriage. Mama didn't want to bring more humiliation on her parents than she already did when she had her first outside marriage. Another reason she'd stayed was because of the stigma. As the first child, she'd worried that becoming a divorcee might affect Aunty Jire's chances of getting married. Suitors might say that she mustn't have been suitably trained for her future role as a wife, like her elder sister who couldn't stay in her husband's home. I realised Mama had stayed for many, many reasons. And in the end, she paid the ultimate price.

***

Easter came and passed. The first week of the school holiday was the most difficult.

Exhausted from a full day of home tutor sessions, I could hardly sleep in anticipation of Tutu's response that never came. Anxiety replaced my restlessness and I became a nervous wreck. Every evening, I stalked her page wishing I had access to her friends' list so that I could write to one of them for information about her. Whenever my internet connection was bad and I couldn't log onto Facebook, I would be agitated. Many times, I typed a new message to her which I always ended up deleting instead of sending. I couldn't understand why she didn't reply. Could it be that she hadn't logged into her account since I sent the message? Could it be that she no longer used the account? Could it be that she didn't want to have anything to do with me?

Aunty Stella called me the weekend before school resumed but she didn't have any positive news about Papa's whereabouts. She'd been able to contact a few of his friends. One of them was a former neighbour of hers from Obalende with whom Papa had attended St. Gregory's College. It was at this neighbour's birthday party that Papa met Mama who had been invited by Aunty Stella. Unfortunately, the neighbour had no idea of Papa's whereabouts; they hadn't set eyes on each other in nearly a decade but had heard from a mutual friend some three years before that Papa was living in Germany. Despite all the hurt Papa had caused me, it gladdened me to know that he was well and alive. In a queer way, that night after the call with Aunty Stella, I thought of Papa in a good light and allowed myself to explore memories of him when he was happy and called me "Lami baby."

The wait for Tutu's response continued for another two weeks after school resumed. Then one Saturday, after I returned from tutoring all day, I logged into my account and saw a response sitting in my inbox. My heart began to pump blood twice as savagely as it always did every time I signed in and saw the little red message notification. My palms grew cold as I clicked on the message. The first thing I noticed before reading was how extremely short the reply was.

"Hello. I'm sorry I don't think I'm the person you're looking for. I don't have any sisters but four brothers. I wish you good luck with finding your sister."

I felt the blood drain from my face and my world grow dark, as though grey storm clouds had suddenly overshadowed the bright sun. I stared at the words for a long time in silence. Strangely I found myself missing Papa at that moment. I wished that he would come looking for me and for the first time, he would hold me, console me and promise to bring us all back together and make our lives better forever. But I knew it wasn't possible.

After all the years that had passed, we would never be able to live together again, whole as a family. A most alluring dream, but impossible to fulfil.

TWELVE

Past, Before the separation

Papa had never once kissed or held me in his arms. He'd never told me he loved me. He'd never told any of us. Mama had said that his father had been strict with him. Perhaps, he didn't know how to love us because he'd not been loved himself.

Papa had become an orphan at the age of fourteen when his father died in a road accident and his mother died of hypertension five years later. Mama Jide, who had been nineteen when they turned orphans, became a father and a mother to her younger siblings. Mama Ola, on the other hand, suffered illusions. She believed that she and Papa were twins. Several times, she told us how a twin—a boy and a girl—had died after Mama Jide was born. She was certain they were she and Papa. She'd said that they'd both decided to return to the world separately, with a two-year gap.

Papa spoke fondly about his sisters. He even seemed to prefer their children to his. Many times, I searched for answers as to why he played *loving father* to Mama Ola's children, the way he never played or laughed with us. Many times, I wondered why we were so unlovable to him.

On some Sunday afternoons, when Papa was in a happy mood, Sunny Ade's sonorous music would be playing on the record player. He would sit on his favourite sofa with a bottle of chilled beer on the table next to him. He would ring his bell to summon Lara, Fola and myself. We would rush to the sitting room and stand before him with our heads down and our hands behind our backs.

"What are you all doing in your rooms?" he would ask while smoking tobacco from a pipe and belching loudly, intermittently. It was one of those questions we intuitively knew didn't require a reply.

"Why are you people always running to your beds once I am in the house?" he would shout and we would jump with fear, praying that his temper would not be ignited. "Do I look like a wizard or a cannibal?"

"No Papa," we would chorus.

"Sit," he would order and we would scramble to find a spot on the rug, far away from him.

I preferred to hide behind the sofa by the door so that he couldn't see my face completely. If Mama was in the kitchen and the aroma of meat cooking with curry and thyme filled the house, he would ask her to give him some pieces before they went into the pot of boiling tomato soup.

"Iyabo, fun mi ni eran bibo," he would shout while absent-mindedly caressing his belly.

After serving some in a dish placed on a silver tray, Mama would often call for me to take it to him. I hated being the one chosen to do this task, but Mama said that I would make a good wife because I served Papa on my knees. However, it wasn't the only reason why she always nominated me. It was also her plan to subtly make Papa like me. I would carry the tray to him with grave solicitude.

Going on my knees, I would carefully place it on the side table, then push the plate of meat to one side and transfer his glass cup and a bottle of beer onto the tray. During this time, I would be saying silent prayers that I wouldn't spill his beer and make his delicate good mood melt away. Sometimes, he would look at me as I served him and say, *Lamy, Lamy. Lamy baby.* Then he would give me a wide smile as he moved his head and body to the beats of the juju music playing on the turntable.

His smile had the same effect on me as Lara's. Their smiles made the muscles in my throat contract in glorious spasms, forcing me to smile deep from within. Once I set his food before him, Papa would take a piece of meat to his lips without caring that it was still steaming. Sometimes, when Mama joined us in the living room, he would get up and start dancing. She would break into a smile and he would reach out and pull her close to him.

Slowly, they would dance together like they were alone in the room. I used to love watching them dance, huddled together, holding each other as they swayed to Sunny Ade's music wafting through the flat. It was on days like these that I believed that he once loved Mama and that love was a beautiful thing.

THIRTEEN

Present day

The upgrading of Mama's grave was completed before the end of April. The security guard sent me grainy photos. Her tomb had been face-lifted with black marble-like tiles to match the headstone. I wanted to go and see it for myself, but I'd promised Mama that I would have united my siblings by the time I returned to see her and I was still no closer to my goal.

On Sunday, Aunty Stella called to give me more updates. A man who'd attended secondary school with Papa had contacted other classmates and had discovered that Papa had left Germany for Spain. He'd promised to continue to fish out information although he believed that his best chance would be during the school's next alumni gathering which was held every year in August.

"August?" I asked hoping I'd misheard.

The man had promised that he would ask around at the gathering and try to get Papa's Spanish phone line. There was no way I would sit and wait around for four months. That night, I rolled back and forth in bed, slipping in and out of sleep, having the same nightmare over and over again. In the nightmares, Papa was pulling at Tutu's hand as she cried, saying that she wanted to stay with me. Mama Jide, who held Papa's wrist, was pulling too. I held on to Tutu's wrist with both hands and pulled with all my strength, but they were stronger. I didn't want to let go but my hands eventually slipped off Tutu's. Then I woke up, drenched in sweat and breathing heavily as if someone had been chasing me for miles.

Ada was at home when I returned on Monday evening. We'd not seen each other since Friday morning when we parted for work. I was eager to share a new idea that had come to me earlier in the day with someone. I'd turned it over and over again in my mind all afternoon and I couldn't think of anything better to trace my little sister. After changing out of my work clothes, I stood at the kitchen door and watched Ada look through the cupboards to see what she could put together for dinner.

"Indomie?" she asked.

"Not for me," I said.

"Ma chérie, you're the only one in the whole country who hates Indomie."

Ada was my best friend, still, there were many things about me she didn't know. Many things about my past I'd not shared with her. I didn't tell her or anyone else why I hated noodles. I'd not eaten it since the last one I cooked for Tutu on the day Mama Jide took her away. Back at the university, I would rather starve than eat it. I couldn't be around the smell either. It brought back memories of that day, of Tutu's leftover soggy noodles, of the heavy silence in the flat that followed her departure, and of the deep loneliness I'd felt in the room I once shared with my sisters.

But Dodo didn't make me feel sick, it was a sort of comfort food and the smell brought me bittersweet memories that I didn't despise as it was Mama's favourite dish. One day, I'd begged her to let me fry some for her. When I burnt them, she didn't scold me or throw them away. She ate the burnt dodo and even thanked me for making her dinner.

"An idea came to me last night," I said to Ada.

We were sitting at the round table to eat the jollof pasta we'd prepared for dinner.

"What idea?" she asked, twisting her fork into the pasta.

Steam billowed from the plate on our table as we waited for it to cool. The news was airing on the TV, but we were not actively watching it.

Ada always wanted to watch the 9:00 pm news. Her mother insisted that she watch the news at least once a day, and follow how things were unfolding in the country. The woman believed that Nigeria was a time bomb and that a civil war would break out soon, due to the increasing political instability and the insurgencies in the northeast and southeast posing a great security threat. She wanted her daughter to know when to pack her bags and cross the border before the bomb detonated and the Seme Border closed.

"I'm contemplating a trip to Ibadan this Saturday to run some advertisements in a local newspaper," I announced.

"Advertisements? What for?"

"To locate anyone who might have information about Mama Ola. Surely, someone must recognise her. A neighbour, a coworker, someone from her church, or even a parent of her children's friends."

Ada held her pasta-clad fork in mid-air and blew on it to cool it down. The pasta unrolled from around it and fell back onto her plate. When I finished sharing my thoughts, she started to nod.

"It's a brilliant idea," she said.

Throughout our entire dinner, we muted the TV and talked about my idea. I'd spent my lunch hour making a list of the most-read newspapers in the city and their advertising rates. I planned to cancel all my classes on Saturday and leave home early.

"I'll come with you," Ada said, surprising me.

"Are you sure? What about Andrew?"

"What about Andrew? I'll tell him I'm going with you to Ibadan. I'm sure he can survive a weekend without me."

"Ma chérie!" I squealed, rising to embrace her. "You are indeed a wonderful friend."

I felt relieved that I wouldn't have to make the trip to Ibadan alone. The thought of spending time together, just like old times, greatly lifted my spirits. We hadn't had the chance to do something together since New Year's, and adventuring to Ibadan might be the last opportunity before I departed for France.

As I cleaned up and washed the dishes after dinner, a text message from Wale arrived. Finally, he'd returned onshore. I stared at the message, reading it over and over again. I had to be careful how I responded. I'd failed with Lara and Fola. If I got it right with Wale, perhaps, as the elder brother, he might take it upon himself to bring us back together after all these years of being apart.

He wrote, 'What's wrong with our relationship?'

I dried my hands and went into my room to text him back. "We're not close like brothers and sisters should be like Mama would have expected us to be."

Perched on the edge of my bed, I fixed my gaze on my phone screen, waiting for his response. There were things I didn't understand about Wale until after Mama died. I knew he'd wanted to live with us at Lawani Street, but I'd always thought he was lucky to live in Dolphin Estate, away from Papa and his cyclonic wrath.

After Mama died, I realised how hard it must have been for him growing up away from his mother and his siblings. He didn't experience being woken up on his birthday by tickles under his feet, the smell of baking cake pervading his nostrils and Mama's melodious voice singing *Happy Birthday To You*.

His reply arrived a few minutes later. "That's because we all live in different cities and we all have our own lives now. Do you want us to leave our present life and move back to Lagos so that we can be the type of family you want?"

"I didn't say that. I meant that we could call and check up on each other. We could try to find Tutu."

"Leave Tutu where she is!"

"Does that mean I shouldn't attempt to reconnect with her? Should I act as though I've never had a little sister?"

"She has her own life and should be able to decide who she wants in it. Let her decide."

I called him immediately, hoping for a direct conversation, but he didn't answer.

"I can't talk now. I'm busy."

"Could you please call me as soon as you can?"

"Ok!"

He never called back.

His rejection didn't surprise me much. Unlike Lara and Fola, Wale and I didn't share many childhood memories. Still, I'd hoped he would want to know where Tutu was after all these years. I couldn't understand why he didn't care, why they didn't care. Didn't they know that living in London didn't guarantee happiness?

***

Ada and I headed to the motor park very early in the morning on the first Saturday in May. We bought drinks and snacks and then boarded a bus going to Ibadan. We sat on the last row of the white bus, in between a young woman and an elderly man who got the window seats. Just as the bus left the park, the driver hit a massive pothole, sending everyone into the air. My head struck the roof before I landed back in my seat.

"You just shifted my womb," a woman in the front of the bus said.

"Do you want to send us through the roof?" a man asked.

"Small, small. Olóyún, ópọmọ ò," another woman said, even though she wasn't carrying a baby on her back or in her womb.

The driver offered his apologies and then began to lament about how it had been just a year since the road was repaired, yet the potholes had already reappeared.

I reached into my handbag and retrieved a novel I had brought to read during the journey. Ada had also brought fashion magazines, but we ended up chatting instead. We talked about how much fun we'd had while at university, even with less money attached to our names. We reminisced about the *prison foods* we'd cooked, the Sean Paul dancehall parties we'd attended, the cheap canteens where we'd dined and the nights we talked and laughed until well past midnight before drifting off to sleep. We both agreed that life had been simpler and more enjoyable when we didn't have to work for money.

The bus eventually reached the final stop, about three hours after we departed from Lagos. Ada and I immediately began searching for a newspaper stand. We bought different newspapers from an elderly vendor stationed near the entrance of the motor park. Afterwards, we stood in one corner, examining the announcements section to determine which of the local newspapers I would choose for running the Ad. Ultimately, I opted for a weekly newspaper that had the highest number of missing-person announcements.

Ada and I occupied the back seats of a cab, sharing the vehicle with two other passengers. The cab driver blasted loud local music on the radio, making it difficult for Ada and me to converse without raising our voices. As we passed houses and a bustling marketplace, I felt like I was in a time warp, moving through the historic city with its brown tin roofs and red earth.

Upon our arrival at the newspaper office, we spoke to an editor who instructed us to wait for the man responsible for the weekly announcements column. About an hour later, we found ourselves seated across from the man in a spacious room, filled with dozens of individuals at their small desks, either typing on computers or talking on the phone. The man patiently listened as I explained my quest to locate Mama Ola. He then inquired if I had a photograph of her for publication. I hadn't considered that. Nonetheless, he agreed to publish a notice without a picture, requesting information from any readers who might know Mama Ola.

There was an official missing person's report on his table with the photo of a young man. He had the look of someone who had seen too many hard times. I found myself wondering about his whereabouts. Had he grown weary of his life, risen one day, and simply walked away from everything he knew without a word? Had he relocated to a different city or given up entirely? For the first time, I was thankful that Mama Ola had sent me away at the right time rather than bringing me with her to Ibadan. If I had accompanied her, I would have been far from Dolphin Estate, missing the chance to see Grandpa before his passing, much like I had missed saying goodbye to Grandma. I never would have met Ada, never would have pursued my French studies, and my life in Lagos would have taken a completely different course.

Before heading back to the motor park, Ada and I asked the gateman at the newspaper office where we could find a good restaurant to eat some local food. He directed us to a small buka he said sold the best Abula in the area. Amala always reminded me of Papa because it was his favourite food and Mama always made it whenever she wanted to please him.

Ada wanted her Amala on one plate and the soups on another, but the woman who served the food refused, asserting it was a sacrilege to separate the meal onto different plates. We were served in stainless steel bowls, fresh from a large pot that still had a fire burning underneath. The amala was covered with a combination of soups—gbegiri and ewedu—referred to by the locals as abula, and various pieces of goat meat were artfully arranged on top. To our surprise, we discovered there were no spoons or cups provided. We washed our hands at a kitchen sink situated in our corner and settled down to eat. The Amala appeared darker than what was served in Lagos and also tasted differently. It was so spicy, causing our noses to run, and we ended up downing two bottles of Malta Guinness each. Drunk with the spice and with full bellies, we left the Buka laughing and giddy with excitement, as though our food had been spiked.

***

I returned to Lagos with new hopes and couldn't wait until the following Saturday when the first announcement would go out. I felt certain that someone who knew Mama Ola would see the newspaper announcement and contact the editor in a matter of days. Mama Ola would then lead me to Papa or Mama Jide, who would then lead me to Tutu.

As soon as we returned home, Ada packed up a weekend bag and went to Surulere to spend the rest of the weekend with Andrew. Nico and I spent about an hour on the phone talking about my Ibadan trip. When he invited me to join him and his friends to visit the Epe fish market the following morning, I agreed without a second thought. I didn't want to be by myself. I thought a trip with him to the fish market would keep my mind busy the entire day until the new week began and I could fill the waiting time with work.

Nico picked me up in a shiny black van with dark-tinted windows. He was with two colleagues and their girlfriends. They were all French except for one of the girls who was Belgian. We sat two by two on each row. Nico and I sat on the first one, right behind the driver. Lekki Phase 1 was generally quiet on Sunday morning—the Christians were in church worshipping while the others were still in bed catching up on sleep. Traffic was slow on the way out of the estate. On Bisola Durosinmi Etti Drive, we tailed a police van and a huge armoured SUV, escorting a man in running gear, jogging down the middle of the street, until we could find an alternate route to reach the main gate.

The sky began to collect and pile up clouds above us as we exited the estate and sped down the Lekki-Epe expressway. Excitement was in the air as the journey to Epe began. It was like being on a bus with children going on a school excursion. I was surprised to find out that I didn't understand everything Nico's friends said because of a few seconds delay in the time it took me to register their words. The actors and presenters I watched on TV Cinq didn't speak as fast.

"She was asking if you've ever been to France," Nico said, repeating the French girl's question. He and I were sitting sideways, facing each other so we could also see those at the back. We were leaving Ajah, moving past big houses with different colours of galvanised roofs to small houses with zinc roofs that turned brown with rust.

I hadn't known that I'd been spoken to. I laughed nervously as I said, "You guys are speaking too fast for me. Before I grasp one sentence you've moved on to the next."

"That happens to me when I'm around people speaking English," the Belgian girl's boyfriend said.

They all agreed and it should have made me feel better, but it didn't. I was a French teacher and needed to do better. I looked past Nico out of the window. A dense blanket of grey clouds had formed over the sky.

"I think it's because you always translate what you hear first to English," Nico said softly so only I could hear. I shifted my eyes to his. "You're afraid of misunderstanding."

I nodded.

"It's about trust in myself," I murmured.

"Yes."

For a brief moment, we stared into each other's eyes as though we were passing across some deep message too delicate to be spoken. Then I pulled away to meet the French girl's gaze.

"No, I've never been to France," I said. "Cotonou is the only place I've been to outside of Nigeria."

"Then you must come to Porto Novo with us next Saturday," the Belgian girl said.

There was a hopeful glint in Nico's eyes which was quickly extinguished when I explained that I had to work on Saturday.

After a three-hour drive to the heart of Epe, we finally arrived at Oluwo. We found the market and a parking space not too far away from the entrance. As we strolled to the market, we passed other White people who were already leaving, some of whom made eye contact and nodded greetings to us. There was no gate fee charged, but some local touts at the entrance insisted we give them money.

The market overlooked a lagoon. Gust of wind brought the smell of fish and the first fat drops of rain. Everyone began to hurry about, bustling and walking fast as thunder crashed in the distance, followed by a bolt of lightning that spread across the dark sky. Customers gathered around every shop and stall, haggling and negotiating prices with the vendors.

We moved along the shops to see the things on display before deciding what we would like to buy. Different kinds of sea animals were exhibited on tables, in baskets and freestanding bathtubs—giant snakes, big snails, pangolins, crocodiles, monitor lizards and alligators. Some were alive, others dead and dried. The Belgian girl took pictures of everything with a small pink Nikon camera. Nico took some pictures with his phone to show his parents.

The wind picked up, rattling roofs loudly, threatening to transplant them. The sky grew even darker, and people began to leave the market in a hurry. Nico and his friends decided to cancel the boat ride around the mangrove, buy some fish and head back home. We separated after agreeing to meet up at the van.

Nico and I shopped together. I bought some shark meat, grass cutters, prawns, shrimps, crayfish and periwinkles. Nico bought some lobsters, crabs, tilapia and orange fish. Our outing turned into a nightmare in a matter of minutes as the rain began to fall and we waited for the trader to clean Nico's order. He was happy to test his English with the vendor, asking her about her job. Her husband was a fisherman and they had been married for thirty years, selling fish together for the same number of years. Her parents were fishermen as well, just like her father's parents.

The woman handed me a black bag containing Nico's order, but he took it from me immediately.

"You're the woman," the woman said to me in Yoruba. "You're supposed to carry it."

I smiled kindly and nodded as we left.

The rain suddenly began to fall in great torrents. We stopped to take shelter by an empty wooden stall. None of Nico's friends were in sight.

We watched the wind swing a roof sheet on a stall. I looked around us and noticed that all the traders were women. The men went out early to catch the fish and the women sold them, assisted by their daughters.

Fishing was a family business transferred from generation to generation in the town. As we stood there waiting for the rain to relent, it came down sideways, wetting my trousers and shoes. When it finally slowed down a bit, Nico and I decided to run to the car. He grabbed my hand and we made a run for it, but the rain immediately resumed, pouring down with a deluge. We stopped by the side of one of the buildings with rows of shops close to the entrance and stood with our backs to the wall.

I stole glances at Nico who watched the rain like it was his first experience. My stomach lurched each time our gaze met. He was always smiling at me like I was a wonder. I'd been trying to deny that I liked him more than I should, more than I wanted to. I was scared of becoming vulnerable if I allowed myself to open up and fall in love.

The challenge with love lies in the necessity to reveal one's inner self; its complexity arises from leaving you exposed and susceptible to being hurt. I was terrified of getting hurt again. I was scared that he could get tired of me someday. I'd heard that White people grow weary of love quickly and once they lose interest, they would get a divorce, and that they didn't understand the concept of 'for better or for worse'.

A bolt of lightning struck as the rain relentlessly hammered against the steel roof above us. I shuddered, crossing my arms over my chest, aware of my nipples pressing against the damp fabric of my tank top.

"It's starting to get cold," I said. I was trembling all over, and my teeth chattered.

"I'm sorry. This isn't how I imagined it."

He appeared genuinely saddened that our outing hadn't gone as planned. I forced a smile and attempted to avert my gaze from his eyes, but found myself unable to look away. I felt a wave of sensation poured through me, causing my pulse to race. I'd never experienced anything like it before—the rush of fear and excitement combined. I thought it was because we were standing too close, so close, that I could smell him, his sweet masculine scent. It was a break from the smell of fish that had clogged my nose since we arrived.

His head began to move closer and closer to mine. When I felt his breath on my face, instinctively, I shut my eyes. All of a sudden, there was a loud noise. I opened my eyes to see a ripped piece of tin roof that had flown off the other building with rows of shops, landing on the ground. We both burst out laughing. Just then, Nico's phone rang. His friends were already in the car. He asked them to come pick us up at the entrance. When the van appeared, we held hands and ran towards it, laughing like little children.

***

My hopes of seeing Tutu again were soon dashed like all the others. The announcement was published in the Ibadan newspaper for three consecutive Saturdays, but none of the responses I received yielded any significant or serious results. I was greatly disappointed.

How was it possible that not one person knew Mama Ola or her children? Could it be that she never relocated to Ibadan? Had she lied so that she didn't have to keep in touch with people? The mere thought that I may never reconnect with Tutu made me feel sick to my heart.

Every attempt at finding her had fallen through. Was I going to spend the rest of my life chasing after my tail?

My last hope of finding Tutu before leaving for France was through the man Aunty Stella had spoken to. But I knew even that wasn't certain. If he indeed succeeded in finding someone who had Papa's contact information at the alumni meeting, there was no guarantee that Papa would put me in contact with Tutu. So, I continued to punch Tutu's name into the Facebook search engine daily, continually hoping that she'd created an account since the last time I checked.

For each failed search, there was a new crack in my heart.

Then one Saturday afternoon, Aunty Stella called me to give me some good news. One of Papa's old classmates had his Spanish telephone number. I couldn't believe it. I hadn't been expecting any news from her about Papa until August. As I scribbled the numbers on a piece of paper with shaky hands, I felt a surge of different emotions well up inside of me, of which none was joy.

My heart skipped many beats as I remembered how much the sound of Papa's voice terrified me. I'd always thought that when I eventually got his number, it would be easy to pick up the phone, call him and demand Tutu's whereabouts. As I stared at the number in my handwriting, I discovered that I was scared to death to speak to my father, despite the many years of separation. I didn't need anything from him for myself, yet, the fear I had for him was still there. It was similar to the fear that used to grip me as a child when I needed to stand before him to request something for school. It hadn't decreased with time. If anything, it seemed to have increased over the years as it lay dormant.

"I tried the number," Aunty Stella said. "I only got voicemail. One thing is certain—it's his number. It was his voice on the answering machine."

After she hung up, I stared at the telephone number and couldn't bring myself to dial it. I'd waited many weeks for it and with it finally in my hands, my courage failed me. I considered writing down what I wanted to say but soon shook off the idea.

Maybe I should call him once my heart stopped pumping furiously so he wouldn't hear the fear nestled in my voice. I clutched my phone and held it close to my chest. Should I just ask him for Mama Jide's number and pretend that I didn't care about all those years at Mama Ola's place when he never returned to see me? I'd gone to bed every night hoping that the following day would be the day he would come for me and say he'd completed the construction of his house. I had wanted him to say we could all live together as a family again, even if Mama wouldn't be a part of it.

For a long time, I sat there in the silence of my room, debating on what to do. Questions buzzed in my head, making me doubt the whole point of everything. What if he stands in my way and refuses to tell me how to find Tutu? What would he gain from stopping me from seeing her? I was his child as much as she was his. I had the right to be in contact with my little sister. I'd waited a dozen years to find her and didn't want to wait for a second longer. *I should do it now.*

My fingers shook as I dialled. My mouth felt dry. I put the phone close to my ear. The call went straight to his answering machine and his voice came on. Aunty Stella had been right. It was surely Papa's voice. Twelve years and his tone hadn't changed at all.

A while later, I tried his number again and still, it was sent to his answering machine. I tried again and again as my anger mounted. After the fifth attempt, with a deep sigh, I put the phone down and cried until I fell into a profound sleep that led me once again to the darkroom.

FOURTEEN

Past

I liked the sound of Papa's laughter—*kikikikiki*—like the engine of a car that refuses to start. It was different from the laughter of the rich men who came together to drink beer and pepper soup every Saturday evening in the next compound. When these men laughed, it was loud and hearty—*hahahahaha*—giving the impression that the rich never cry.

Thursday nights were nights Papa was sure to be in a good mood and his happiness would be contagious. He would arrive home from work as early as 7:00 pm. It was a sacrilege for him to be elsewhere as his favourite TV drama series *Checkmate* aired at 8:00 pm. Mama would be happy too because Papa came home early. She would wear a body-clinging short gown and pull her hair in a ponytail. We all would also be in good spirits as we were allowed to go to the living room to watch TV even though Papa was there.

When I was nine, one Thursday, Mama returned home in time to begin dinner preparation. She decided to make amala—one of Papa's favourite dishes. I hated amala because of its black colour, and because when it got cold, it developed a thin hard layer that always scratched my throat when I swallowed it. But I was happy Mama was preparing it. Certainly, Papa's favourite soap opera and meal would make a relaxed evening for everyone.

"Have you all listed the things you're going to ask your father?" Mama asked us while she was cooking.

"I don't need anything," I heard Lara say in a grumpy voice.

"Me neither," Fola joined in.

"Just the toilet rolls I told you about," I said. "Tomorrow is the last day to bring six rolls for the new term."

"Don't tell him tomorrow is the last day," Mama advised. "If he doesn't give you the money to buy them this evening, I'll give it to you and then when he gives it to you, you'll return my money."

About an hour later, I was on my knees, arranging Papa's food on a table before him. I unfurled the amala from a transparent plastic wrap and filled his glass to the brim with chilled water.

"Lami baby," he said, showing his beautiful set of teeth—perfectly aligned and as white as snow.

I smiled shyly, reluctant to look into his eyes and see how they sparkled when they weren't radiating an elemental fury.

"You'll make a great wife," Mama said from where she was sitting. "See the way you're taking care of your father."

Papa ignored her. I picked up the bowl of water and raised it so he could wash his hands. Then I handed him a napkin to dry them with. He grabbed the remote control and increased the volume of the TV. *Checkmate* had just begun. Mama was sitting on the single sofa opposite the TV. Lara and Fola sat at her feet. I was by the sofa, half hiding behind it, watching Papa without him being aware of it. His eyes had bulged from having worn glasses almost all his life and his well-groomed beard had timid shades of grey. He was good-looking for his forty years.

When the *Chief Fuji* scene came on, as always, his three wives were arguing. Papa's *kikikikiki* rose and filled the room. The others laughed too without stifling their voices. I, on the other hand, wasn't watching the screen like everyone else. Rather, I was busy quietly reciting how I would approach Papa with the toilet paper request. Every time he laughed and gasped for breath, I tried to figure out if the scene was funny enough to make my request when the next advert came on. Just when a very funny scene was playing and I was certain that it was the right one I'd been waiting for, the electricity supply was cut off.

"Ha!" Papa said at the same time as most of the Lawani Street residents who had been enjoying their favourite soap seconds ago.

Lara rose and switched on the rechargeable lamp for Papa who was still eating. Mama rose too. Her long hair was parted in the middle, combed back from her face and caught in a rubber band. She looked slightly older than Papa despite the seven-year difference. She took a torch from one of the drawers of the long buffet table and left the living room to start the power generator. We all followed her. At the door, Mama asked me to go back to fill Papa's cup with water and then tell him about the toilet paper.

"Let me tell him after you switch on the generator," I protested.

"No, go and tell him now. He's still in a good mood," she whispered, pushing me towards the living room.

Fear immediately morphed my heart into a tennis ball, hitting it hard against my ribs. Reluctantly, I returned to the living room, knelt before

Papa and filled his cup again. I could hear Mama pulling the generator's rope.

"Papa, tomorrow is the last day to take toilet rolls to school," I said slowly.

"How many are they asking for this time?" he asked in a slightly irritated voice.

"Six rolls, sir."

"Half a dozen? From four to six rolls?" He raised his voice but he was still not fully angry, just irritated.

"Yes, Papa."

The generator started. I felt some relief. I waited anxiously to hear the sound of the change-over switch box but instead, the generator went off. I began to get worried. Papa would miss a lot of scenes and it might put him in a bad mood. Some minutes later, Mama appeared at the door.

"I think the plug is bad again," she said. "The generator won't start."

Papa didn't say a word. Mama sat again. Fola stood behind her. I remained on my knees before Papa.

"Have you heard that her teacher is asking for six rolls of toilet paper just for this term?" Papa said. "I am sure those teachers take them home to their family or sell them."

The anger I'd feared could now be heard in his voice. Mama said nothing. Fola fled the living room. I knew it was time to get out of Papa's presence too before his anger which had gathered into an avalanche would roll down on me. I got up to leave.

"Come back here and clear this table," he shouted.

I held up the bowl of water so that he could wash his hands. It wasn't the toilet rolls that annoyed him, but the generator that wouldn't start and the missed scenes from his favourite soap opera. He got up, picked up the torch and went to start the generator himself. Mama followed him. I escaped to our room after clearing up the table.

Lara was lying on her bed humming a soft sad tune. I sat at the study desk and watched Papa through the transparent window louvres that opened up onto the balcony at the back of the flat. Mama held the torch and pointed at whatever Papa was doing. He pulled and pulled, but the generator wouldn't start. Finally, he gave up and there was a silence that grew sinister with every passing minute.

A while later, Mama came into the girls' room to tell Lara to go and light up the lanterns. When Papa shut the balcony door with a loud thud, I thought that the hinges would give way and the door would fall off. After he stomped down the corridor into the living room, Fola sneaked into our room. We didn't say anything to each other and didn't hear Mama's steps until she reappeared at the door a second time.

"Come to the dining table and eat," she said in a low voice.

It was a bad sign that Mama herself whispered and tiptoed. A moment later, we were sitting around the table in the dining room. A large kerosene lantern placed at the centre of the table cast flickering shadows on the walls. Mama prayed before we began to eat. When Papa was home, we didn't talk or laugh at the table; we ate silently and returned to our rooms. But that evening, Fola decided to lighten the mood by singing, 'Ireti, give us food o'—a song he'd just learnt from one of the funny scenes of the soap opera. Mama and I burst out laughing. Papa must have heard us because he appeared at the door.

"Why are you eating dodo when you gave us amala to eat?" he asked Mama. "Why can't you eat the same thing as us? You give us whatever you want and then prepare something nice for yourself."

"But you know that I cannot eat what I cook the same day because it nauseates me. That's why I asked Lara to fry some plantains for me. Besides, amala is your favourite food; it's why I prepared it for you."

Papa's eyes rested heavily on Mama, accusingly. For several seconds, he was quiet as if he was trying to control his anger while sweat dripped from his hairline. Suddenly, his eyes shifted to me. His eyes were wide open and anger danced in his pupils like the orange flame on the lantern's wick.

"And you, Olamide," Papa said. "I am not going to give you six rolls of toilet paper to give to your teacher who is a thief. Tomorrow, I am going with you to your school. I must talk to your teacher and the principal. I am going to tell them that even at home we don't use toilet paper to clean up."

Then he stormed back into the living room.

***

Papa was always the first to leave the house every morning. He worked as an accountant at a cement factory. But on that Friday morning, he decided to go to school with me, and he took his time to get ready. He opened the bonnet of his Volkswagen Passat and began to inspect the motor oil and brake fluid. Afterwards, he opened his boot and brought out a transparent 1.5-litre plastic bottle with some water in it.

"Go and top it up," he ordered, handing it over to me.

I raced to the tap at the other side of the compound to fill the bottle. When I returned, Papa had closed the bonnet and the boot. He had also started the engine to warm it up. He wasn't going to fill the coolant or the windshield washer. As he drove out of the garage, I ran past the security guard and after Papa's car afraid that he would leave me behind. Not that I minded, except that I would get to school late and would spend the rest of the morning working on the school farm as punishment if Papa didn't go with me.

Papa stopped in front of the next house so that I could get in. Still carrying the plastic bottle of water, I opened the back door but he screamed, 'Get to the front, my friend. I am not your driver.'

I shut the door and took the passenger seat—Mama's place.

All night, I'd been unable to sleep, hoping that Mama had somehow found a way of convincing Papa not to carry out his plans. In the morning, she whispered to me saying, "I did my best but he wouldn't change his mind. Don't worry, all will be well." I wished she hadn't forced me to ask him for money. I wished she would stop forcing me to appear before Papa for anything at all. Most times, it always ended badly.

When we arrived at my school, Papa parked outside the gate. I dropped the bottle of water on the car floor and stepped out at the same time as him.

"Where is the bottle of water?" he asked as we arrived in front of the school gate.

"I left it in the car."

"Go and get it, you idiot," he thundered.

As we walked back to the car for the bottle, my heart began to race with panic. I was certain that he wanted the bottle so that he could empty the water on the principal or my teacher.

"Lead the way to your class," he said after the gateman let us in.

I walked quickly ahead of him. The assembly was over and no one was roaming the compound. Fresh white blooms had fallen under the frangipani tree which had broom marks across the sand around its roots. We walked past the Chemistry Lab, past the pigsty that was being cleaned by students who had arrived late, and then finally, we arrived at the entrance of my class.

"Give me the bottle!" he ordered.

I handed it to him. He checked if it was tightly screwed before he confidently sauntered up the three steps that led into my class. All the students stood up, chorused "Good morning sir,' and then sat down again. Aunty Janet walked towards us with a huge smile that vanished when she saw that Papa's frown remained steadfast.

"Good morning sir," she said. "You must be Olamide's father."

"Good morning," Papa replied in a clinical tone.

"I hope there is no problem." When she looked at me for answers, I dropped my eyes to my *Bata* shoes.

"There is a problem," Papa said. "I would like to know who has asked my daughter to come to school with six rolls of toilet paper."

"It's the new principal, sir."

"Before it was four per term, now it's six. Is it that as they grow older, they use more toilet paper? If there are over thirty children in a class and they all bring six rolls each, are you saying they use one hundred and eighty rolls a term? What happens to all the leftovers at the end of the term?"

"Sir, I know you are upset. I would advise that you speak to the principal. Unfortunately, she's not in school today. She'll be back tomorrow. She's in a better position to respond to your questions. Normally, when the term ends, what is left of the rolls is sent to the principal. When we run out of stock during the term, we use the remainder that is kept in the store."

I lifted my head and turned to look at my classmates. Some were eavesdropping; some were talking; others were giggling. Pero, my best friend, whom I shared a seat with waved at me. I dropped my eyes to my shoes again. I was wondering how long it would be before Papa would leave. Just then, he handed the bottle of water to Aunty Janet. She accepted it without questions.

"Give this to her when she needs to use the toilet." I heard him say. "We use water in our house to tamba. She does not need tissue." Then turning to me, he barked, "Get to your seat!"

I jumped and fled to my desk as he stormed off. All day, I didn't dare to look at my teacher's face. I felt the need to apologise to her on Papa's behalf, but I didn't. The whole class gossiped and laughed at what Papa had said. That day, I got my nickname, *Tamba*.

FIFTEEN

Present day

There was abundant rain in June. For days on end, it rained non-stop and we experienced a power cut for more than twenty-four hours. By the end of the month, I had received offers from the Universities of Bordeaux, Strasbourg and Grenoble. I chose Grenoble. I could now allow myself to dream it. I'd been too afraid to do so for fear that it wouldn't happen. Life seemed to always want to steal whatever made me happy.

Ada was happy for me even though it meant that she had to start looking for another flatmate. I applied for a student visa to study and began to prepare to relocate to France in August. I informed my boss and colleagues. The children were disappointed when they heard that I was leaving the school at the end of the term. I got more friend requests on Facebook from them. I joined interviews to help the Director find another French teacher. The exercise took longer than expected. Many of the candidates didn't speak French fluently. With the summer break fast approaching, the Director had no choice but to employ a young university graduate and pay for a conversation class for her at Alliance

Française on Saturday mornings. Nneoma was her name. She was serious and eager to learn, but wouldn't be ready to handle the post all by herself by the time the school resumed for the new session in October.

In the following days, Papa's number continued to go to voicemail when I rang it, but I was too busy to worry too much. I had a lot on my plate as I prepared for my relocation. I sold things I would no longer need and gave out others. Ada offered to help keep the ones I'd love to come back to. It was during this time that Aunt Stella called to tell me that the alumni meeting of the old boys' association had been cancelled that year.

"What?" I said, disappointment washing over me like a wave. "But why? Why this particular year?"

I felt my heart sink in my chest. I'd been hoping that one of his friends would have his new telephone number or house address.

"But I was still able to get some news about your father for you."

I fell silent. My heart thumped in my chest in anticipation of the news.

"One of your father's friends organised a big party yesterday to celebrate his birthday, and most of those who would have attended the alumni meeting were present. Unfortunately, none of them knew the whereabouts of Papa in Spain."

My heart sank a second time at the news. Once again, my hopes were dashed. The only new information I got was that he was married to a Spanish woman of Jamaican origins. Did he tell her about his former life? About his four children back in Nigeria, and the one in the UK? Did he ever think of us?

"Did you never consider the possibility that even if you reconnected with him, he could refuse to tell you anything about Tutu?" Aunty Stella asked one Saturday evening.

Her question made me break down and cry. Of course, I knew there was no guarantee that he would tell or give me anything useful. If he was still the same man I knew, he could refuse to tell me anything about her just to hurt me, and there would be nothing I could do about it.

"There's something I would like to talk to you about," she said after she'd consoled me. "It's not something you might like to hear, but it's in my duty as your godmother to tell you."

"What is it, Aunty?" I pulled a wad of tissue out from the box on my night table and blew my nose into it.

"When you told me you were trying to find your sister, I immediately offered to help you. I was sure that I could trace your father through his childhood friends. Unfortunately, my efforts have also yielded nothing. I consecrated weeks, whereas you've spent months searching. I'm sure your mother is very proud of you wherever she is now. She knows you've tried your best. However, I believe it is time for you to let go."

"What?" My jaw dropped. I couldn't believe I'd heard her right.

"I mean live your life and let time do its own thing. Eventually, your sister will come looking for you when the time is right."

"What if she doesn't even know we exist."

"One day, we'll find someone who knows where your father is and things will unravel from there."

I started to cry again. She too was asking me to stop searching for Tutu. I felt disappointed in her. If she lost her child, would she stop searching? Did our culture not say a dead child is better than a lost one?

"I can't just sit around doing nothing. I have to continue searching for her. When we eventually reconnect, I need her to know that I never stopped looking for her."

"Have you ever thought about the possibility that when you find her she may not be as ecstatic as you are?"

"Perhaps." I sniffed and squeezed my eyes shut as if to force out imaginary tears.

"You've been separated for so long and she has her own life now. After you gave me your siblings' contact, I reached out and tried to get involved in their lives, but they've been unreceptive. I've had to come to terms with the fact that it isn't their wish."

"Tutu will be different." I pushed back a fresh urge to cry.

"Perhaps yes, perhaps no."

"We won't know until we find her."

"You can't always force destiny, Lami. You need to learn when to let go. It'll happen if it will."

"If she was your biological daughter, would you stop searching?" I asked, slightly irritated.

"I wouldn't. People would certainly tell me what I'm telling you, but I wouldn't listen. Still, it has to be told. I owe it to your mother to advise you the way she would have advised mine had the table turned."

I started to cry again as I rejected her advice in my head. I couldn't stop searching for Tutu. I couldn't stop hoping. Hope was all I had left.

"But I promised Mama," I said, choking back a sob. I shut my eyes. They felt so dry and itched badly.

"She won't hold it against you if you don't fulfil such a difficult promise. I knew your mother well enough to know that she would want you to live your own life, a happy fulfilling life."

"I'm happy… and I'll be happier if I find her."

"Surely, one day you'll see her again but when? Today? Tomorrow? Next year? Next decade? Nobody knows. In the meantime, you need to enjoy your youth and your health."

I broke down afresh. I felt emotionally drained. Letting go seemed impossible. It sounded to me like forgetting. How could I explain to Aunty Stella that since that day when Mama Jide drove away with Tutu in her car, a part of my heart flew away with her and never returned? How do I tell her that every time I thought about Tutu, I saw her with glittering eyes, looking up at me and saying, *kawee me* the way she used to do when she was a child? Sometimes, I imagined her as an adult, looking at me with sad eyes and saying, *Carry me*.

"If your siblings don't want to come together as a family, it's fine. They're probably trying to start their own new families. Start afresh too," Aunty Stella said. "I'll be fifty next year. In my life, I've seen friends become family and family become strangers. It happens all the time. Family is important but you can't always force it. One thing I want you to know is that you're a part of my family. Remember that my doors will always be open for you."

"Thank you, Aunty." I pulled out another handful of tissues from the box and blew my nose that was running like a faucet. I wished that my eyes would run half as much as my nose. It would have provided a cathartic release I needed in that moment.

"You're a young woman and you have your life ahead of you. Go to France, study hard, meet people, read a romance novel in a café, travel with friends and see Europe. Most of all, find love. You're like a daughter to me and I'm giving you the same advice I would give my daughter. Time is fleeting. Don't forget to live your own life while Tutu is living hers. This is the time to enjoy your youth. If you don't do that now, it'll not wait for you and before you know it, it'll be too late."

After we hung up, I lay in bed and cried some more until I developed a headache. I couldn't completely stop searching for Tutu. The only means left to continue the search was through Facebook, and also to keep calling Papa's number with the hope that he'd answer it someday. I needed to have hope, to grab anything worth holding on to, to have something to live for. I hoped desperately that she would create a Facebook account soon.

Or perhaps in three years after she would have turned eighteen, she would create an account and try to find us. And I'll be right there, waiting for her.

**

The following evening, when Ada returned from spending the weekend with Andrew, she sat on my bed, watching me try on all my clothes. She'd insisted on helping me decide what to take with me to France and what to leave behind or give to the orphanage.

"What do you think?" I asked, wearing a pair of black satin Cargo Joggers.

"Mais oui. Good for summer."

Then I changed into a high-waisted pencil skirt. "What about this one?"

"Naaaa, too teacherly."

I threw my head back and laughed. I was happy I wasn't home alone like the night before when I'd cried my heart out to fatigue. Ada was the only one who could make me smile or laugh even when my heart was heavy with sadness.

"It's too tight. You can't twerk in it." So she jumped, squatted and began twerking, her buttocks popping out and in.

I glanced at our reflection in the mirror and attempted to twerk. She stopped dancing and began cheering me on, "Go bébé, go bébé." She was right. The skirt was too tight. Just then, my phone began to ring. I reached for it.

"There's something I think you should know," Aunty Stella announced right after we exchanged greetings, sounding just like she did when she made a similar announcement the day before. I sensed a slight urgency in her voice and left Ada in my room.

"What is it Aunty," I said, shutting the bedroom door behind me.

"I've been thinking about it seriously for some time now and my husband agrees that you deserve to know."

"To know what?"

"What I want to tell you is going to be difficult to hear but you're an adult now and…"

Her long sentences with carefully chosen words reminded me of many scenes in my life, of many instances when bad news was delivered to me. My heart thumped with so much noise I wondered if she could hear it over the phone. I placed a hand over my chest and waited in fear of the words that she was about to pronounce. I feared she would say that Papa was battling cancer at a hospital in Spain or that Tutu was dead.

"Your father is not Tutu's biological father," she dropped the bomb.

"What?"

"I hate telling you this way, but it's been eating me up for many weeks now. I needed to tell you. I thought you deserved to know."

I sat on the sofa and stared at the dark screen of the TV. She couldn't possibly be telling the truth. Tutu couldn't have been adopted. I'd seen Mama pregnant. I touched her belly and felt the baby move under my hands. Could she have been exchanged at the hospital?

"Are you still there, Lami?" Her voice cut through the invasive thought.

The dogs from the next compound began barking loudly. The security guard yelled at them, just as dogs from other compounds joined the barking.

"How can this be possible?"

"It's a long story which I'd planned for when we were face to face, and not like this."

"Who's her father? Is he alive or dead?"

"He's alive. He's the owner of the company where your mother worked."

"Mr Durojaiye?" I gasped.

"That's him."

"Oh, my God! I cannot believe this."

"Do you know him?"

"I know him. We met him a few times."

"He was at your mother's funeral."

"I don't remember seeing him there, but I do remember the last time I saw him. He came to see Mama during the time she was sick." He had given us a brand new fifty naira note each and then he carried Tutu on his lap. "Did he know she was his?"

"He didn't. Your mum didn't tell him. She couldn't tell anyone."

"How could Mama cheat on Papa with a married man?" I felt my stomach lurch. "She used to warn us all the time about the consequences of dating a married man."

"Mr Durojaiye had been separated from his wife for six years when they began to see each other. Your mother was miserable with your father and they were already sleeping in separate rooms permanently. She'd finally made up her mind to leave him. Mr Durojaiye truly loved your mother and she was about to ask your father for a divorce but nothing went as planned. By the time she learnt she had cancer and had a few months to live, leaving your father was no longer necessary."

I gave a long-drawn-out sigh.

"I'm sorry for telling you this way, over the phone, but since I don't know when we'll get to see each other…"

"Why did you have to tell me at all?" I cut her. "Why must I know? I would have preferred not to know. How do I tell my siblings? How do I announce it to Tutu when I reunite with her?"

"You don't have to tell them now. You'll know when the time is right. If you saw Tutu today, would you tell her such? It would not be wise. If your father learns the truth today, he would consider her a bastard and ask his sister to throw her out. You know what he's capable of. This is something she can only be told when she becomes an independent adult who can take care of herself. When she can make for herself the decision on whether to go and look for her real father or not."

"Oh Lord, this is too much for me to process. Do you know where he is now?"

"He was appointed as a special adviser to the Osun State Governor a few years back, but I don't think he's still into politics."

I felt many emotions all at the same time. Could this be the reason why God didn't hear our prayers for Mama because she'd committed adultery? Could her sickness be the wages of her sin? After I hung up the phone, I rose and returned to my room. Ada was no longer there. I sat on my bed, turned on my laptop and googled the man's name. Using the image function, I stared at the few photos of him the search had pulled up, wondering if he'd truly loved Mama. Would they have lived happily ever after if Mama didn't die and they'd gotten married? Would he have accepted and loved all her children? Reaching for my wallet from inside my handbag, I took out the baby picture of Tutu and placed it beside his face. They looked hardly alike. Could Mama have been wrong about who Tutu's real father was?

When I returned to the living room, I told Ada everything. I needed to tell someone. I felt deeply hurt and betrayed by Mama for hiding the truth from everybody. How would Tutu feel knowing she'd grown up without her father and with people she had no blood relations with?

"I wish Aunty Stella never told me," I said to Ada when she returned to my room. "I didn't need to know. How do I inform the others?"

"Bébé, I think you shouldn't," she advised. "If I were you, I would never talk about it.'"

"But Tutu deserves to know the truth."

"Yes, she does, but just like your mother's friend said, she doesn't need to know now."

***

Mr Durojaiye's recruitment firm was situated in Ikeja, off Allen Avenue. His office address had been easy to find online, as well as the location when I got off the bus at Ikeja. The door was still closed when I arrived there around 7:00 am. I texted Ada to let her know when I got there and about an hour later the receptionist arrived. The receptionist didn't have permed hair, wasn't wearing makeup and was dressed in a shapeless green satin dress. I could tell that he had remarried, and was almost sure his wife had employed his receptionist.

The receptionist let me sit in the waiting room even though I didn't have an appointment. I'd intended to spend the whole day at the entrance waiting for Mr Durojaiye if I wasn't allowed in, or until he agreed to see me should he refuse at first to speak with me. Because I didn't know how long I would have to wait, I'd gone with a novel and a *Gala* snack in case I began to starve. Yet I hated *Gala* sausage rolls. Not because there was no longer sausage in them like in old times, but because they reminded me of good childhood memories, of periods when Mama was still in our lives like meaty fillings still lined the inside of the pastry snack.

In the waiting area of the office, from where I was sitting, I caught a glimpse of Mr Durojaiye when he arrived and walked past. The receptionist followed him into his office and when she returned, she smiled and said he would receive me immediately. My heart started beating fast. I couldn't believe it. He must have recognised my surname. He still remembered Mama after all these years.

I took a deep breath before knocking on his door. My heart continued racing as I stepped inside his office. The air conditioner was humming loudly and the air was stuffy. He looked up from his agenda and beckoned me over to sit in one of the chairs on the other side of his desk. I shut the door quietly behind me and approached him as confidently as I could feign. He had white fluorescent lights on and the thick curtains were drawn. The space smelled like the past, like history—of old books and documents. A framed photo of him and a woman sat on his desk. In it, he wore a tux, and, a white wedding dress that showed an ample amount of cleavage. They were not young lovebirds. They both looked to be in their fifties.

When I began by apologising for not making an appointment before coming, he cut me off and said it was okay. He told me he remembered me and my siblings. I watched his face closely. A dozen years and he hadn't changed much in stature, but his hair was almost all grey. Would he have accepted Tutu had he known about Mama's pregnancy? Would he have asked her to abort it? Would he have married her had she dared to leave Papa? Would he have been a good stepfather to us? How had he felt when he heard about Mama's sickness? How long before he remarried after Mama's death? I had so many questions, but I couldn't bring myself to ask them.

"I remember the first time I saw you," I said. It was a passing thought, one which I'd had no intention of thinking aloud.

He raised an eyebrow, but his face remained unreadable.

"I came to the office with my mum. She was going to work a half-day so she could take me to a dentist appointment in the afternoon." I paused and noticed that the humming of the air conditioner was quieter. I wasn't expecting him to remember such mundane details. "When you saw me, you asked me if I was a boy or girl. My hair was cut short. You said I looked like a boy."

A small smile appeared on his lips.

"My mum was happy when you said so. I had thought she planned it with you because she'd been trying to get me to start making my hair again."

"I can't remember any of it, but I'm sure she didn't ask me to say so." His voice had grown a little friendlier. "I must have been wondering why a girl had her hair cut like a boy."

"I didn't think you would still remember my mum." My voice was low, but he surely heard me.

"It's impossible to forget her," he said. "She didn't deserve to die young."

I looked away from him, to his table, to the agenda opened before him. I could feel the temperature in the room beginning to go down.

"What can I do for you?" he asked all of a sudden. "I'm heading to the Island in fifteen minutes. I have a meeting in Ikoyi."

"I won't take much of your time, sir," I said. Then I suddenly didn't know where to start. I'd thought it over many times, and it had seemed that letting him know that Tutu was his daughter was the right thing to do. He caught me staring at the framed photograph.

"My wife too has cancer,' he said. "The doctors say she would not make it past 2008, but she's still here fighting."

"I'm so sorry to hear that." I didn't know why he told me that, confiding in me about something so private.

'We got married when we were both twenty-one, got a divorce after two decades, only to remarry half a decade later."

"I'm so sorry," I said again as I realised that his confession was a sign to me that it wasn't the right time to tell him about Tutu.

"How are your siblings?" he asked.

I gave him everyone's location in Nigeria. "Tutu was sent to London after the burial. I haven't set my eyes on her since then."

He nodded as I spoke, but he didn't seem to know who was who. He didn't even seem to have an idea that Tutu was his flesh and blood. He said he was glad to hear that we were all doing well, even though I hadn't said anything to him about what we were doing in life.

"So, what can I do for you?" he asked again.

I decided I would come another time, perhaps when I returned to Nigeria after my studies. He had enough on his plate already, it didn't seem right for me to add more.

"I read an article about you and thought to come and see you."

"Are you looking for a job?" he asked.

I told him I had a job and would be leaving Nigeria soon for a Master's program in France.

"You told my receptionist that what you have come for is urgent."

"Yes, sir, I... I..." I stuttered as he watched my face.

"Is it about your Masters?" he asked.

I nodded foolishly. He opened a drawer, pulled out a cheque and started to fill it. I shuddered at the coldness of the conditioned air circling the room. Goosebumps broke out across my skin, seeming to cover every inch of me. When he stopped writing, he told me things weren't going so well at the moment, and then he handed me the cheque and asked me to wait until the end of the month to deposit it in the bank. I thanked him for his help and rose. He opened his drawer again, brought out his business card and handed it to me.

"Call me once you've gotten your visa. I'll pay for your flight ticket."

SIXTEEN

Past

Papa wasn't at home when we returned from the 10 o'clock mass at St. Dominic Catholic church on a Sunday in April. I was eight that year and we still attended the Catholic church. Like every other Sunday when Papa was away, Mama allowed us to eat lunch in front of the TV while watching one of our favourite movies.

After plaiting my hair and Lara's, Mama went to the salon to style hers. A few minutes after she left the house, we heard loud honks. Although it was unusual for Papa to be home at such an hour on a Sunday afternoon, we were certain it was him as the guard opened the garage gate. We'd memorised the sound of his car's horn so well that if several cars honked at the same time, we could tell if he was amongst them or not.

Immediately, Fola switched off the TV and then we both dashed into our rooms. From my bed, I heard Papa unlock the front door padlock, open the burglary gate and the entrance door, and shut them behind him. Several minutes later, the time it took him to change into casual wear from his usual Sunday traditional attire, he began to ring his bell. First, he rang it twice and Lara who had been expecting to be summoned had gotten up and stepped out of the room, leaving the door open. My heartbeat began to slow down as it always did when the bell stopped after the second peal. Unfortunately, the bell immediately started to ring again and then stopped after the third peal. The shallow rapid breaths and tightness of my heart returned and then worsened as I climbed down the narrow ladder from the top bunk bed. I wondered what he wanted me for since it was Lara who served his meal whenever Mama wasn't home.

By the time I stepped outside our bedroom, the bell had started all over again and Fola, who needed no magician to tell him that he was next, came out of his room. Our eyes met briefly. I saw the fear in there and knew he could see mine too. Together, we walked down the corridor towards the living room in silence. There, I tiptoed in weak little steps and stood on my feeble legs behind Lara, hiding my face from Papa, lest he remembered my shortcomings.

"How long since she left?" I heard Papa ask Lara.

"It's been a while, sir. I didn't look at the time. I wasn't in the living room when she left," she replied politely, her hands respectfully behind her back.

Fola and I had our hands behind our backs too and our heads bowed. I stared at my feet, praying that it shouldn't be the day when Papa would remember that I didn't shed tears when I cried.

"What did I tell you about knowing the exact time things happened?" Papa shouted before immediately asking again. "Who put on the TV?"

Trembling, I looked up quickly and down again. No one said anything. It was Fola and I who'd been watching *Seven Lucky Kids* while Lara had been in the room, writing one of her many letters.

"I asked who put on the TV," Papa asked again. Although he didn't shout the second time, his voice raised goosebumps on my skin.

"Mama," Fola replied.

Papa wasn't duped, he shouted, "Who was watching the TV?"

"We were, sir," Fola replied.

"Who are we?" His eyes had become a raging fire.

"Lami and I," Fola responded again.

"I touched the back of the TV and it was hot. I know you just put it off. Do you people think I am stupid? You take me for a fool. You think I will not know that you have been watching TV instead of reading your books."

I was so terrified of what was to come, I bit hard on my lip to stop myself from falling as I was shaking badly. I could sense his temper bubbling inside him from the way he spoke, for he chose his words deliberately to light the fuse of his anger bomb. We didn't know how long before he would finally explode, causing a consuming conflagration. All we knew was that Mama was not there to protect us.

"Are you not supposed to be reading your books?" he asked, looking from me to Fola and back.

"We have read them, sir," Fola replied.

"You have read all of them and you have nothing else to do but watch TV? Have you all done your chores?"

"Yes sir," we all chorused.

He was talking about the daily chores he wrote for each one of us on sticky notes, which he stuck on the refrigerator door. He would often rewrite them and switch chores, increasing or decreasing them, depending on whether we were on a school holiday or not.

"What time was the electricity restored?" he asked.

It was another question that pressed a flame to the fuse. I tried to remember what time the kids who lived in the face-me-I-face-you bungalows in the compound behind the house screamed *up NEPA*. I couldn't tell what time it was exactly, but it was before 2:00 pm. My eyes fell back to my feet. I was still so terrified I suddenly wanted to pee so badly. Papa rose, pulling his khaki shorts up by the waist as he approached us. I suppressed the urge to take a step back or make a run for the door.

"How many times have I told you, people, to always be time-conscious?" he asked.

"All the time sir," we said in unison.

Papa came and stood in front of me.

"You, why are you wearing trousers?" he asked me.

I looked up and he slapped me hard across the face. I staggered backwards and put my left hand on my burning cheek. At the same time, I was holding my pee tightly inside me. I dropped my head and kept my eyes fixed on my feet, too afraid to meet his eyes and see the hate they held for me.

"Did I not tell your mother that I don't want my daughters to wear trousers? She can if she likes, but my daughters will not wear trousers in my house."

At that point, my bladder felt as though it would burst. I knew that he would kill me if I peed on myself, yet I was too afraid to tell him I needed to go to the toilet. He walked past me and into his bedroom. A moment later, he returned with a bamboo stick and we began to move to one side of the living room as if to give clear passage for an ambulance. He kept approaching us, taking one step at a time as he held the bamboo stick at both ends and bent it, forward and backward, as if testing its flexibility. I began wiping my palms on the hip of my trousers, getting ready to receive strokes of the stick.

"You people were watching TV instead of reading," he said accusingly.

"I was not watching TV," Lara retorted, taking a step backwards.

"You don't know what time your mother left the house. You don't know what time the electricity was restored. What if something happened and you are being questioned by the Police? How will you give vital information if you don't know what time things happen?" he asked, approaching Lara.

By now, we all had our backs close to the door, but it was locked and we had nowhere to go.

"Now, why I called you all here is that I saw Mr Mensah, and he told me that he saw you people lying by the roadside in Abule-Ijesha trying to catch tadpoles from a dirty stinking gutter."

When he said that, my heart seemed to collapse and the need to pee disappeared completely. It was as though I'd just been told that I had less than an hour to live. What I'd feared the most during the last week had finally become reality. My fears had indeed caught up with me.

We'd always asked Papa for a pet, but he'd refused. 'I didn't have any pets when I was growing up,' he'd replied, the same way he'd said, 'I didn't have a bicycle while growing up' when we'd asked him for a bicycle. Fola always wanted a rabbit, but Papa had said he didn't want animals in his house. I'd also dreamed about owning a kitten many times, but I'd never voiced that dream to anyone. I knew that it would never happen. So, when we discovered that tiny fishes lived in some dirty gutter in Abule Ijesha, we decided to catch them and give them a better life.

One afternoon after school, Lara, Fola and I took some bowls and went to Abule-Ijesha. Fola laid by the roadside to catch some, using a bailer. I held the bucket where he poured in what he caught. We were on a small relatively unused road and we were not expecting to see anyone we knew. Lara, who instructed us on what to do, hadn't seen Teacher Mensah until he walked up to us.

"What are you doing here?" Teacher Mensah asked, looking into the bucket I was carrying.

Fola stood up and began to dust his shirt and shorts. "We are catching fish for our aquarium."

"Don't you know these are frogs?" Teacher Mensah asked, his eyes wide in their sockets.

We shook our heads.

"Does the odour not bother you?"

"No," Fola said.

"And you," he said to Fola. "You were practically lying by the gutter with your head almost inside. You want to take these stinking tadpoles to your house?"

"We'll change the water and take care of them," Fola replied.

"Pour them back into the gutter now!" he ordered.

Quickly and without any hesitation, I emptied the contents of the bucket into the stagnant canal. After I was done, he said to us, "Get out of here, you dirty cocoons."

Silently, we walked back home like we'd just lost a competition. A week earlier, we had stumbled upon a large, circular vase discarded near our neighbour's trash and decided to repurpose it as an aquarium. We'd cleaned it up and prepared a home for the fish we would catch. We filled it with water, layered with freshly washed sand and then hid it in Fola's room. We intended to nourish the fish with a diet of *garri* and breadcrumbs, to give them a healthier environment than the murky waters of the gutter where they resided.

That afternoon, as we walked back home not saying a word to each other, what worried me wasn't the fish we didn't have for the aquarium, but the fear that Teacher Mensah might report to Papa.

"I don't care if he tells," Lara had said as she washed her hands at the tap close to the parking lot. "The most Papa can do is beat us."

"We should have begged him not to tell Papa," I said regretfully.

Fola shrugged and said, "Let him tell if he wants to."

"Let's tell Mama so that she can talk to Teacher Mensah," I suggested.

"No need," Fola said. "He might not see Papa anytime soon or might not even remember when he does."

Ever since this incident, I'd dreaded every night when Papa returned home. A month later, when Papa didn't talk about it, I thought my prayers had been answered. I'd prayed that Papa's path should not cross Teacher Mensah's, and if it did, that Teacher Mensah should have forgotten by then. So, as Papa stood over us shouting and flexing his cane, I wished I'd run back to look for Teacher Mensah to plead with him not to tell Papa. I wish that I'd told Mama so that she could have spoken to Teacher Mensah about it, this way, he wouldn't have had any need to mention it to Papa whenever they met.

For having defied his authority to own a pet, Papa compelled us to stand on one leg and bend forward until we touched the ground with only one finger. The other hand had to be placed behind our backs and the other leg extended straight behind us. This torturous punishment was called *pick pin,* and to get it right, you had to maintain balance on one finger and one leg as though picking up a pin.

In my mind, this was one of the most pervasive and excruciating forms of punishment that had ever been devised.

***

Lara, Fola and I remained in the *pick-pin* punishment position as Papa ate and until Mama returned from the hair salon. When we shook, wobbled or changed legs or fingers, Papa flogged our backs with the long bamboo cane. Despite Mama confirming that she'd permitted us to watch TV, Papa still wouldn't relent. When he decided to let us go some three hours later, we each received twelve lashes of the bamboo stick.

Papa liked the number twelve. Perhaps it was because there were twelve months in a year or because Jesus had twelve disciples. Or, perhaps because he liked the words *one dozen* which he repeated over and over again when he told Mama what to add to the monthly grocery list. But Papa never let me go at the same time as the others. I always got more strokes of the cane, a double dozen or a triple or much more. He was always hoping that one day he would beat me hard enough that I'd shed tears. He never could understand that my dry eyes weren't an attempt to defile him, that I just couldn't, no matter how hard I tried.

"Say I will cry," Papa screamed as he flogged me.

"I will cry," I repeated after him. Still, the tears wouldn't come and mucus didn't count.

I was lying on the three-seater sofa as he whipped my back and buttocks. He continued until the cane broke in two. Then he picked up a belt.

"I'll cry, Papa." I pleaded, "Please, Papa." But my pleas hardened him, instead of reaching into his soul and finding mercy where it was hiding. "I am crying, Papa." I continued to plead as the lashes stung my skin, but he still didn't stop until he was breathless and the leather of his belt had gone soft. He took a moment to catch his breath, then he opened the living room door he had locked after he dismissed Lara and Fola, and went into the kitchen to get the big wooden spatula.

"If you kill her, I'll testify against you in court," Mama said to him, standing in his way and trying to take the stick away from him, but he pushed her out of the living room and locked the door again.

"Is it her fault that she can't shed tears? Did she create herself?" Mama shouted as she banged on the door.

I fell off the sofa onto the rug, screaming, after the first strike of the spatula landed on my already-ravaged buttocks.

"Please Papa, please. I love you, Papa." I begged.

"I don't love you, you tearless girl, you witch. You must cry."

I curled up into a ball and covered my head and face as the wooden stick struck my bones. I waited to die, but certain pains, as gruelling as they may be, couldn't kill.

"You evil child. You must cry. You must shed tears," Papa continued to shout as he struck harder and faster. "You don't want to cry, abi? By the time I am finished with you, the evil bird in you will fly away and never return."

"You're a wicked and heartless man," Mama continued to shout through the locked door.

The louder my cries, the louder Mama's shouts and the faster Papa struck while repeating *you witch*. I tried to sail away, to escape the present and Papa's strokes, but the physical pain was too real to be ignored. When he finally got tired of hitting me, he said, 'Get up and transfer to your corner' as he tried to straighten his bent waist. He let the spatula drop on the floor. He removed his glasses and wiped the tears trickling down his face with his wrist. The front of his singlet was soaked with sweat.

"Éméré," Papa spat in disgust as he put his glasses back on.

I struggled to get up, staggering as every part of my sore body throbbed with pain. I'd learnt a long time ago that no matter the number of strokes I received, and the length of time I spent in purgatory, I would never be able to pay my debt. Papa would never love me because I was the black sheep, the tearless girl. Despite all the extras I did to make him overlook this flaw— this imperfection—it was simply impossible to make him hate me even a tiny bit less.

In those days, I lived each day in constant fear. I tried to stay out of trouble so that Papa wouldn't remember that I couldn't shed tears when I cried. When the others decided to do something that risked angering Papa, I instantly became their conscience. I would remind them, in Papa's words, that he would beat the living daylight out of them and strike the hell out of me. If one of us did something wrong and Papa wanted to know who was responsible, I'd consider telling him the name of the culprit. However, I never did. Aside from the fact that Mama forbade us from telling on one another, the courage to become a traitor, to save my head alone, was simply beyond me.

"It is better he punishes you all than only one of you," Mama would say. She would line us all up and give us each a stick from the broom. "Break it," she would say, and we would, easily. And then, one after the other, she would give us the whole bunch of sticks tied together and repeat her command. None of us would be able to break them altogether, no matter how much force we applied. "You see," she would say. "When you stick together, no one can break you. They can only succeed when you're separated." Afterwards, she would make us repeat after her, over and over again, "United we stand, and divided we fall."

But Papa always flew into a mad rage when we didn't snitch on each other. Then he would punish us all. Except me. I always had to pay more wages than the others, because my cries couldn't be genuine without tears.

SEVENTEEN

Present day

August arrived with more rain and power outages. As I prepared for my trip to France, I didn't know how to make peace with not having any news about Tutu. Thoughts of our separation continued to leave me with a sore heart. I tried to convince myself that she was fine and that Mama Jide was a better mother to her than Mama Ola was to me, but I still couldn't stop worrying about my baby sister. I couldn't bring myself to relinquish all hope of finding her, no matter how distant the hope may be.

In the second week of August, my passport was finally returned to me, but without the student visa. I had been denied. I couldn't believe it. I'd received three admissions, but the French Consulate refused to give me a long-stay visa to pursue my studies in France. Had they no idea that when I returned to Nigeria it would be to propagate their language and culture?

I felt betrayed. I felt like I deserved the visa for everything I had done for the language. For the love of the language, I'd dumped Sciences for Arts. I'd been a mockery of many. When I met other Science classmates from secondary school and I told them I'd gone on and studied French, they would say with surprise, "You went to the University to study the French Language? But what happened?"

I wanted to prove to everyone that being a teacher didn't mean that I was condemned to poverty and that being a French teacher was not a self-curse. The only way I could do that was to get employed in international schools that paid in foreign currency. To get employed by these schools, I needed to have a Master's degree from France. I'd painstakingly saved for the project. I worked six days a week, every week, and barely allowed myself any luxury. I made my hair and always took a homemade meal to work for lunch.

I called my representative at Campus France who'd worked on and approved my visa application before I sent it to the Consulate. He told me my application had been rejected because the French Consulate didn't think that I was financially capable of studying and living in France temporarily. I thought I'd presented evidence of sufficient funds for my tuition and living expenses for the entire duration of the course. The Campus France representative suggested that I find a sponsor who lived in Nigeria or France and then re-apply the following year. The rejection stung. I'd been hit back-to-back with a variety of disappointments since the year started. Still, nothing prepared me for the visa denial. I'd given up my job, gifted out most of my belongings, and gotten someone who would rent my room from October.

"I can't believe they denied you," Ada said when I gave her the bad news.

I looked up at her from where I was lying in my bed, with the covers pulled up to my chin.

"It feels like I'm in a bad dream," I said.

"I'm sorry, bébé."

A sob escaped from between my lips and I covered my face with my hands. Where do I start? How do I pick my old life back up? I felt her climb onto my bed and lay down next to me.

"What are you going to do now?" she said, stroking my hair.

I uncovered my face. She looked so sad like it was her dream that had just been cut short. I sniffed and choked down another sob.

"I have to start looking for another job."

"Why don't you go back to your former school and see if they'll take you back?"

I shook up my head. "I can't go back there."

"Why?"

"Nneoma. She'll be fired because of me."

"Bébé, why are you worried about her? You need your job back."

The following day, I left home early and went around distributing my CV to private schools. By the end of the week, I'd lost count of the number of CVs I'd deposited in Ikoyi, V/I and Lekki environs. Most schools were closed for the long holidays, and their administrative departments were as well. The few that were open were there for half a day only. I would have to wait until they reopened to find out if they needed a French teacher, or if one of them who didn't already teach French as a subject, would want to give it a try. Ada announced to the new flatmate that the room would no longer be available in October and returned every naira she'd received. Thankfully, a contract had not yet been signed. I felt guilty for dashing the woman's hopes, but that faded quickly when her brother threatened Ada with personal violence.

"I escaped trouble," Ada said to me. "Imagine if she had already moved in and we'd had a disagreement. She would have brought in her thug of a brother to beat me up or even strangle me in my sleep."

When Nico returned in September and I gave him the news, he was just as upset as Ada had been on hearing it too. He offered to be my sponsor in France.

"Reapply immediately!" he said. His eyes were wide, almost golden green in colour.

I shook my head. "It's too late now."

We were sitting on the sofa in his apartment, facing one another.

"Resubmit your application," he insisted. "I'm sure you'll get it this time."

"My representative advised waiting another year before reapplying. If I do so immediately, they may find it suspicious and I'll end up having two rejections on file."

"Promise me you'll apply to Sorbonne and let me act as your sponsor in your next application."

"If we are still friends."

He reached for my hand. "Why do you think we will stop being friends?"

I shrugged. "Life happens, you know."

"Lami, we'll stop being friends only if you want... only if you cut me off..."

I shook my head quickly. "I won't. I was wrong back then. You're a good person and a good friend to me. I don't ever want to lose our friendship."

He relaxed against the chair and smiled as though he knew that I meant every word.

***

A week after school resumed in September, I still hadn't gotten any job offer that paid a decent wage. I reached out to the parents of the children I used to teach on Saturdays, informing them that my admission had been delayed for a year. Fortunately, they were happy to take me back. I also took up after-school classes for two brothers in Ikoyi. With nothing else forthcoming in teaching, I began hunting for administrative jobs on the Internet. At night, I had difficulty staying asleep for more than an hour, so I catnapped on and off, living more in the unconscious than in the conscious.

In the second week, I received a phone call from one of the private schools to which I applied. I was asked to speak to a French man over the phone. He interviewed me for about 25 minutes asking more questions about my background and motivation than about my education and job experience. The following day, I got another call from the school, informing me that I'd been selected with seven other people for the next stage. I was invited to visit the school the following Thursday, for a face-to-face interview with a panel of five people. After this, I was one of three people selected for the final stage. The last interview took place the Tuesday after. My anxiety only lasted two days before I got news of an offer for the job. A few moments later, while still basking in the news, my phone rang again. It was the director of my former school. He'd found out that I was still in the country when my prospective employer called to inquire about my performance.

"Why didn't you call me to tell me?" he asked after I explained what happened with the visa. "You know I would re-employ you in a heartbeat."

"I know sir… It's why I didn't call… I wanted you to give Nneoma a chance."

"Even you know that Nneoma isn't fully ready."

"She only needs time. She'll be as competent as I was, and even more."

"Listen to the offer I have…"

"I've already been offered a position by…"

"Lami, I'll offer you a ten per cent increase if you return to your job for one year. I want you to keep training Nneoma. It'll not be good for your career if you leave your new employer after a year… I'm sure you haven't told them your plan to leave them soon."

I felt his words melt my reluctance away. "Let me think about it," I said.

"What is there to think about?" he asked. "Call them and tell them you got another offer. They're still in the recruiting process, they'll find someone else easily."

The next morning, I was back in my former workplace. When the kids arrived at the language class for French Culture and saw me, they were all surprised and happy. They covered me with kisses and hugs, and showered me with uncountable "Vous nous avez manquez Mademoiselle Lami."

A different kind of happiness comes from working with kids—from their innocence, their unselfish love and their untainted view of life. I wished that I could see myself the way they saw me. I also wished that I could see life the way they saw it, but I knew life better. I knew that once you find happiness in what it hands you, it would immediately want it back. It would pump you up with joy and still go ahead to puncture you. Life can make you no lasting promise of joy.

During my lunch hour, I dialled Papa's number, not expecting him to pick it up. Instead of the usual recording of his voice that always came up, I got a generic computer voice saying that the number was no longer in service. I tried again and again, but still got the same message. Could he have changed his line? I was back to square one and didn't know what else to do to find him.

I tried Papa's number again when I returned home and got the same digital voice, saying the same thing. My heart sank into my stomach. His voice was the only proof I'd had in years that he was alive and it was the closest I'd ever been to finding my sister. Since getting his phone number, I'd called him over a hundred times, not once leaving him a voice message. I feared that if I left a message and he found I had his number, he could change his line so as not to speak to me. Now that his number was disconnected, the leftover hope that I'd had of finding her, completely drained away.

That day, staring at my phone as I listened to the digital voice, I finally decided I had to move on from Papa's rejection of me. I had become an adult and didn't need him for anything other than to reconnect me to Tutu if he was willing to. It didn't matter anymore if I never saw him again, if he never came to my wedding, if he never realised how much pain he'd brought me and my siblings. I was going to stop trying his number, and hoping it would be reconnected. I was going to stop asking

Aunty Stella if she had any news from any of his childhood friends. I was going to stop thinking about what he was doing if he was happy with his Jamaican wife and if he ever thought of us.

I tried to make peace with God, to stop being angry that he didn't answer my prayers. He didn't give me tears for my eyes. He didn't cure Mama from the cancer that had eaten her up alive. I accepted His decision to have made me different and I accepted His decision to take Mama. In the end, I wasn't doing too badly without my mother. At twenty-four, I wasn't burdened with an unplanned pregnancy. I wasn't married to a violent man like my father. I wasn't doing drugs and abusing alcohol. I was independent and able to fend for myself.

"Ma chérie, why don't we spend the holiday in the UK?" Ada suggested when she returned from her weekend with Andrew. I told her that Papa's phone number no longer worked.

"UK?" I stopped mashing boiled plantain inside a pot of bean porridge.

"I have a distant aunt we can stay within Manchester. When we get there, we'll ask around about how to find Tutu."

For a second, it seemed like a great idea. I could try to find Tutu, but how? It's not like I would recognise her if we sat side by side on a train. I couldn't walk into a police station and ask for help. Would two weeks be enough to find her before I had to return to Lagos to resume work?

"Chérie, I just got a visa rejection. I want to lay low until my next application." I continued mashing the plantain as white steam rose and vanished into the air.

"Damn France! I'm sure the UK will give us a visa. Some of my colleagues got six months when they applied for a tourist visa for the first time this year."

"They are bankers and I'm a teacher. It's not the same thing."

"Don't be negative, bébé,' she said in a less exciting voice. 'I'm sure you'll get it. You need the visa to dis-virgin your passport. It will help during your next French visa application."

I paused to meet her gaze. "You don't seem to realise that my life fell apart with that rejection. I lost three admissions. I'd given out half of what I owned and if not for God and you, I would have also lost my job and my accommodation."

"I know bébé and I'm sorry it happened to you. I was just thinking that the fact that you submitted a virgin passport might have been a factor. It was why I asked you to come to Lome with me last Christmas so it's no longer brand new when you applied for a visa with it. Also, you need a break, bébé. This year hasn't been a walk in the park for you."

***

November arrived with record heat across the country. The sun scorched us during the day and the heat enveloped us in the evenings. Ada counted the days before our UK visas arrived. She began planning to spend the Christmas holidays in Manchester. I, on the other hand, refused to allow myself to get carried away with any expectations, not from life or in the powers of fate and faith. I'd been faithless for too long to begin hoping for such a miracle. I'd learnt to be wary of dreaming of good things. I'd concluded that if I hoped too high, then I would fall dangerously low when disappointment inevitably set in.

Despite all my futile searches since my promise to Mama, I knew that as far as Tutu's matter was concerned, I would still reach out and grab anything that felt like hope, like a newborn would instinctively grab if it felt a finger, any finger in its palm. Every night before going to bed, I continued to connect to the internet to check my Facebook account.

After Nico returned to Lagos that November, I went to watch him play football on Wednesday. His skin had taken a lighter shade and his hair had been cut short. As always, he was clean-shaven. After the match in which Nico's team lost 3–2, he came and sat beside me on the bench. His Adam's apple bobbed as he drank from a sports water bottle and his chest rose and fell from all the running around the pitch. He held my gaze when he stopped drinking and tried to catch his breath. His hair had darkened with sweat and his jersey was sticking to his body.

"You played well," I said.

He smiled up to his eyes. "Thank you. I was happy that you came."

For a moment, we remained silent as we watched his friends talk and laugh as they analysed the game and reminisced about the tackles. One of his friends burst into a guffaw and fell on the pitch. Two others chased themselves around. We watched them in silence, listening to their laughter resounding in the air.

I stole glances at Nico and his smiling face made warmth unfurl inside me. I was happy to see him. I'd missed him in October even though we spoke nearly every day. The truth was that I liked him too much and the thought kept scaring me. What would happen when he stopped liking me? What would happen next after his contract in Nigeria ended? Would I survive another rejection if he broke my heart?

During the ride to my place, he offered to go with me on Saturday to see my childhood homes. It was Papa's birthday and Mama's death anniversary. And I had no intention of returning to the cemetery before fulfilling my promise.

On Saturday morning, Nico picked me up in his SUV. We started by going to Dolphin Estate which was closer to Banana Island, than to Lekki. The estate that had once been considered a posh area now looked like a slum. It was an eyesore in Eti-Osa, one of the richest local government areas of Lagos. Each block of flats had parking areas right in front, and instead of cars, rickety kiosks had been erected in many of the spaces. Some sold provisions, some sold foodstuffs and some sold cooked food. Others were shops for dressmakers, hair stylists, video cassette hire and shoe repairers.

The tumbledown look must have depreciated the real estate values in the area and had we delayed selling off the apartment after Grandpa died, we would have had to let it go at a loss. I was embarrassed Nico had to see the area in this bad state. After showing him the flat, we drove to the street where there'd been the baboon that had no hair on its buttocks. The prison cage was still there, but empty of its prisoner. I forced myself not to be sad, thinking that he must have died. Years back, he had already been old, and imprisoned for far too long. I hoped that wherever he was, he was free and happy.

After we left Dolphin Estate, we took the Third Mainland Bridge and headed to visit my main childhood neighbourhood. To my consternation, Lawani Street was nothing like I remembered it. For a moment,

I thought that I had the wrong address. The street looked dilapidated. The building itself seemed run-down. Its dark green colour had faded shabbily and the paint was peeling off the wall. Like when we were in Dolphin Estate, we didn't stop or get out of the car. A flood of emotions washed over me as Moses cruised by slowly, me pointing to the balcony where I'd stood and watched Mama Jide drive away with Tutu.

As we headed back to Lagos Island in silence, we drove into a traffic holdup on Herbert Macaulay Way. Young and old men and women in colourful T-shirts hawked snacks, drinks, CDs and phone cards along the barely moving lanes. I could hear the traffic cacophony despite the windows being rolled up, and despite the radio playing R&B songs. Drivers cursed one another out, okadas and motorists honked at each other, sirens screamed at motorists to clear the way, traders haggled as they jogged after making their trades, and beggars lamented into the rolled-up windows of flashy cars in the hope of being given money. As I watched these scenes, in my mind a shift was happening as it dawned on me that the life I had known had become a mirage; it no longer existed.

Eventually, we reached the Third Mainland Bridge which was free of traffic and drove through to connect Lagos Island. The odour that Makoko emitted had changed over the years, going from pungent to putrid. The smell permeated the vehicle and didn't fade before we descended from the eight-lane bridge. It was another confirmation that the past was gone forever. Still, I was sick with nostalgia, with the feeling of moving fast through life, the same one that used to overwhelm me as a child when Mama drove us through the bridge.

That night, I had a hard time falling asleep. I couldn't stop thinking about how the past I'd imagined was no more and how I had to stop looking backwards. In the following days, I worked on making peace with my past, particularly my childhood. I began making intentional efforts to live in the present and accept reality. I stopped allowing my mind to wander back in time. I accepted that I couldn't have changed who my father was. I had no control over the things he did and couldn't change how things had turned out with a progenitor-like him. But I could do something about the present and the future. I could stop my childhood trauma from continuing to affect me and keep me from living. I could free myself from its web to enjoy my life to its fullest.

EIGHTEEN

Past

When I was seven, I was chosen to audition and then selected to take part in the Christmas Carol. Every member of the choir was asked to wear long white socks for the occasion. Mama was proud that I would perform on stage in front of an audience, but when I told her about the socks criteria, she said, "Ask your father for the money."

"You know he won't give me," I said to Mama after I'd asked Papa once and he pretended not to have heard me.

"He'll give you," Mama insisted. "He likes doing things at the last minute. Keep asking him until he gives it to you."

Every other day, I would inflate myself with courage before going to stand before Papa. Then I'd subtly remind him that I needed money for the long white socks. Still, he would ignore me and I'd scurry down the corridor, back to my room before his mood turned sour.

"Let me wear the socks you bought for me to wear to church on Christmas day," I pleaded with Mama the night before the program. "I promise that I'll not get them dirty."

Mama had already bought our Christmas attires so that she wouldn't pay more at the last hour which was when Papa always gave her his share of the cost.

"Go and ask your father for the money," Mama repeated. "If he gives you, then I'll give you the socks and replace them. If he knows I've bought your Christmas attires already, then he won't give me his share and I really need that money to offset other expenses."

I mustered up all my courage until my lungs felt bloated and my chest expanded. I dawdled to Papa who was in their bedroom and asked him once again for money to buy a pair of long white socks. He looked away from what he was doing at his reading table, setting his eyes on me before saying that he'd wanted to give the money to Mama, but he'd forgotten all about it. He sounded really sincere, saying that since the Christmas Carol was the following day, it was too late to buy one.

"Wear what you have," he concluded.

"The headmistress wants us to wear new long white socks. My school socks are no longer very white and they stop halfway up my calves."

"I am sorry for you then. It's too late and there's nothing I can do about it now."

"It's not too late," I blurted. "Mama has brand new socks."

I told him to ask Mama to let me wear the ones she'd bought for me for Christmas day. So, he returned with me to the sitting room where Mama was watching TV and asked her to give the socks to me. When Mama refused, Papa returned to their bedroom and began to turn everything upside down, looking for the attires Mama was hiding. Mama rose from her chair and went into their bedroom.

They began screaming and shouting at each other. Minutes later, Papa began whipping Mama with a belt. It was no surprise to either Lara, Fola or myself. Many times, over the years, we'd witnessed Papa slapping or punching her, or even beating her with a belt. It always ended up with him throwing her things out. So, as we stood outside our bedroom doors, we were waiting for Mama to come out and tell us we had to leave.

When Mama's scream got louder, we all ran to the living room. Lara tried to open their bedroom door, but it was locked. She began to hit the door while Fola and I cried. Through the locked door, Papa asked us to return to our rooms. He went on to say that if he came out and we were still there he would pounce on us so that we wouldn't know what side to sleep on that night. I was the first to sprint down the corridor to the girls' room. My last experience in purgatory was barely a month before and I didn't want to go back there.

We waited in our rooms until Mama came to get us. Her upper lip was swollen, and as usual, Papa had thrown her things out. She sat on Lara's bed and cried for a while; muffled sobs that echoed in my ears. She pulled me close as she cried, dispelling any fear I might have that she was angry with me.

Lara and I quickly packed our clothes in our school bags. It'd happened several times before that we no longer needed Mama to pack for us in her leather suitcases. As far as I could remember, Papa always sent Mama out of the flat every time they fought. Their rifts always started with arguments and shouting, then sometimes would escalate into a physical fight. After they wore themselves out from warring, Papa would ask Mama to leave his home. He didn't care what time of the night it was. Neither did he care that she left with us. He knew someone from her family would come to beg him to take her back, under the guise of helping the couple settle their rift. He knew whoever would come would not have the courage to apportion his own blame to his face. In these conflicts, Mama had to admit to being the culprit for him to have her back under his roof.

That night, much like other times, I was happy we were going away, far away from the flat, purgatory and Papa, I also felt guilty for my role in starting the fight. It'd been a peaceful evening, and there'd been peace in our home for days. I scolded myself as I looked through my side of the wardrobe for the clothes to take. Papa came out of their bedroom as we were leaving. We were now standing outside the flat, waiting for Mama who was trying to connect the padlock to the bolt on the burglary gate. Papa stared at me, a surprised look on his face.

"Lami, are you too going with your mother?" he asked just as Mama snapped the padlock shut.

I nodded and he flared up, unlocking a torrent of fury.

"Is it not because of you all these things happened? I was fighting for you and now you want to go with your mother. You are an evil child."

He shouted through the burglary gate, his voice echoing in the stairway. I stood still, trembling on my thin legs as Mama, Lara and Fola began to descend the stairs, and until Papa banged the door. The insults he heaped on me sat heavily upon my head, weighing heavier than the school bag on my back. I didn't understand why he was surprised I was going with her. I always went with her. He should know he had no chance if we had to choose between Mama and him.

"Let's go," Mama said, looking up at me from the lower landing.

We waited under the stairs while the security man went in search of a taxi. It wasn't midnight yet, so he found one quickly. By the time we arrived at Dolphin Estate that night, one of Mama's eyes had swollen shut, puffed up like *puff-puff*. Uncle Kay gave up his bed, as usual, and went to sleep on the sofa in the living room. Lara, Fola, and I gathered on the bed with Mama. Tutu wasn't yet born then. I stayed awake for a long time listening to Mama groan every time she moved as she tried to find the best sleeping position. I'd seen the belt marks all over her body as she was changing into her pyjamas. As I lay there, staring at the golden light reflected from the street lamp on the wall, I wished that we never had to go back home.

In the morning, Mama called her office and made excuses for not coming in. Despite the built-up anticipation, I didn't go to the Christmas Carol program either. I didn't care about it anymore. We spent the Christmas holiday at Dolphin Estate because Mama and Papa didn't settle their rift until the following year. I was sick from the moment I learnt that we were returning home to Papa. Whenever we had to return home after one of their fights, I always fell sick and would throw up everything I tried to eat.

During the next two days, I suffered from stomach aches and a high fever. It was impossible to keep drugs and food down. When we returned home, I made myself invisible. I didn't want to be seen by Papa. I feared that he would remember my betrayal. As the day passed slowly, each peal of the bell made my heart beat faster and faster, and only gradually slowed if a fourth one followed the third.

NINETEEN

Present day

Six weeks after Ada and I applied for UK visas, we received our passports back. I got a big surprise and Ada, a big shock. She was denied, but I was granted a six-month visa.

"Fuck the UK," Ada said, looking up from her passport. "They must be feeling special with their freezing temperatures."

We were in the living room, still in our work clothes. I stared at her, holding my passport up in my hands. I couldn't believe it. I'd been certain she would get it and I would be refused. Indeed, she earned more than I did, but I had more money in my account—the funds I'd put aside for my studies, my inheritance from Dolphin Estate, the funds Mr Durojaiye gave me and all the money I'd saved from my salary ever since I started working. Apparently, it had been sufficient for a UK tourist visa, even though it fell short for a French student visa.

Ada took another glance at her passport before flinging it on the dining table and falling onto the sofa.

"I can't go without you," I said, meeting her gaze.

"Why not? You can still stay with my aunt in Manchester. She won't mind."

I stared at the dark screen of the TV. This was supposed to be a girls' trip. We were supposed to be discovering a white Christmas together. We were supposed to create the same memories.

"No way I'm going without you. What will I do all day long?"

Later, as I lay in bed, my thoughts turned to the visa. Though I was saddened by Ada's rejection, the sadness quickly dissipated in the face of my own elation at being granted a visa. It still felt surreal. I retrieved my passport from the bedside table drawer and gazed at the visa. Placing the passport over my heart, I closed my eyes. I would be in the same city as Tutu. But, could I travel to London by myself? Without Ada?

Opening my eyes, I remembered a university classmate who had relocated to London with her family. We were friends on Facebook. I should contact her. Suddenly, I realised that the power was out and that everything was pitch black. I jumped up and grabbed my phone from under my pillow, the light from the screen chasing away the darkness around me. Outside, generators roared to life, their engines devouring the tranquillity like ravenous beasts. I paused, realising that I had been in the dark for a moment without panicking. My nyctophobia had been chased away, albeit briefly, by a moment of happiness.

On Wednesday after work, I rested a bit at home before heading to Fantasy Land to watch Nico play football. After the match, we walked slowly around the pitch, going in circles. The sun had set, and the sky was already hosting the stars. Smiling up at him, I told him I'd stayed in the dark for several seconds without panicking. And while he was still smiling at the good news, I told him my UK visa application had been granted. His eyes twinkled, competing with the stars. I felt like a proud little girl showing off her report card to her parents.

"I haven't quite decided whether I'll go to London yet," I said. "Ada and I had planned to go together. She's no longer her usual bubbly self since she was denied the visa. I don't know what to do to make her feel better."

Nico nodded as though in sympathy. "She's a strong person. She'll get through this."

Two of the players shouted their goodbyes to us. Nico and I smiled and waved at them. It was a beautiful night. An occasional mild breeze stirred the stuffy air from the blistering heat of the day. A small group of players were still standing in the middle of the pitch, their sports bags hanging from their shoulders or on the floor beside them.

"It's a year since we met," Nico says all of a sudden.

We stopped walking and stood facing each other. Two of Nico's teammates ran around us chasing each other and laughing hard. I smiled and followed them with my eyes.

"How time flies," I said when my gaze met Nico's again.

I told him about the dinner with Tunji that had ended badly the night we'd bumped into each other at the entrance of Eko Hotel. His friends stopped by us to give Nico his sports bag and say goodbye.

"I want to take you out to dinner for your birthday," Nico said when we were all alone.

"Because of what I just told you?"

"This way, Tunji will no longer be your last date." He reached out and took my hand.

"C'est un rencard?" I looked up from our hands.

"Oui, Lami. So, will you go out on a date with me?"

My eyes found my feet. Then I bit my lip. He reached a hand up and with a finger, tipped my head back up until our gaze met and melded. My heart raced as he searched deep inside my eyes. I wanted to look away, shut my eyes, and refuse him access to my soul, but I couldn't pull away.

He leaned closer and my eyes fluttered shut. All I could hear was the loud beating of my heart. I opened my eyes when he brushed his lips against my forehead. Just then the bright field lightning was shut down, leaving our vision to the mercy of the yellow security lamps. Nico started to chuckle. I joined in. He bent over to pick up his sports bag from the ground and slung it over his shoulder. Then he grabbed my hand in his as we walked to his car.

"7:00 pm, Saturday," he said when we arrived at my place.

"Where are you taking me?"

"You'll have to wait to find out." A teasing smile appeared on his lips. I smiled back and unbuckled my seat belt.

***

Nico was on time to pick me up on Saturday evening. I wore a black, knee-length dress that Ada opined was more appropriate for a formal ceremony than a dinner date. Nico wore a suit jacket without a tie, which gave him a casual look. He took me to the Asian-Fusion Restaurant at Eko Hotels and Suites on Victoria Island where I'd had dinner with Tunji. We got a table close to the big windows. The sun had set, but there were orange streaks still painted across the sky. A waiter in a waistcoat came and took our order. While we waited for our dishes, we had a drink—Malta Guinness for me and an espresso martini cocktail for Nico—and shared the events of our day.

I could tell that Nico was ill at ease because he avoided meeting my eyes many times as we talked. I waited restlessly for him to pop the question, formally asking me to be his girlfriend. My restlessness must have added to his nervousness because he kept blushing and showing dimples. By the time our dishes arrived, he still hadn't asked me out as I'd suspected he would.

The food was good. The dim lights gave an elegant enchanting aura and the sweet soothing jazz piano composition that played in the background made it a perfect night to *be asked out.*

"I have a gift for you," he announced suddenly.

I protested as he produced a small box from inside the pocket of his jacket which he hung on the back of his chair. He placed the wrapped gift beside my plate.

"What is it?' I asked, eyeing the cute box. I pushed away the empty dessert plate, picked up the gift, and began to unwrap it.

"Earrings?" I asked, looking up at him from a little black leather box.

He said nothing.

I pressed the clasp and the lid flipped open to display a chain and heart locket made of gold. It had beautiful paisley scrollwork on the front side of the pendant. Engraved on the reverse side were the words, "Always in my heart."

I read it aloud, looked up at him and asked, "What's this?"

"It's a photo locket that can take two pictures on the inside."

We both knew that his response was not what I was referring to.

"Is it for me?" I asked, still bewildered.

He nodded.

"Are these real diamonds?" I asked again as the stones sparkled even in the dim light. "It must have cost you a fortune."

"Yes, they are real diamonds. There are twenty-two of them."

"Oh my God Nico! This is so beautiful. It's an incredible gift, but it's too much, I cannot accept it."

I opened the locket and couldn't help but imagine which of Mama's pictures I was willing to cut to insert inside. Afterwards, I put the chain and locket back gently into the black box, set it down on the table, and pushed it towards him.

"It's a birthday gift."

"The dinner itself is already a gift. You didn't have to bother."

"It wasn't a bother. I wanted to get you something very nice. I thought that you might want to carry a picture of your sister and your mum with you wherever you go," he said as the waiter arrived to clear the table.

I wanted to say, "I just want you to ask me out formally." Instead, I said, "Nico, I'm so sorry, but I'm afraid I can't accept this gift. It's too expensive. I mean it's very beautiful, but it's just too much."

At that moment, another waiter arrived with the bill. Once Nico took care of the bill, we made our way out of the restaurant. On our way to Lekki, he asked me if I'd decided about going to the UK alone and staying a few days in London.

"I'm considering it seriously," I said.

Although I'd eventually accepted to let life take its natural course as Aunty Stella had advised and not force things, I couldn't help thinking that I could find Mama Jide through a newspaper announcement in

London. So, I told Nico about my plans to run adverts in a London newspaper if it wouldn't be too costly.

"Why don't you come to spend Christmas with me in Paris?" he said all of a sudden. "We'll find a newspaper in London together and have the announcement published. As soon as they find your sister, we'll fly to London. It's an hour away by flight." The words rushed out of his mouth like they burnt his tongue.

"You want me to come to Paris?"

"Yes. You can apply for a French tourist visa and come to Paris. You won't be by yourself in London without Ada."

"It's barely three months since I was denied a visa at the French embassy."

"You were denied a student visa, not a tourist visa. It's not the same thing."

I shook my head. "They'll deny me again and it'll be on their file when I'll have to reapply for a student visa."

"You'll be asking only for two weeks. You don't have to do anything. I'll handle it. Don't worry. I'll invite you. I'll give you an invitation letter. Two weeks is nothing. They can't refuse that."

I stared at him, thinking, wondering if it was a good idea. I wasn't sure I was capable of spending time alone with Nico without revealing too much about my feelings.

"Lami," he said a little firmly. "You won't be denied this time around. You have a valid UK visa on your passport and I'll be inviting you."

We lapsed into silence as Moses sped down Ozumba Mbadiwe Road. Flashy cars, some with diplomatic plate numbers, sped past us.

"I don't want to force you," he said, as we approached Lekki roundabout. "You've always said you don't like spending the holidays alone. If you don't mind spending it in cold Paris with me, then you are welcome. You can have my room, and if you don't feel like going to Brittany for the New Year, you can stay back at the apartment when I leave. You're not obliged to come with me."

"I don't know…"

"We can visit the Louvre. You've always wanted to see it." He suddenly sounded excited as if I'd already agreed to his proposition.

"Give me some time to think about it," I said, apologetically.

***

The night before Nico left for Paris, he invited Ada, Andrew, and me to a parlour party he was organising at his apartment. He also invited the sequined girl, Gina, and her friend. After apéro and a few games of pool, we went out dancing at a nearby nightclub. The club was packed and the music was deafening, but we still managed to have a great time dancing. I was so happy to see my friends being friends. After leaving the club, Nico and I returned to his apartment. He insisted I took his bedroom, like the first time I had spent the night there.

Later, as I stood by the light switch of the adjoining bathroom, I took a deep breath and plunged myself into complete darkness. My heartbeat quickened, and I immediately turned the lights on again.

"I can do it," I told myself.

I turned the light off again and counted five seconds until I turned it on again. My fingers were cold and my mouth was dry.

"I did it," I said to myself again. "I can do ten."

I flicked the lights off again and reached eight before summoning the light again. Beads of sweat formed on my forehead. I didn't want to push my luck, so I left the bathroom door ajar and climbed into bed. In the same room where I had gone crazy when I found myself enveloped in thick darkness, I had been able to tolerate eight seconds of darkness of my own will. I fell asleep smiling, proud of my progress. I had faced my fear and won.

The next morning, we woke up early so that Nico could get to the airport for his flight. We didn't talk about his invitation for me to spend the holiday in France the night before, and we didn't talk about it again that morning until about an hour before he had to leave.

"I've been thinking about something that may help find your sister," Nico said after he set his luggage at the door.

"What?" I turned in my seat to face him. I was sitting in one of the high chairs around the island.

"Would you permit me to hire a private investigator in England who can find your aunt?"

I paused, fixing my eyes on him as excitement began to build up inside me. It was such a stroke of genius. Why hadn't I thought of it myself? In that eureka moment, I realised how brilliant he was and how grateful I was to have met him again that night at the Eko Hotel entrance gate. Had I taken one of the hotel cabs, we would have missed each other and perhaps never seen each other again.

"It should be easier to find someone in Europe than in Africa. Do you have her picture?"

"You mean my sister? I have a picture of her at two." I rose, retrieved my handbag from the sofa and rummaged inside it for my purse. Then I handed him the picture. "It won't be of any help. She may have grown darker, fatter, and her face might have completely changed."

He stared at it for a long time before looking up to meet my eyes.

"She has your eyes," he said.

"Lara, Tutu and I all have our mother's eyes."

We discussed his plan throughout the entire journey to the airport, and it seemed almost too good to be true. Could this truly be the one solution that would ultimately lead me to find Tutu?

"You really want me to come to meet your parents?" I asked after he said we could spend New Year at his family house in Brittany if we found Tutu before.

"I've talked so much about you to my parents. They'll be happy to meet you."

"You already told them about me?"

He nodded.

I averted my eyes from his and focused on the scenery ahead. We had just reached the airport. I met his gaze again and told him I would be happy to meet them. I also told him I would be the happiest person alive if Tutu was found before Christmas. I heard the sound of the doors unlocking. Moses, who had parked the vehicle, opened his door and stepped out as though to give us privacy, even though he didn't speak any French.

"If you give me her full name and the name of your aunt with whom she lives, maybe she can be found before Christmas and you could have a beautiful Christmas gift," Nico said.

When he offered to foot the bill for finding Tutu, I declined his offer, telling him that I would use a part of my savings.

"No, keep your tuition fee," he said. "I suggested the private investigator. Let me do this for you please."

"No," I shook my head. "I'd rather pay for it."

"Fifty, fifty. Let me be part of this important event in your life."

I leaned towards him and threw my hands around his neck.

"Thank you so much," I whispered. "You are so kind but I can't accept it."

He removed my hands from around his neck gently and leaned back to stare into my eyes. I could feel my lips curling, changing shape. I looked away because I didn't want him to see my face crumple up as I cried.

"You are the one who is kind and who brings sunshine into my life. Because of you, I feel at home in Nigeria. My family is far away, but I don't feel lonely. You're my only family here."

He put his hands around me, pulling me close for comfort.

"No one has ever told me that," I said. "No one has ever made me feel this way, as if I'm needed."

With Ada, I was the one who needed and depended on her. She was strong and intelligent, and I always felt like I was the complete opposite. Hearing Nico, who had other friends in Lagos, both Nigerians and non-Nigerians, say it was me who made him feel at home, I felt like I was useful for something in our friendship. Calling me his family made me realise that family wasn't only those whom one shared a bloodline with. It was okay if Lara, Wale and Fola didn't want us to rebuild our relationship. I had Ada, and now Nico. And it was more than enough for me.

"If you don't get a French visa, I'll come to meet you in London and we'll find a detective."

I swallowed a sob as I nodded and threw my arms around him again. "Oh, Nico, you must be an angel."

TWENTY

Past

Days after we returned home from Dolphin Estate, I knew to continue to watch my back as I could tell that Papa hadn't forgiven me for what happened with the white socks. A week later, on Saturday evening, the moment that I'd feared the most arrived. A secret that I'd been keeping was finally uncovered by Papa.

When I received my report card in school and saw that I had the second position, I panicked. It'd been the first term of a new class and I'd lost the top spot to a boy called John. I knew Papa would be angry. I'd always been top of the class since I started primary school. I'd always worked hard to retain the position because I wanted to please Papa. Then it became something that I knew he would be upset about if ever I lost it. I'd studied hard for the exams and couldn't understand why I'd arrived second. I feared Papa would blame it on the Christmas carol preparations. So, when I discovered that John had only done slightly better than myself, I thought that perhaps the information would make Papa less angry. But the more I thought about it as the hours passed, the more scared I'd become. So, on my way home, an idea came to me as I passed in front of a bookshop. I ran home, broke my piggy bank, and went back out to buy a red pen. In the toilet, I shaded the position from two to one. It was badly done, and I began to fear that Papa would suspect that I did it myself. Later that night, as he looked at the report card, he asked why my teacher had painted my report card like a five-year-old.

"She made an error," I said. "She wanted to write one, but wrote two and had to correct it."

Papa believed me. He scolded Lara and Fola for not being among the top three in their respective classes. Then he praised me, saying I'd never gotten anything lower than the first position. He announced that I would be the only one to get a Christmas present. I never got it, maybe because we spent Christmas in Dolphin estate or because I was the instigator of the white socks rift. Not that I cared. I never had any intention to ask him if he forgot, knowing what I'd done. What I'd never contemplated was that Papa would bump into my teacher and speak to her about the untidy report card.

Papa was furious when he found out that I'd come second that term. He ordered me to *pick pin* and flogged my back every time the leg that I was supposed to hang in the air touched the ground.

"If you cry with tears, I will let you go," he said, from where he was sitting in the living room.

Amusement seemed to flicker in his eyes. He knew I couldn't, no matter how hard I cried. I prayed to God for a miracle. I couldn't understand why I had plenty of spit in my mouth and mucus in my nose, but no tears in my eyes.

When Papa felt like I'd had enough, he whipped me. Twelve strokes on each hand, and another twelve on my butt. As always, he locked the door of the sitting room so that Mama couldn't interfere.

"I beg you, don't kill that girl." Mama banged on the door, wailing along with me. "What she did is wrong, but does that mean you should kill her?"

"Get up and transfer to your corner," Papa said after the final lash of the whipping on my buttocks.

I got off the sofa and staggered like a drunkard to his bedroom. There, Papa opened his wardrobe and pushed his jackets to one side, revealing a little stool. Papa had said he got a carpenter to build the stool specially for Mama, to turn amala in the kitchen. But it ended up being a stool meant for me to sit in purgatory, one that Mama borrowed when she needed to make amala. As I grew older, Papa thought I'd be more comfortable in purgatory if I was sitting on the stool and no longer on the floor of the wardrobe.

Trembling, I watched Papa shut the wardrobe door. I could tell he'd switched off the lights when there was none spilling into the wardrobe from around the door. Horrified of the dark, I began to panic because I couldn't see my hands. I couldn't tell if it was just the dark or if I had gone blind. Fear laid its grip on me and wouldn't let me go. The thickness of the darkness also hung to my spirit, pulling and holding me down.

"Don't let them take away my sight, oh God," I would pray with a tearless sob every time I was in the darkroom. "I would rather be deaf or dumb, but don't let me be blind please!"

The dark room was the place I dreaded most in the world. But Papa always made me sit here, in purgatory to think about what I'd done and why I'd stubbornly refused to shed tears until I would be forgiven and allowed to return to the girls' room. Sometimes, I could be there for up to an hour. Other times, I could be there most of the night or even until the following day. And some other times, I was there all through the weekend.

In the dark room, my eyes would strain as they searched for anything to assure me that I hadn't gone blind without knowing it. I would feel my eyes with my fingers, wondering why my lashes weren't wet, wondering if I was truly a witch but didn't know it yet.

In the dark room, my tummy would growl hungrily, and I would salivate as I imagined my siblings eating quietly at the dining table without me, afraid of making any noise with the cutlery. In my mind's eyes, I would see my empty chair and my plate hanging clean on the plate rack in the kitchen. Then I would console myself as my stomach continued to make loud gurgling sounds.

"Don't worry, Lami. It's just another night without supper. It won't kill you."

When Wale was visiting and I was in purgatory during the day, he would sneak into the dark room to see me when he could. He would bring me a small piece of bread and give me a little cross which he always carried with him. He would place the pendant cross in the centre of my palm and gently help me tighten my swollen fingers around it.

"Jesus will take away your pain," he would say, and gratefully, I would hold on to the cross as if my life depended on it. After he left, I would kiss the cross several times, like Grandpa used to do to his, and would only give it back to Wale after I left purgatory.

Whenever Mama had the chance, especially while Papa had gone to use the toilet, she would sneak into the room to give me painkillers which I would chew without water. Sometimes, she would bring me one or two Okin biscuits. Before leaving, in a brief second, she would stroke my head and I would cling to her clothes, after which she would hastily retreat. It became a routine, some sort of comfort. Another thing that eased my distress was the touch of her trembling hand as she rubbed my head. I could sense her fear. Alone in the dark room, I would reassure myself that it was okay to be afraid. If Mama could be fearful, then it was okay for me to be too.

It was in that dark room that I'd let my guard down, opening myself up to a legion of fears. Many of my anxieties took root in that very place: a deep-seated phobia for darkness, the terror of losing my sight, the fear of being a witch without knowing it, the persistent fear of never being able to shed tears, the constant worry of never gaining Papa's approval, the haunting fear of being rejected by my siblings, and a myriad of other concerns.

As the years passed, I carried these countless fears with me everywhere until I began to suffocate under their weight. I wanted to shed them, but I didn't know how to ward them off on my own. They grafted themselves upon my spirit until they became a part of my personality—a part of me.

These fears fed on my anxieties and grew bigger and bigger, shadowing me through my journey from childhood to adulthood, while transforming and adopting other fears along the way: The fear of rejection, stemming from my inability to earn Papa's love. The fear of death gripped me after Mama's passing. The fear of abandonment, an unhealed wound from losing my mother, which was deepeened by my breakup with my first boyfriend in university year. The constant fear that something unfortunate would occur whenever I chanced upon a little happiness.

TWENTY-ONE

Present day

December had longer nights. The sun rose late, gathering its full strength at noon before gradually yielding to an early sunset. The circle went round and round, turning days into weeks. As the month drew to a close, despite daily practices, I still couldn't endure more than ten seconds in pitch-blackness without giving in to panic. To my disappointment, my nyctophobia wasn't fading as quickly as I had hoped.

During that month, I juggled between exam preparations and the school Christmas concert. Still, I was grateful these things kept me occupied and prevented me from dwelling on my visa application, sparing me the anxiety of potential rejection. Finally, the end-of-year exams came and passed. The French Carol was a success. A Schengen visa was pasted into my passport. Fortune smiled at me. I was going to France.

The days before my flight were foggy in my memory. I'd been too dazed to truly comprehend that I would be spending the holiday in Paris, that I would hire a detective to find Tutu and that I would go to the UK to see her. My life felt too good to be true so my mind rose in my defence, constantly reminding me that nothing good lasts long. I, thus, started waking up daily expecting something to go wrong that would make my trip to Paris impossible. Many times, I'd open my passport just to stare at the Schengen visa, hoping that the surreal feeling would leave me. Because I'd been sure I would be denied, I hadn't allowed myself to dream about what it would mean to spend the holiday in Paris. With everything I'd been through, I'd made myself believe that rejections were more difficult to handle when expectations were high.

It wasn't until I landed in Paris and spilt out from the plane with other passengers that everything truly became real. As I walked on French soil and followed the signs to baggage claim, the weight of reality continued to sink in. I was indeed in the Paris of my dreams, the Paris of my books, the Paris I'd seen only in images on Google; the Paris I'd taught the children about; the Paris Nico described to me over the phone when he walked its streets at night; the Paris that was believed to allow one die fulfilled just from beholding it.

After picking up my bag from the carousel, I walked toward the exit on shaky feet. With each step, my heart thumped hard against my ribcage. For some reason, I was suddenly seized with the fear that Nico wouldn't be there. Where would I go if he didn't show up? Amidst throngs of people who were waiting in the arrivals area, I searched the ocean of eager faces and there he was, waiting, just as he had said. He was wearing a dark brown winter jacket with the hood up. When he saw me, he pulled down the hood and smiled. He had, without a doubt, the most beautiful dimpled smile I'd ever seen. Relieved to see him, I rushed into his arms and we hugged for a long time as though we were lovers who had been apart for many months.

Nico had arrived thirty minutes before my plane was due to land and had come with a black doudoune that had faux fur around the hood. He'd also brought leather gloves and a scarf for me. In the middle of the hall, I changed from the jacket I was wearing to the black doudoune. Afterwards, he helped me with my luggage and we exited the airport holding hands. Even through the gloves, I could feel the warmth of his hand and the joy he felt at having me in his country.

Some forty minutes after we left the airport in a taxi, we arrived in a beautiful and calm residential area in a place called La Defense. The buildings didn't have high fences, electric barbed wire, or security guards. We didn't see anyone out in the street, nor around or inside Nico's building. As we walked toward the elevator, the only noises I heard were those of our shoes and the rollers of my luggage against the black and white marble floor. Nico's apartment was on the fifth floor. The corridor smelled like hotel restaurants—a melange of different home-cooked food. My stomach growled as I inhaled the aroma, even though it wasn't anything close to the smell of Nigerian spices. I was starving. I'd fallen asleep before the flight attendants served food on the plane and no one had thought to wake me up.

Nico's apartment was at the end of the corridor. He'd left the heating on and the temperature was very comfortable. Standing by the door, I looked around the room as I removed my extra clothing—gloves, scarf, bonnet, and jacket—until I felt lighter. Like in Lagos, his living room had an open-plan kitchen, but with more elaborate furnishing and not enough space for a pool table.

"It's so nice here. I'm not going to step out of this apartment until it's time to go back to Lagos," I joked, rubbing my hands together to get the blood flowing freely again.

He laughed. "You won't stay all locked up during your stay here. I've got activities lined up that you'll like."

Walking behind him in socks and his indoor slippers, he showed me around his apartment with the intruding daylight giving it a radiant glow. It had just a bedroom which he'd prepared for me, and which I tried to decline, but he wouldn't hear of it. He prepared the bathroom so I could have a hot bath. When I stepped out of the bathroom, the aroma of food was floating in the air. Nico served cucumber, avocado, and cold smoked salmon for starters, after which we had baked pasta.

With lunch over, we set up the Christmas tree he'd bought and hung glittering silver snowflakes and shiny ball ornaments all over it. He placed a glittering silver star tree topper at the top of the tree and hung a garland over the entrance door. He told me it was the first time he was setting up a tree in his apartment. He said it was so I could get the full experience of a Parisian Christmas holiday. Each year, he spent Christmas with his family in Brittany, and so had never needed a tree there. As for me, the last time I'd decorated a Christmas tree, it had been with my mother and every one of my siblings, and I had believed that I was one of the happiest children in the world.

As Nico parked up the empty boxes of the tree and its decorations, I logged into Facebook on his laptop and sent Ada a message, telling her that I'd arrived safely, and giving her Nico's home number. After a dinner of potatoes cooked in melted duck fat and red wine, Nico and I sat side by side, browsing various websites in search of British private detectives. We came across several agencies and numerous detectives, but it was challenging to discern which ones were reputable. After some deliberation, we selected five and I proceeded to email each one, briefly explaining what I required.

To my surprise, about an hour later, I received a response from one, Detective Barrot. He asked for all the information I had regarding Mama Jide. I couldn't believe it; I hadn't expected any response until after Christmas. I promptly replied, explaining that all I had was her maiden name, as neither Papa nor Mama Ola had ever mentioned her married name. Given that her first child was named Jide, everyone simply referred to her as Mama Jide or Big Mummy. Detective Barrot responded immediately, mentioning his hourly charges for the job and indicating that insufficient information would result in a higher fee. I requested a day or two to see if I could gather more information that might help in the investigation.

That night, while Nico slept on the convertible sofa in the living room and I had his big soft bed all to myself, I couldn't fall asleep, despite the fatigue from my six-hour flight. The email exchange with Detective Barrot hadn't gone as I'd imagined, and my new hope of finding Tutu had suddenly been shaken from its new foundation. I didn't have any way of getting any more information. I decided I would let Detective Barrot start his search anyway. If Tutu still hadn't been found by the time I exhausted the amount I put aside for this cause, I'd ask him to stop then.

***

Breakfast was a bowl of chocolate, fresh chocolate au pain and a croissant. The croissants tasted nothing like the ones I bought from a French boulangerie in Lagos. It melted on the tongue like butter on a hot pan. I watched in amusement as Nico spread butter and jam on both sides of his sliced baguette before dipping it in his bowl of coffee.

The sun still wasn't up by the time we left the apartment at 10:00 am. I wanted to shop for warm clothes. When Nico told me that the mall was only about a twelve-minute walk away, I suggested going on foot so that I could get a closer view of the city. The road had lanes for pedestrians, cyclists, vehicles and trams. Every other minute, tramways moved past us in both directions. Despite the gloves and the bonnet, my fingers went stiff with cold and my brain felt numb. Still, I enjoyed the walk to La Défense station. I was amazed when I found out that each of the buildings around had a name. To distract myself from the stinging cold, I named areas in Lagos where trams would reduce traffic congestion and improve the lives of Lagosians.

Les Quatre Temps shopping mall was inside the station. Nico opened and held doors for me as we walked in and out of stores. He was generous with his time as I tried on clothes in the fitting room. All of the jumpers I chose had turtlenecks to protect my neck from the cold. Nico gave me his opinion each time I asked for it and he insisted on carrying my shopping bags.

At noon, we lunched in a small Italian restaurant inside the mall and bought an international calling card from a Tabac shop. I needed to call my siblings. I needed to find out if they had any information about Mama Jide. The first thing I did when we returned home was to check my email, but there was still no response from the other detectives. I called Lara's number, but it didn't ring. Her phone was switched off. Next, I called Wale's number, but it was also unreachable. When I called Fola, to my surprise, he picked up after the first ring.

"How many times did we even see her?" he asked when I asked him if he remembered anything about Mama Jide. "All I remember is that she's a nurse and she had four children then. I think her husband was a taxi driver. I remember that he once cheated on her with another woman who had a Nigerian restaurant in London."

"I can't believe you remember that. I remember Mama saying she lost a lot of weight from fasting and praying for forty days so that the woman would stop enticing her husband with food."

I tried Lara's number five times before bedtime, but it remained out of service.

The following morning, I tried it again before Nico and I left the apartment. Still, it didn't ring.

I had my first experience on the tram that morning. It moved slowly and noiselessly along the centre of the road. I couldn't understand how Lagos State could generate billions yearly and couldn't build tramway networks. Thugs in Lagos motor parks and roads were making enough illegal revenue from motorists to fund the tramway. At the station, we took the metro. It was my first time on a train and in an underground transport. I'd seen old trains running through colonial-era railways in Yaba, but I'd never been on one.

We spent the morning at Musée Grévin. Although I was eager to return home so I could try Lara's number again, I forced myself to enjoy the moment. The realism of the wax figures of several celebrities was mind-blowing. There were famous people in music, film, sports and even politics. Some of the statues stood side by side, and some had decor around them that made them seem extremely realistic. Nico took pictures of me standing by Naomi Campbell, Celine Dion, Barrack Obama, Picasso, and Ray Charles. I couldn't wait to show the photos to my students who would be amazed by the vivid likeness. I took photos of many of the pop culture icons. They'd be useful in French culture class about the museum. One final photo, this time for Nico. He couldn't pass up a chance to pose with his football legend, Pélé.

We had lunch in a nice restaurant close by. The delicious onion soup for starters was particularly enjoyable. I had coq au vin and roasted potatoes for the main course. The dessert was cheesecake. Nico always ordered a different dish from mine so that I could try whatever he ordered. I took a small bite of his melted goat cheese and honey off his fingers, a sip of fish soup off his spoon, and a taste of his salmon and roasted asparagus from his fork.

"How do you turn dark chocolate into white chocolate?" he asked after he fed me a mouthful of his mousse au chocolat.

I swallowed. "I don't know."

"You turn on the light," he said, smiling and I burst into laughter.

After we left the restaurant, we strolled to the Palais Garnier. Standing before it, I paused and stared in awe at the enormous structure. It was indeed a work of art—its big glass dome, its golden statues sitting on top, and its baroque-style facade and pillars. I thought the exterior was super impressive until I got inside and beheld the stunning masterpiece. So ornately decorated, its luxurious beauty hurt the eyes. So lavishly styled, that I lacked words to describe its opulence. Its designer must have slept and caught a glimpse of where angels rested after running helter-skelter around the earth, doing God's errands, saving men from men.

On our way out, Nico took a picture of me with my hands outstretched in front of the Palace. A couple, in the middle of taking a selfie, paused and offered to capture a photo of Nico and me. In return, we helped them take their picture as well.

The sky had turned dark by the time we returned home. Although exhausted from the two-hour visit to the Opera Garnier, I felt fulfilled. After the blood in my fingers started to circulate again, I borrowed Nico's laptop to see if I had any new emails or Facebook messages. There was still no word from Lara and her continued silence worsened my worry. There was also no response from the other detectives. I called Lara's number again. It was still switched off. I was hoping that she, being older, would remember something about Mama Jide that would be helpful to Detective Barrot. While Nico took a nap, I wrote to the detective, explaining that I was still trying to get more information.

***

Christmas Eve was cold and windy. By now I'd given up all thought of meeting the sun in France. After breakfast, Nico announced that we would be spending two nights in his friend's apartment on Passy in the 16th arrondissement. His friend worked in Libreville. They both had each other's apartment keys so whoever was in town could watch both apartments.

"He has a great view of Paris from his windows," Nico said.

I kept staring at him, not understanding why we needed to change apartments.

"Why can't we just stay here?"

"Trust me, you'll like it when you see it."

He was right. The apartment was on the seventh floor and had a superb view of the Eiffel Tower which I was yet to visit because we'd saved it for Christmas day. Taking in the sumptuous view, I understood why Nico wanted us to spend two nights there. I looked away from the window and turned around slowly. The apartment was beautiful with its open floor plan, lavishly decorated with modern furniture. Everything was beige—sofa, curtains, lamps, centre rug, small marble fireplace.

After we'd settled in, I dialled Lara again without success. I'd lost count of the number of times I'd tried. Where was she? What could have happened to her phone? Why hadn't she checked her Facebook messages either? I worried that she might be unwell and in the hospital. It was possible she had an accident or had her phone stolen. I pushed away those negative thoughts.

Nico and I walked along the river Seine, past several bookstands, but we didn't have time to stop until we arrived at Musee d'Orsay. I was glad to be out and occupying my mind. There was panic growing inside me because of the silence from Lara's end, and also because the information I hoped to get from her was delaying the search for Mama Jide and my reconnection with Tutu.

Following lunch in a small restaurant near Musee d'Orsay, we spent the remainder of the afternoon exploring the museum, immersed in its rich collection of art and history. Everything there had its special history; the building itself was once an abandoned train station condemned for demolition before being renovated and converted into a museum. There was something special about being there with Nico. It felt as though we were sailing through a magical world as we toured each room, each corridor, and each floor.

The fifth floor was my favourite. It housed great pieces of impressionist paintings of some of the finest artists of all time. It was overwhelming being up close to the works of Manet, Cézanne, Monet, Sisley, Degas, Renoir and even Van Gogh. It was like an invitation into the second half of the 19th century, the era of Impressionists and post-Impressionists, the most important period in the history of art. I had a fascination for portraits: self-portraits and portraits painted by another artist; portraits of family members and friends; personalities, ordinary people and even slaves. It was a peek into their lives, a window through which I felt close to them, as though I'd known them personally, as though if I reached out and touched the paintings, I'd feel and even smell them.

Many times, I'd wondered what Papa had done to all those photos in frames Mama had hung all over the flat in Lawani Street There used to be a beautiful portrait of Mama in the living room. She was dressed in green and white Buba and Iro Aso Oke and sparkly green gélé. Her makeup was perfect and her red lips smiled as though she would live forever. It was the only thing I would like to recover if I knew where Papa had taken all our belongings after we left Lawani Street

"Look," Nico said, pointing to a painting.

My eyes followed his finger and I was blown away when my eyes fell on Gustave Courbet's *The Stormy Sea*. I must have spent ten minutes just staring at the beautiful seascape painting: the high waves, the two boats on the shore and the low thick clouds. The knife work reminded me of the storm that had swept through my life after I was denied a student visa—going forward had felt impossible, and going backwards as well. Without a job to go to in the mornings, I'd felt so vulnerable, as powerless as the scared little girl Papa abandoned at Mama Ola's place a dozen years back. In front of the painting, I bit hard on my lips to hold back a sob. I'd promised myself I would no longer be retracting my steps backwards or digging into the past.

Turning towards Nico, our eyes met and he smiled. A soft dimpled smile that filled me with a sense of peace and calm, reminding me that the storm was over and the raging waves had calmed down. Was he my last bus stop? Was he my forever man? Could I truly be more fortunate in love than my mother? Did I truly deserve a man like Nico?

It was night when we finally left the museum. So, we went in search of a restaurant nearby to have dinner. Holding gloved hands, we walked down a beautifully illuminated street that was lined with trees with leafless branches, decorated with hundreds of golden lights. From the sidewalk, we caught a glimpse of an apartment where two little girls with long hair, holding make-believe microphones, were singing and dancing in front of a huge Christmas tree. The adults seemed to be enjoying the spectacle. Some of them clapped their hands, while some others had their phones pointed at the girls. Memories of Mama singing in the kitchen while using ọmọ orogùn, stuck with hot Eba or Amala as a microphone rushed into my mind. Mama would give Fola and me big spoons so that we could sing in duets or as a group. As though Nico could tell that my heart was heavy with these memories, he squeezed my hand and I held on tightly to his.

We found a cosy bistro where we had a quiet dinner before heading home. I grew more worried when I found no messages from Lara and her number still wouldn't go through. Nico suggested placing a newspaper announcement to locate Mama Jide if we still hadn't heard from Lara after Boxing Day. However, I no longer felt confident about that route because I didn't know her married name.

I made myself some tea and stayed in the apartment alone while Nico went to get some groceries. In his absence, I sat and listened to nothing. Silence engorged the apartment. When I'd drunk my mug halfway, I reached for my phone and tried Lara's number again. Her phone was still switched off. I contemplated informing Wale and Fola, but I feared I would be raising a false alarm. She could have just misplaced her phone or had it stolen.

I looked around the room and giggled to myself. I'd always loved tall windows when I saw them in movies, but right in front of my eyes, I found them funny. They looked like doors, starting from the floor to the ceiling, but leading nowhere. The one before me now didn't have a balcony, still, it had wrought-iron balcony railings to keep people from falling out of the door window. I'd never seen any of such in Lagos.

After I emptied the mug, I got out of bed and went to the window. I would never have imagined that one day, I would look out of a window and see the Eiffel Tower. The surreal feeling returned as I continued to stare at the tower which somehow didn't disappear. It stood there. Tall. Proud. Imposing. It was there long before me and it would still be there long after I'd left Paris. I looked away, down at the rooftops of the buildings, further down at the facades, and then below at the people walking past on the street. I wondered what my life would be like as a student in Paris. Would it continue to be as magical as that of a tourist whose days here were brief? I wondered what it would look like to live in the city of love with someone whom I loved, with our days unnumbered.

Suddenly, my heart began to quicken its pace. I felt very afraid as I realised that I couldn't keep lying to myself that I hadn't fallen in love with Nico. I returned to bed and crawled under the covers. What I'd feared the most had happened—falling in love. Love meant happiness, and once life discovered I was happy, it was sure to try and steal that from me.

TWENTY-TWO

Past

One Sunday, when I was six, while Mama was at the salon, Papa summoned Lara, Fola and me to the living room using the bell by his favourite sofa. Like always, during the journey from our rooms to the living room, my mind raced like a sports car as I tried to figure out what we'd all done wrong. To the best of my knowledge, our weekend chores were all done. We'd pumped water into the tank and filled the two giant drums on the balcony at the back of the flat for days when there would be water cut. We'd done all our schoolwork. We'd washed and ironed our uniforms and shined our *Bata* school shoes with wine wax. Still, Papa had a talent for always finding flaws despite our best efforts.

On trembling legs, I stepped into the living room at the same time as the others. I knew that whatever we would get punished and flogged for, my cross would be heavier, and my nails thicker. I bowed my head and put my hands behind my back as we filed in and stood before him.

"Is that not your mother?" Papa asked.

I raised my head to find him pointing to the TV. The back of a woman was frozen on the screen. The image was from a music video by Shina

Peters, a juju musician, and we'd seen it several times since its release. Indeed, the woman was wearing a top similar to one of Mama's.

"No," Fola said.

"It's not Mama," Lara concurred.

Papa said nothing. Calmly, he pointed the remote control to the video cassette player and backtracked the video.

"Can't you see that's your mother?" Papa said as the scene played. He still wasn't angry yet.

It was true that the woman looked like Mama with her back turned to the camera. She had the same skin colour tone and jerry curls as Mama, but her hair was shorter, and she was also not as tall as Mama. When Fola and I had teased Mama about being in the music video she had found it amusing. But Papa didn't find it funny.

"You must be blind. Get out of my sight now before I pounce on you," Papa screamed at Lara when she pointed out that Mama was taller than the woman.

Fola and I weren't allowed to leave just yet. Papa continued to insist that the woman was Mama. It was as though he was looking for a reason to pick a fight with Mama when she returned from the salon. He began to say that Mama was a prostitute who went to night parties to dance with strange men. When Fola insisted that it wasn't Mama as we'd already seen the music video several times with her, he flared up more and sent us out of the living room. As I lay on my bed, I thought of how funny Papa's accusation was, especially because Mama had never slept outside of the house except whenever they fought and he sent us packing to Dolphin Estate.

When Mama returned about an hour later, Papa started accusing her as soon as she stepped into the flat. They raised their voices at each other. Lara left our bedroom door open so that she could hear their arguments. Fola did the same with his. Mama told Papa that her own top had long sleeves while the woman's had short sleeves, but he insisted that she must have cut it short or folded it in. Mama asked him how she could have folded it in without it being obvious in the video, or how she could have cut it short and sewed it back without traces of it on the top. At this period, she hadn't even started learning how to sew.

Suddenly, while they were still arguing, Mama called Lara and me into the living room and asked us in front of Papa if it was her. Lara said she had already told him it wasn't her, mentioning that Mama was much taller and the woman was slimmer. Papa ordered us out of the living room once again. The argument continued, escalating through the loudness of their voices and the harshness of their words.

"Òpònú ni ẹ́," Papa screamed.

"Yet you chose and married that very stupid person with your eyes open."

"Apọ̀dà ni ẹ́."

"It was you who came and married me, yet I'm the one who is confused."

"You are nothing but a cheap prostitute. What kind of a mother goes to juju parties to dance and shake everything."

"You're a liar and a very wicked man. You know very well that it's not me, but you like to sow confusion wherever there's happiness. Whenever you come home, we lose peace. What kind of a father are you that your children hide in their rooms whenever you're at home?"

They continued trading insults, switching between Yoruba and English until I fell asleep. Sometime around midnight, Mama woke me up. Papa had thrown her things out. She asked if I wanted to come with her. I flung off the covers and almost jumped down from the bunk bed as I scrambled out of bed. Lara and I hurriedly began to pack some clothes into our school bags while Mama went to fetch Fola.

Mama told us we could stay back, "It's me he is sending away, not you." Neither Lara, Fola, nor I ever opted to stay back. Who would protect us from Papa's wrath if Mama wasn't there? Who would ask Papa to temper justice with mercy when I did something wrong? Who would come to see me when I ended up in purgatory? Mama didn't have a car at that time, and taking a taxi wasn't an option because, at that hour, they had all closed for the night. Because Mama's parents didn't have a landline telephone, we couldn't call them either. So, Mama called one of her aunts who had a car, and a landline telephone, and lived close by.

We left the flat and waited for Aunt Nike by the staircase with the security man. Fola and I were happy. We played *shadow puppets* casting shadows of birds, rabbits and dogs on the wall under the stairs. Aunt Nike honked once when she arrived. A moment later, the security guard was putting Mama's suitcase and our school bags in the car boot. Lara, Fola, and I climbed into the back seat, while Mama sat in front with Aunt Nike. The security guard waited and watched us leave. Fola and I waved at him until he was out of sight.

The following morning, Mama called her office to tell them she wouldn't come in. We spent the rest of the week with Aunt Nike. Because we were pampered all day long, I always wished that we never had to return home. I used to feel guilty for wanting Mama and Papa to fight so that he would throw her out. For wherever we sought refuge was always better than being at home.

On Saturday morning, Aunt Nike and her husband went early to Lawani Street to talk to Papa. When they returned and confirmed that we would return home the following day, I began suffering stomach aches and burning up with a fever. I threw up everything I ate and was unable to fall asleep until dawn. It was no surprise to anyone because it happened to me every time we had to return home to Papa.

I always wished so hard that Mama would say, 'Enough is enough. I'm never going back to him.' But these back-and-forths continued for many years until Papa discovered a new way to punish Mama without her family having to interfere to settle their disagreement. He began sending her out of their bedroom to the dining room which Mama converted into a temporary bedroom and reconverted back to a dining room after they settled their dispute.

As we grew older, we assured Mama she didn't have to stay with Papa for our sake. We would suggest going to live in Dolphin Estate or renting a flat in the estate or around it. She always had many reasons why she couldn't leave. Her salary alone wasn't enough; she had to wait until she got a promotion. Also, there was no way she would leave us behind. She'd tried it before and her heart couldn't take it. She'd rather die than leave us behind once more. After she got a promotion, she began to say she worried that Lara and I might have a hard time getting married. She believed that no one would want their son to marry into a family where a man wasn't the head of the family.

"Your father knows this. He'll wait patiently for that day and when you will have come looking for him to stand in on your special day, then he'll refuse to honour you with his presence."

TWENTY-THREE

Present day

"Réveille-toi," Nico whispered. "Réveille-toi, Lami."

I blinked my eyes open and saw Nico perched on the edge of the sofa bed where I'd been sleeping. The apartment was bathed in soft light from the floor lamp next to the TV.

"Quelle heure est-il?" I asked, my voice heavy with the fatness of deep slumber.

"It's a little past six. It's time to start preparing. The taxi will be here in an hour."

At 7:00 pm, Nico and I left the apartment and took the birdcage elevator down. It was drizzling and windy as we climbed into the taxi. The pavements glistened with rain. The glass of the window fogged up from the steam of my breath. When I shivered, Nico asked the driver to turn the heating up. Without making a sound, I muttered my thank you to him and settled back in my seat. Half an hour later, we arrived in Palaiseau, where Nico's friend lived. Max and Nico had been colleagues in Total Paris. Then Max was sent to Malaysia. He was spending the holidays in France with his Malaysian girlfriend, Sandy.

We found them waiting for us at their front door when we got out of the elevator. We exchanged kisses and I gave the champagne we brought to Sandy. She was taller than every one of us and had long dark flowing hair and high cheekbones. The aroma of food floating in the air when we got out of the elevator had come from their apartment. The golden-brown turkey sat on a silver platter surrounded by roasted potatoes. Max and Sandy talked about their life in Malaysia and all the places they'd visited in Asia.

Nico also told them about Nigeria. He spoke about the different beaches he'd been to in Lagos, and also about the Epe fish market. Memories of that rainy day rushed through my mind and I could almost perceive its fresh fish odour as Nico described the different types of sea animals we saw. When he began to talk about the point-and-kill restaurant Andrew and Ada had taken us to in Ebute Metta, I held my breath, thinking he would mention the part where we had to hurriedly leave because the canal suddenly started to stink. Thankfully, he left that part out. All he talked about was how tasty the catfish was and how he regretted not finishing his dish because it was too peppery. If I'd been asked about Nigeria, I might not have been able to say so many nice and funny things that would make a non-African want to visit.

Our taxi arrived at 12:30 am. As we took the elevator down, Nico said to me, "I thought I was dreaming when I saw you empty your glass after the toast."

"I'm just so happy," I said a little too loudly. It nagged at the back of my mind that I might be tipsy, especially as I giggled at the loudness of my response. He leaned close and gave me a gentle peck on the cheek, causing my face to heat up as my heart fluttered around in its jail.

Before bed, Nico and I exchanged gifts. I gave him a silver pendant that looked like a razor blade and a necklace made from genuine leather. I'd bought it in Lagos along with two identical silver cuff bracelets with 'Forever Sisters' written on the front. I planned to keep one of the bracelets for myself and give the other one to Tutu when we eventually met. In return, Nico gave me a pink waterproof camera and said that I would need it to take pictures when Tutu and I met. My throat swelled and I nearly choked on the welling emotions. I threw my hands around his neck and embraced him, thanking him. I loved the gift, but what I loved most was his optimism. His words meant so much; they watered the bud of hope in me.

It was still dark outside when I awoke. I pulled out my phone from under the pillow. It was a few minutes past 3:00 am. I rolled over and lay on my back, dragging in a long, weary breath. My heart felt heavy as the stiff skin on my face crumpled when a sob burst out of my throat. My dry lower lip split and bled, but my eyes remained as dry as limestone. Desperate, I muttered a prayer to God.

"I've not asked you anything in years, not since Mama passed away. I don't want to leave Europe without finding my little sister. I've tried everything I can on my own and failed. Therefore, I beg of you to lend a helping hand. Please, locate Tutu and reunite what's left of my family."

For a long time, I lay there unable to go back to sleep, closing and opening my eyes as my thoughts shifted gears, changing direction each time. After some time, I tiptoed to the toilet past Nico who was sleeping on a mattress topper. On my way back, I stood at the window, staring out over the City of Lights. My eyes swept across the buildings with busy balconies—potted plants, French flags, Christmas lights. When Nico stirred in his sleep, ruffling the covers, I made my way back to bed and pulled the blankets up to my chin. Some moments later, I was fast asleep.

***

Nico and I spent Christmas morning alone at home. Outside, the weather was frigid, clear and dry. We left the sofa bed open and had breakfast in it, in front of the TV, like lovers. We were friends doing lovers' things, laughing like friends and smiling like lovers. I'd never been so close to or happy with any man. At noon, we cooked ourselves lunch—lasagna bolognese with bechamel. Nico proved once again to be a top chef. I loved every minute of that quiet afternoon we spent together in the palm of the apartment. We were sufficient. Just the two of us. We didn't need other people to create memorable moments.

I tried Lara's number several times, but she was still unreachable. I refreshed my Facebook inbox every other minute, hoping to find a message from her. But there was nothing. I was starting to panic. What if something had happened to her? What if she was in trouble? I didn't know what to do.

After an agitated nap, Nico suggested we go out for a long walk to work off my restlessness. We had to be back by 7:00 pm when the capon he'd ordered for dinner would be delivered. I was grateful for his suggestion. I needed to get out of the house and clear my mind of its worries. We went to the Champs Elysees, one of the most famous and beautiful streets in the world. With my new camera, I took as many pictures as I could of the Arc de Triomphe before I lost feeling at the tips of my fingers.

Then we began walking down the avenue that stretched to la Tour Eiffel for a close-up view. We went past the trees lining the sidewalk, past the brand stores, past the cars gliding up and down the eight lanes. It started to grow dark and wickedly chill. Still, there were droves of people strolling along the avenue. I'd never seen so many dogs and so many different breeds of them. Neither had I ever had to dodge so much dog poop. Some people simply walked their dogs, while others carried them in their hands like babies. There were many couples—lovers holding hands or walking with their arms wrapped around each other.

Out of nowhere, a strong intuition washed over me and I began to wonder if Tutu could be nearby. Could it be possible that she was vacationing in Paris? Perhaps alone or with friends. She was certainly too young to be with a lover. My eyes swept across the many faces moving past us, scanning for young Black girls. Would our eyes recognise each other? Would there be a flutter in my heart or a knot in my stomach if my gaze met hers? There were several Black people, pretty young black girls, looking stylish, lightly dressed in colourful jumpers, nicely fitting jeans and jackets that were unbuttoned. Most often, my eyes met theirs, and in there, I could almost hear the unspoken, *I see you, Sister*. Some offered me a smile like I wasn't a stranger, and I smiled back. It was strange—the feeling of connection, of kinship, of sisterhood.

As we approached the Eiffel Tower, I hooked my arm around Nico's. Seeing it at a distance from the apartment was one thing, but being up close was another. I was struck by its grandeur. The closer we got, the more impressive it became. At the foot of the tower, as I stood gazing up at its towering height, the wind began to pick up. I shuddered, almost dropping my new camera when a strong gust of wind blew past us and almost knocked me off my feet.

"We should start heading back home," Nico said when he noticed that I was shivering and shaking at the same time.

Pulling my frozen lips into a smile, I turned around slowly, giving my surroundings a final look. At that moment, I made up my mind that Paris would be my first choice of city when I would reapply for my Master's program. I would come back to see the Eiffel Tower with Nico when the weather wasn't so unwelcoming. I even dared to hope that I would have found Tutu and that she would come to see me in Paris, and together, we would visit the top of the Tower.

"Let's go home," I said, hooking my arm in Nico's once again.

We took a taxi back home and seated in the back, I suddenly began to miss Lagos. Its harsh sun, its smell of the Atlantic Ocean, and its bustling traffic noises. Had we been in Lagos at this moment, we would have been able to stroll around Banana Island in tank tops and shorts. I made a silent vow to never again complain about the weather—too much sun or too much rain. We had it easy in Lagos. When it rained and we got soaked, we could still let our clothes dry on our bodies without losing feeling in our fingers and toes. Our noses didn't sting when we breathed. Our faces didn't turn stiff with cold, and neither did our mouths produce steam like chimneys.

The capon arrived a little before 8:00 pm. I helped Nico set the table. He swapped the lights for three white candles whose orange flames made the table glow. Then we sat down to eat. I tried not to cry as Nico said a prayer before we dove into the meal, including in it, a request to God to bring Tutu to us.

As we ate, I realised it was my happiest Christmas as an adult. I also realised that happiness was too fluid and flexible to come from just one direction. It could take whatever way or form if only we'd recognise it. In my new realm of awareness, I recognised it in hearing Ada laugh until she cried. I recognised it in Nico's tap-dancing while cooking. I recognised it in the memory of Mama, Fola, and Tutu dancing to loud music from Mama's stereo player while Lara smiled sheepishly.

That night, I promised myself to always remember that happiness resided in all these little things and more and to let that be a mental armour whenever I found myself in places where I no longer had the desire to live.

"Lami," I heard Nico call.

I opened my eyes to realise I'd dozed off in front of the TV.

"I know you're tired," Nico said. "If you want to sleep early, it's fine with me. But I have a surprise for you now. Come," he said, reaching for my hand. "Come and see."

I threw off the blanket I'd wrapped around my legs and got up from the bed. Then he led me to the curtain-covered window.

"Close your eyes," he whispered.

My trust in him defeated my fear of darkness, so I did as he instructed. I began counting in my head to keep the fear at bay until I heard him pulling the curtains back. I made it to eleven seconds before he said, "Okay. You can open your eyes now."

"Wow!" I exclaimed as I watched a dazzling view of the Eiffel Tower, sparkling all over with golden pearls of light. I wanted to throw the window wide open, stick my head out, and scream like Eddie Murphy's character in *Coming to America*, 'Good evening, Paris!'

"I wanted you to experience this," Nico said gently, standing behind me.

I turned to look at him. "Thank you," I whispered, wishing we could stay this happy together, forever. "It's such a beautiful experience."

In silence, we stood side by side, taking it all in. I'd never felt so calm, so peaceful, so loved. I wanted us to stand and watch the golden light all night, but a few moments later, the glow suddenly died out.

"It'll come back on every hour for five minutes until one in the morning," Nico said. "If you're still up at one, you can watch the last feature when it twinkles."

"Wake me up again if I fall asleep," I said, checking my phone for the time.

I'd been asleep only a few minutes, but it had seemed as though I'd been at it for hours. I tried to call Lara again. Her phone was still off. I fell into another deep worry about her whereabouts, but I continued to push out the horrible fears from my mind. Over and over again, I repeated to myself that she was well and not lying in a hospital or a morgue. I called Ada and we talked for long minutes, long enough for the nagging worries to settle again like dust.

After the call, I checked through my emails and Facebook messages, but still, there was no response from Lara. I decided to focus on replying to messages from friends who'd sent me Christmas greetings. One of the messages was from Uncle Kay. When I clicked to read, my heart skipped a beat when I realised it had been sent by Lara.

"Merry Christmas, Lami!" the message read. "I don't currently have a phone. My compound was robbed by armed men. It was terrible. They took my phone but didn't harm me. I'll tell you more later. Anyways, guess what! You won't believe what I'm about to tell you: I found Tutu on Facebook. I saw Mama Ola yesterday on my way to Uncle Kay's place. She lives in Agbara, not Ibadan. She said she spent last Christmas in London with Mama Jide, and that Tutu, who they call Anna, is now a big girl! When I got home, I searched on Facebook and found her. She's now Anna Ajayi. I have just sent her a message. All this while, we didn't think of searching for her with her baptismal name and Mama Jide's surname. Can you imagine? I also have news about Papa. I'll give you the full gist when I get a new phone."

I froze, unable to believe what I'd just read. Had my luck turned so much that my nightmares had now given way to such wishful dreams? I dug my nails into my skin until I felt pain. No, this was no dream. Afraid that I might have imagined what I understood of the message, I started to read it all over again. This time around, I read slowly, letting each word sink in. After the second reading, my heart began to thump at the tip of my tongue. I wanted to scream but my voice had disappeared. I wanted to run but my legs were immobile. I stared at Nico who was by the dining table, putting some Nesquik in two white mugs etched with red hearts. I needed to remember this moment forever—the moment when a thirteen-year-old dream came true. I needed to remember exactly how I felt when I realised that my little sister had been found alive and well. I stood up and walked over to Nico who was stirring the contents in the mugs, using his two hands at the same time. He paused what he was doing when I came and stood before him, wearing a puzzled look.

I threw my arms around him and gave him a tight hug. I held my breath, holding back a sob that was threatening to burst from my throat.

"Ca va?" he asked.

I let out a sob. Within seconds, I was crying like a child on his shoulder. He held me and rubbed my back as I clung to him. We stood this way for a long time.

"I found her," I whispered when my voice finally returned.

"Who? Lara?"

"No. Anna."

"Who's Anna?" he asked, pulling back to look me in the face.

"Tutu," I sobbed. "I found Tutu. Her baptismal name is Anna."

He wore his confusion on his face. I was smiling now, through all the emotions I was experiencing, as it continued to dawn on me that I wasn't dreaming.

"Lara found her on Facebook. She took up her baptismal name and my aunt's marital name. She changed her surname. That's why we never found her."

"This is such great news," Nico said, pulling me back into a hug. He swirled me around until I screamed that I was dizzy.

"Yes, it is. It's so unbelievable. Lara sent me the link to her Facebook page," I said, still a bit dizzy from being twirled.

He led me by the hand to the sofa bed. Then I clicked on the link in Lara's message. Anna Smart-Cole's page immediately came up. Tutu had grown into a beautiful young girl. In her profile photo, she was sitting on a black leather sofa, wearing an orange and blue striped, armless turtleneck. She didn't have any makeup on, and her nappy hair was combed back. She looked happy and healthy; plump with glowing skin.

For many minutes, I studied her facial features, scanning for proof that she and Mr Durojaiye were of kin, but she looked nothing like him. Could Mama have been mistaken about the identity of Tutu's father?

The problem was, she didn't look anything like Papa either. Nothing from her picture suggested that she was a *Davies*. Did she have chicken skin with brown spots behind her thighs like Papa and I? Did she laugh making the *kikikkikiki* sound? Did she enjoy boiled pieces of meat like Papa? Only a paternity test could reveal the truth. I didn't care whose daughter she was. All that mattered to me was that she was my sister. She had the same upturned eyes, a trait from Mama's side of the family. She was certainly the daughter of my mother and I loved her unconditionally. I clicked on the message button and began to type.

"Anna, it's Lami. Do you remember me? I'm dying to hear from you."

After sending the message, I began to worry that the message was too short and wished that I had explained who I was.

"What if she doesn't remember?" I asked Nico. "What if she deletes the message because she doesn't know who I am? What if she thinks I'm one of those distant family members who add people on Facebook just so they can ask them for money?"

"Let's be hopeful. If she doesn't reply in two to three days, you'll send another message. This time around, you'll introduce yourself in full."

"Two to three days?" I exclaimed. "I can't survive such torment."

Immediately, I sent Anna a friend request, and another message explaining who I was. Then I went back to staring at her profile photo, hoping she'd reply before she went to sleep. Nico rose and began rummaging through his backpack. Then he returned to sit beside me, placing something on my lap. It was the little box containing the locket he'd given me as a birthday present, which I'd politely declined.

"Now that you have found Tutu, you can't refuse it," he joked. "You don't have a choice."

"No, Nico. You already gave me a Christmas gift."

"I know, I got you the camera so that you can take a picture of your sister that you can insert in the locket. It would make me very happy if you accept it. I chose it especially for you."

I stared at him, knowing if I refused it a second time, I would hurt him. He'd chosen the gift with the belief that I would find Tutu. I'd been afraid that if I boldly displayed my belief like him, life would make sure it didn't happen. He'd bought me a camera when there was no hope that I would find Tutu. I stared at him and wished he could see just how much my heart swelled with gratitude for him, and just how much a tender love for him had blossomed in there like a fruitful tree in spring. Every day we'd spent together since my arrival in Paris, I'd known him more, appreciated him more, and loved him more.

"Thank you, Nico." I turned around and lifted my braids. He put the necklace around my neck, fumbling with it as he tried to clip the ends together.

"It's so beautiful," I said, throwing my arms around his neck. "I'll cherish it forever."

TWENTY-FOUR

Present day

Nico and I stayed up until late into the night. I told him stories about each of my siblings as we sat on the sofa facing each other. At midnight, there was still no response from Anna. An hour later, we stood at the window and watched the lights of the Eiffel Tower as it came on and started to twinkle. The light danced on and off, bouncing all around the structure, glowing against the night sky. Inside me, I was dancing too, swirling around in a waltz, in the ballroom of my head, and saying to myself, "Dreams do indeed come true."

"Do you know why I'm afraid of the dark?" I asked after the tower lights had gone off.

Nico shook his head. He was now sitting across from me at the dining table.

"I told you so many things about me, but not what I want to tell you now. It's something I've never told anyone before. Not even Ada."

He didn't say anything, but he reached out across the table and took my hand. The way he gently squeezed it was worth more than all the words he could have woven together. As I stared at our hands, I felt my heart swell with love for him.

"When I was a child, my father used to lock me in the dark in his room, inside his wardrobe." I forced myself to meet Nico's eyes. "He would say that I was a witch. My crime was that when I cried, tears didn't run down my face."

"Your father said you were a witch because of that?" he asked in dismay.

I nodded and dropped my eyes. A sense of shame washed over me.

"When was this?" he asked.

"All the years before my mother died."

"My aunt's son had this issue when he was a baby a few years back. I remember her always being worried, calling my mother almost every night about the same issue. Finally, they went to see a doctor and he told them it was nothing."

"Are you serious?" I sat straight up.

"Of course, I am. They saw a paediatric ophthalmologist."

"I can't believe you know someone who cries without tears like me," I said in disbelief. I struggled with the thought that he might only have said it to be nice, to make me not feel bad about myself.

"Not anymore. This happened like four years ago. By the time he was six months old, he had tears trickling down his face. The doctor said it was common. Did you see a doctor?"

"No, I didn't. I was never taken to see one."

We fell into silence again as I tried to think about how different my life would have been had I been taken to see a doctor. If Papa had known that it was normal, instead of his hate, would he have loved me for my intelligence, for having the same skin colour as him, and for sharing his birth month? I held tighter to Nico's hand. I liked the feeling of his thumb as it caressed my hand.

"Why don't we Google it?" he asked.

I looked up from our hands to meet his gaze. "I already did."

"What did it say?'

"That there are different conditions responsible for crying without tears. It can be that one's tear ducts are either not fully formed or blocked."

Nico nodded, his thumb still caressing my hand.

"I used to think I was dehydrated," I said in a little voice. "I would drink a lot of water and then try to force myself to cry with tears, or I would put my saliva on my eyelids and trace it down my face. I desperately wanted to be able to cry tears and I despised myself for my inability to do so. I couldn't even cry at my mother's funeral. I didn't shed a single tear. I have always wondered what the people who were at the ceremony thought. They must have thought I was heartless or that I was happy she died."

"You were just a child. Why would anyone think that? If they noticed, they must have thought that you were in shock."

"I think it might have something to do with the measles I caught as a baby, but for a long time before I googled it, I thought I was suffering from some unknown disease."

"True, it could be true, or there might be several other reasons. One thing I am certain of is that witchcraft is not a factor in this."

What he told me was what I'd wanted someone to tell me all those years, back in that dark room. Although Mama always assured me that it wasn't my fault, she never explained why I couldn't cry. I rose to my feet and approached Nico. When he rose too, I threw my hands around his neck, hugging him tightly and burying my face in the warmth of his neck. I felt so grateful that I'd met him and for his patience when I resisted him. He must be my guardian angel, because how could one person bring so much joy to another person's life, and in such little time too? I remained still against him as his heartbeat vibrated against mine. I understood its rhythms and patterns. I wanted to remember every second of this evening, every feeling too. I wanted to remember this embrace forever. He began gently stroking his hand up and down my back again until I felt warmth spread through me and a shiver run down my spine. I held on tighter as I struggled to control the wild beating of my heart. I felt him tighten his grip too. I knew he could hear the loud thudding my heart made. I moved my cheek against him until my lips brushed against his. He pulled back gently and looked into my eyes.

"Je t'aime, Olamide Davies."

"Je t'aime aussi, Nicolas Troadec."

Then I pulled his mouth down to mine.

***

There was still no response from Tutu when I awoke. None either after I returned from buying second-hand children's storybooks from bouquinistes along the Seine.

I stood at the window and took a last view of the tower before we left the Passy apartment. It was a cold, blustery Boxing Day morning. The tricolour flags of France attached to balcony railings fluttered wildly in the wind. Although I would miss the beautiful view of the apartment, I was happy to return to Nico's.

Back in La Defense, we had baked potatoes for lunch. I had just finished clearing the dining table when the familiar sound of a notification bubble emanated from Nico's laptop. I hurried to check and discovered that Anna had accepted my friend request on Facebook. I just sat there on the sofa and stared at the screen in front of me, imagining her sitting before a computer and going through my wall and pictures. How did she feel when she read my messages? Did she remember me? Was she a quarter as excited as I was, or was she indifferent like she would be to any average friend from school? Many questions for which I had no answers raced through my mind. My palms became damp, and thick heat enveloped me underneath my thick clothes.

As Nico joined me, sitting beside me, I reached for the laptop, set it on my lap, and started browsing through Anna's photos. In one of the pictures, she stood alongside a white girl with blondish-yellow hair, her arm draped around the girl's shoulder as they both beamed at the camera.

"She looks so much like you," Nico said.

"She has the same smile as Mama in this picture,' I said, meeting his gaze and witnessing his happiness for me. "It's unbelievable."

There weren't so many photos of her. Rather, her album was populated with lots of pictures of beautiful landscapes. On her friends list, I found my cousins. There was Tomi, Mama Jide's second child and only daughter, with the name Sharon Ajayi on Facebook. There was no way I would ever have recognised her through her baptismal name and husband's surname had I accidentally found her account in my search. Looking through her page, she looked nothing like that girl who had sat in our living room with a snobbish face some eighteen years back, with legs crossed and hands placed on her knees, one above the other. The girl who had said *No, thanks,* when Mama asked her to go with us to our room so that we could get to know each other.

Unable to believe that I wasn't in some sort of dream or trance, I went through Tutu's photo albums over and over again. I read all the comments on every photo and saved all the ones she appeared in.

Just then a message notification appeared.

"It's her," I exclaimed with unbridled joy, clicking on the message and reading it slowly. Then I read it a second time. I laughed and cried at the same time, and then, I read Anna's message a third and a fourth time.

Hello, Sis,

It's so nice to hear from you too. I intend to come to Nigeria to visit and meet you all after my A-level exams. Here's my number, I'm eager to hear from you.

Anna.

She had called me *Sis*. My joy was boundless. I felt like catching the next flight to London just to hug her tightly. I felt like dashing out into the street and shouting, 'We won! We won!' An explosion of emotions rumbled within me. I had no idea how to contain or control it. I couldn't tell which emotion was the most dominant of all: shock, excitement, fear, or perhaps, all three. After a brief moment of hesitation, I dialled the number and she picked up on the first ring.

"Hello," she said in a soft voice that carried a distinct refined and measured British accent.

"Hello, Tutu. Sorry, Anna. it's Lami," I said in a low voice. Amidst the whirlwind of emotions coursing through me, it was excitement that surged the highest, and I fought to keep it from seeping into my voice.

"Hey! Hello sis," she said. Her voice took a higher pitch.

"Hello," I said again, this time, completely failing to conceal the elation in my voice.

I didn't even know what to say or where to start. I hadn't thought about it before calling. What does one say after thirteen years of separation? Where does one start? What do I leave out? Suddenly, a sob rose in my throat. I put a hand over my mouth and tried desperately not to cry, for all the things they'd taken from us; for the time we could have spent together that'd been stolen from us; and for the pain that'd bruised our hearts when they tore us all apart.

"I've been dying for this day to come," I said.

"Me too. I've dreamt over and over again of this happening, not over the phone though, but in person." There were traces of humour in her voice. My heart smiled. I always knew she wouldn't turn out quiet and moody.

"Me too," I said.

"I didn't see your message until this afternoon. That's why I didn't reply earlier. I also got a message from Lara. I just replied to her too with my phone number."

"She probably hasn't seen it yet. I'm sure she's going to call you as soon as she does."

"Do you have her number?"

"I do. I'll send it to you, but it's not working for now. She's getting a new phone today."

"I'll just wait for her to call me then. What about Wale and Fola?"

I reached for Nico's hand. "I haven't told them yet, but I'll send you their number as soon as I hang up."

"I'm planning to travel to Lagos after my exams next year to spend Christmas with you all. Papa is okay with it. I have some money saved up. It's going to be another whole year of waiting, but now that we've found each other, I think I'll survive."

"Maybe I can fly over to see you..." I intertwined my fingers with Nico's.

"Are you serious, Sis?" she asked, sounding astonished.

"Yes, I am. I'm currently in La Garenne Colombes." I tightened my grip on Nico's fingers. "I already have a visa. My best friend and I were supposed to spend our holidays in Manchester, but the plans changed. I can come if you want... just to see you in person before you come to Nigeria."

"Sis!" she exclaimed.

I was smiling as I hung up. Nico and I untangled our fingers and hugged immediately as if we had both planned it. I could feel his heart beating as fast as mine, both thumping in a harmonious rhythm in an intimate conversation. At that moment, between us, we didn't need vowels or consonants. The warmth of the side of his face against mine sent a sublime, soothing and sweet feeling that coursed through me.

Time seemed to stand still as the feeling took over me, sweeping me completely away. Amidst shared warmth and mixed breath, his lips found mine. I closed my eyes and kissed him back, eager as though I had been waiting forever for this. It felt like paradise—his taste, his smell, his tongue sliding ever so slowly in and out. When we finally broke apart, I hugged him again, holding onto his neck to hide my eyes from his. I was afraid of what he would see if I allowed him to look into them just then.

"What's wrong?" he asked. His voice was soft and warm.

"I need to book a flight," I whispered, still breathless.

***

"Lami, I need to talk to you about something serious," Nico said after we had booked our tickets.

"What is it?" I said, meeting his gaze softly.

"You've had a difficult childhood. When I think about all the things you've told me that you went through, I'm not sure that I would have survived them if they happened to me. I don't know anyone who has lived through so many harrowing experiences," he paused. I raised my brows wondering what he was driving at. He continued, "I know out there in the world there must be many others who have, but I don't know anyone with such baggage of pain and traumas."

He reached for my hands. I looked down at our hands and up at him again.

"I had a beautiful childhood, a happy one," he continued. "I have always had my parents and I met all my grandparents. They showed me so much love. The only traumatising loss I've experienced was the death of my aunt." He squeezed my hands and then added, "I think you should see a therapist who can help you get over all these."

"A therapist?" I asked, fixing him a stare. "What for?"

"To help you overcome the traumatic experiences… you know… to get rid of all the hurt, pain and grief."

"What are you talking about?" I asked, confused. I pulled out my hands from his. "Are you talking about seeing a psychiatrist?"

"No, a psychologist."

"Psychologists and psychiatrists are siblings. One is for serious mental issues and the other is for milder mental problems. Why would I need one? Do I come off as weak or mentally disturbed to you?"

"No. I didn't say that and I didn't mean it that way. You're not a weak person; on the contrary, you're one of the strongest people I've ever met. You're also refreshingly lucid, but since I've known you, I've sensed that you're battling remnants of some crippling pain. The only time you talked about your little sister without giving off some pain was when you discovered her Facebook account."

He reached for my hands again.

"For the first time, you told me about her without revealing regrets and anxiety," he continued.

My jaw dropped. I couldn't believe he had been psychoanalysing me all this while.

"Also, when you talk about your father, there is unforgiveness laced up in your voice."

Dumbfounded, I just sat there and stared at him as he continued talking.

"You and your siblings have done all you could to avoid seeing each other over these years. You're all hurting and trying to avoid the past. It's like not accepting the past... not letting go, not wanting to face it, and then leaving it to spill into the present, dragging it with you into the future. It's time to let go completely."

I pulled my hands away from his again.

But he continued, "Cutting away from each other won't make the pain go away. Running away from the past will not set you free either. You have to stay, stand and face it. You have to accept your mother's death. When you talk about her, it's like you're still mourning her like it happened yesterday."

"No, no, no," I said slowly, in a small voice that became inflamed with anger with every word I spoke afterwards. "Don't even go there. What right do you have to tell me when to stop mourning? I'll mourn as long as I want, and all my life if it takes that long to heal. What do you even really know about me to decide if it's time to heal or not? Do you think you know enough about me to judge me and tell me what to do? You've thought all these things about me and you've never told me. Do you think it's that easy to heal? Do you think I didn't try to move on? Do you know how many times I tried and failed? I've made peace with her death and accepted the pain. This deep feeling of loss will never leave me. It will remain at the bottom of my heart forever. It bleeds every blessed day. I have no control over it, so don't tell me about the end of mourning, and the last thing I want is someone psychoanalysing me."

I stood up after my violent outburst and stormed off, refusing to cry in front of him.

***

A sob broke from my chest as soon as I shut the bedroom door soundlessly behind me. I fell onto the bed to cry my heart out, but my eyes remained dry and unperturbed. Still, Nico's look of horror as I spoke reappeared in my mind to torment me. I must have acted like Papa. I must have displayed his trait. It was why Nico had looked at me the way I used to look at Papa when I watched his anger transform into a rage, right before my eyes, ready to overtake me like a storm. I was my father's daughter. I had in me the thing I hated the most about him. I felt shame envelop me.

Nico was no doubt a nice person. He surely hadn't meant any harm. This was the season of Christmas and we were supposed to be happy. I was seeing Anna the following day, after thirteen long years, and I wanted him to go with me; to be with me. Why had I been so upset? Was it because he was right? Why was I still sad despite having reconnected with Anna? I tried to analyse it, to understand why her reappearance in my life hadn't completely swept away all the dark clouds floating in my sky. My body quivered with convulsive sobs as I lay sprawled in the bed.

It was thirteen years since I last saw Papa, yet I let him have so much control over my life. Every time I thought about him, I replayed traumatic childhood memories and relived the pain that came with remembering. I allowed him to drift in and out of my life through those painful memories. I allowed him to maintain his emotional hold over me.

How long was I going to let him have this level of control over my life? I'd found Tutu, and nothing I could do would bring Mama back. The only way toward a happier future was to completely accept everything my past had been, to let go of everything that I couldn't change. The hurt and pain I'd carried around with me from the past was a burden, a cage that had imprisoned me. I had become a victim of my resentment for Papa. All I had to do was forgive. I shut my eyes and he was there, sitting on his favourite sofa in Lawani Street, watching the TV. His eyes were wide under his thick eyeglasses. His beards were full and neatly trimmed. He threw his head back and laughed, *kikikikiki*.

"I forgive you, Papa. I've found Tutu. I'm at peace now, so you've earned the right to get off scot-free. I release you. You are free. I release you now."

I opened my eyes and my spirit felt lighter. Perhaps, Nico was right and I indeed needed to see a therapist. Perhaps when I returned to Lagos, I'd try therapy to see what it felt like. Just maybe.

I lay there thinking of how to go and apologise to Nico. My words had been hurtful and he didn't deserve them. What would he make of me, of my lunatic display? Several minutes had passed since I left him in the living room, perhaps an hour, I couldn't tell. I rubbed my thumb and index finger over the gold locket he had given me. Suddenly, there was a gentle knock on the bedroom door.

"Lami, are you asleep?" Nico asked.

"No, I'm awake. Please come in." I sat up in bed.

He appeared in the doorway, wearing an apologetic look when I was the one who should apologise.

"I'm sorry,' I said, meeting his eyes. "I regret speaking to you in that manner."

"I'm sorry too." He came to stand beside the bed, his hands buried in the pocket of his jogging pants.

"You have nothing to apologise for. You're right about everything you said."

"I wasn't trying to psychoanalyse you. I just wanted you to see things from another perspective. I was wrong to have brought this up tonight. It was very bad timing."

"It's ok. I'm reuniting with Anna tomorrow… that's all that matters."
"I would like to take you somewhere."
"Now?"
He nodded.
"What time is it?"
"Half past nine. We'll be back in an hour. Dress warmly."
After he left the room, I sat there for a few seconds smiling at myself. Then finally, I got out of bed and pulled on some clothes.

***

When we arrived at Châtelet Les Halles, cold air rushed past us into the station as we walked up the stairs and out into the streets. We headed towards Quai Francois Mitterrand, climbing the few flights of stairs of a wide footbridge made of wooden planks to get to the other side. Luminous lamps lit up the entire length of the bridge, and a beautiful enchanting edifice with an elegant cupola stood at the end.

"Where is this?" I asked, completely enthralled by the magnificent view.

"It's called Pont des Arts. It's very popular for its love locks,' he said, touching the metal grate of the bridge railings which was covered with hundreds and hundreds of colourful padlocks. 'All these locks you see have been put on the bridge by lovers from all over the world."

"Of all the places I've visited in Paris, this is the most enchanting. It's breathtakingly beautiful."

A Black man in a red jacket on the right side of the bridge displayed coloured padlocks on a piece of cloth. I opened my handbag and took out my camera to take a few pictures of the amazing sights. Nico seemed lost in his thoughts as he stood looking down at the Seine. How he looked that night in a radiant glow under one of the lamps will forever remain engraved in my mind: his hood slipping off his head, his hands in the pockets of his jacket and his backpack hugging him from behind. It was as though we were destined to meet on the bridge and he was standing there in the cold waiting for me.

I went and stood beside him, slipped my hand in the crook of his elbow and rested my head against his shoulder. For a long time, we watched in silence long sleek boats that glided majestically on the river below.

"I want you to have dinner with me on one of these boats when we return from Brittany," Nico said. "I'll go ahead and make a reservation online tonight. The last time I was on one of them, I was about six. My parents and I had come to Paris for vacation. That was when I knew that I would live in Paris someday."

"Paris is a beautiful place to live in. It must be glorious to be here on a summer evening. I find Paris more charming at night than in the daytime. One can go out every night and just explore the city. It's bright everywhere."

"I can't tell which I prefer. I like every second of the day here."

"Now I understand why you would rather spend your Christmas here despite the cold rather than in Lagos with its lovely weather."

"I love Lagos too. It's unique. There can't be any other place like Lagos. The two cities are incomparable. Lagos is an infant compared to ancient Paris."

"Can we sit for a while and just admire the view and the people walking past?"

"Aren't you cold anymore?" he teased as we walked over to the closest bench.

"Cold? Are you kidding me? How can one be cold with such a glorious view?"

We sat side by side, our arms entwined. Another young couple who sat on the next bench was making out.

"I wish we could stay here forever." I rested my head on his shoulder.

"And so do I." He kissed my forehead.

We sat quietly watching the few people that passed by or stood to look over the bridge. A woman who wore a doundoune like mine walked by slowly with an elderly woman. They looked like daughter and mother and spoke in low tones. They must have walked over the bridge several times as they didn't seem enchanted by its magic or beauty.

"Where's that?" I asked, pointing to a nearby building with a dome.

"It's the *Institut de France*. If we still have time when we return from Paris we can visit its châteaux and museums."

"It looks like something from a fairy tale, like a palace where a beautiful prince and princess are living with their children happily."

He offered to take a picture of me with the institute as the background. I handed him the camera and rose.

"You'll have to pay me if I appear in your picture," the man selling padlocks said to us.

We laughed and sat down again as I looked through the pictures. Nico put his hands around me and then we just sat there. I wasn't thinking about getting away from the cold.

"It's so romantic," I said. "There's something about this bridge, these lights and this view. Now I understand why people say *See Paris and die*."

Nico looked at me and asked, "You can feel it too?"

I nodded, looking into his eyes and holding his gaze, "You make me so happy. I am happy being here with you. My heart is filled with so much love I think it will explode."

"This is how you make me feel. Every time you are around me, I am seized with so much love. I have loved you from that first night I set my eyes on you and I'll love you until I die."

"Why didn't you tell me?"

"You said you weren't ready for a relationship."

"I know... but you could have tried again."

"I thought you were right. I thought we should get to know each other better and be good friends first and then afterwards, I could tell you how I feel about you. Since you arrived in Paris, I've been thinking about telling you how I feel... I've been waiting for the right moment to tell you."

Smiling, I pulled him closer, pushed his hood back, and kissed him. "I have wanted to do this since the last time."

"Me too," he said before kissing me again.

I liked the taste of his lips and how his cold fingers felt across my cheeks. When we broke off I said, "You know with me, you don't have to hold anything back. I want you always to tell me what's on your mind."

"I promise. I will always tell you."

"What's on your mind now?"

"I was wondering if you would want to be mine forever."

I smiled and nodded. I still wouldn't break his gaze. I wasn't ashamed of what I was exposing. I wasn't afraid that he would see all the love that was overflowing from my heart.

"What's on your mind?" he asked.

"I want to tell you that I want you to kiss me, again and again, and every day for the rest of my life."

"I love you too with my whole heart and with everything in me. When I say I love you, I mean I would love you every day for the rest of my life. I wish I could show you exactly how much. I'll do anything to make sure you never cry again. And if you must cry, I'll cry with you. When you mourn, I'll mourn with you, and when you rejoice, be sure that I will rejoice with you."

I bit down on my lower lip as I held back a cry. His words, although soft, squeezed my heart so tight. We hugged each other and didn't let go.

"I love you too Nico," I said into his ear.

He pulled back from me so that he could look into my eyes, then he went down on one knee on the Pont des Arts and said, "Lami, tu veux être ma copine?"

I looked around, shy that people might be watching us. The couple on the bench further away had their eyes on us. They were smiling and hopeful, sort of transfixed. They watched as if Nico and I were master actors on a stage.

An elderly woman in a brown fur-like coat and cap stopped in front of us. She held a tiny dog in her hands. The man selling padlocks also came close. It seemed as if Nico and all the people around were waiting for my answer, as though he had asked me to marry him.

"Yes, yes, yes Nico I'll be your girlfriend."

More passers-by had stopped to watch. I knelt beside Nico and kissed him. Everyone around us began clapping, as though we had completed the last scene in a romantic movie. It was impossible to count the people as their shadows on the bridge seemed to fall on one another. I hugged Nico tightly and buried my face in the warmth of his neck. I knew that I wouldn't have any reason ever to compare him to my ex, nor ever regret my choice. They were extremely different, and with either of them, the feelings were worlds apart. Before my heart was broken back in university, I had led myself to believe that my ex was the one for me. And here I was, with a heart filled with so much love for someone else. With Nico, my mind could see a bright future for both of us, he and me together. When I was with my ex, I hardly thought about our future together, for thick fears clouded my mind. There was always the fear of losing him, of losing love, and of losing happiness.

"Why don't you buy a padlock to seal your love?" the man selling padlocks said to Nico when we got up and the people who had stopped to watch began to disperse.

"I don't need a padlock to prove to you that I'll stay with you forever," Nico said to me and I nodded approvingly. "I'll never leave your side except if you don't want me there."

"I would never want you to leave," I said and then kissed him again.

"Best wishes," a woman who wore a red-hooded cape coat said to me as she walked away.

"Bonne chance, ma soeur," the padlock seller shouted behind us. I turned and waved at him.

TWENTY-FIVE

Present day

A strange quietness saturated the flat. The silence was eerie. I walked down the long corridor in a long white spaghetti-strap cotton dress. The terrazzo flooring was warm against my bare feet. Nothing had changed since my last night in the flat. A gust of wind arrived from the front balcony, forcing me to shut my eyes. It brushed past me, blowing the skirt of my dress between my legs before escaping through the second balcony door. I shivered just as a door flung open. I heard the sound of glass bottles falling over themselves. I looked around me. There was no one in sight and it seemed like I was alone in the flat. I continued walking towards the living room. Papa's favourite chair by the TV was bare of his presence. The ornate gold Florentine-style wood frame with the picture of the Virgin Mary carrying baby Jesus in her hands was still hanging on the wall at the end of the room.

Standing in front of Papa's bedroom door, a sudden rush of fear overwhelmed me. I reminded myself I was now an adult and that he could no longer send me to purgatory. Still, my body shook uncontrollably. I covered my face with my hands. My ears were suddenly filled with the sound of my own sobbing, but it wasn't coming from my mouth. I paused and uncovered my face. I listened and realised the sound was coming from behind Papa's bedroom door. I reached out and turned the handle. The door parted open, and the sobbing grew louder. I peered into the darkness. A sudden panic engulfed me. I wanted to shut the door and flee, but the volume of the sobbing continued to grow like the rising intro of an orchestra. Turning all the strength I could gather into courage; I pushed the door wide open to allow as much natural light as possible. Then I stepped inside and away from the shaft of light, as I continued to probe the darkness.

"Don't cry, I'm coming, don't cry," I said as I ventured inside.

With my hands stretched out before me and my eyes wide open but unseeing, I took one step after the other. I was terrified, but I didn't turn and run. I arrived on the verge of hysteria but contained it for the child who needed my help. I remained strong and forged on until my eyes adjusted in the dark. When I reached the wardrobe, I pulled the door open and saw her form, sitting on the small stool in one corner.

"Hey," I said and stooped.

I reached out and lifted her chin. In the gloomy darkness, we contemplated each other. An unsettling familiarity stared back at me. I slid my hand down her arm until I was holding her hand. I could hear her unspoken pleas as her grip tightened in my grasp. It was as though we'd known each other for a long time, as though we'd walked through the same valley of trauma. I unclasped our grip and slid my arms around her small frame, hugging her tightly.

"I'm sorry I'm late. I know how courageous and patient you've been. I'm proud of you. I love you." I whispered into her ear. Then I rose, took her by the hand and led her into the brightly-lit living room. "We're free now. He can't hurt us anymore."

***

A beam of light from the security lamps outside poured into the room through the holes in the window shutter. I lay awake, listening to Nico's soft breathing as he slept peacefully beside me. Images of my dream danced before my eyes. The girl was finally free. I took a deep breath and felt at peace, liberated. I realised how it was the first year since Mama died that I hadn't been bombarded with nightmares during the end-of-the-year holiday. Gone were the dreams about Papa ringing his bell and stopping on the third peal, of him taking steps down the long corridor with a bamboo cane, or of him and Mama Jide pulling Tutu away from me while I held on as tightly as I could.

I'd been awake for over half an hour when my alarm finally went off at 4:30 am. Nico stirred in his sleep but didn't wake up. I'd asked him to share the bed with me after we returned home the night before. I crawled out of bed, rushed a bath, and left the bathroom so Nico could use it. I felt excited about seeing Anna as I moved around the apartment getting ready for our trip.

At exactly 5:00 am, we were riding the elevator down. The taxi we'd booked was already waiting, parked right in front of the gate. The driver, a man in his early thirties, chatted with Nico all the way to the airport. To find some quiet time to prepare for the reunion ahead, I created silence in my head and retreated within.

We arrived at the airport two hours before departure. Since we didn't have any luggage to check in, we headed straight for the security checkpoint and joined separate queues to be checked through customs. With his EU passport, Nico's passage was seamless, but he waited for me until I was cleared. At precisely 7:00 am, our plane lifted off for Heathrow. I sat by the window while Nico sat in the middle seat, with the seat near the aisle unoccupied. After the seat belts and no smoking lights went out, I leaned back in my chair and closed my eyes. Nico's hand brushed lightly against mine on the armrests. I opened my eyes and found myself face-to-face with him; he'd been watching me. Our gaze held for a moment before we both broke into a smile.

"Thank you for finding the time to come with me today," I said.

"You know I'll always create time for you."

I nodded.

"I love you, Lami. I'll always love you."

I felt my heart swell up with so much love, it felt as though it would explode in my chest. I threw my arms around him and held him tight.

"I love you too, Nico."

After we settled back in our seats, we continued to hold hands. At that moment, I was undoubtedly one of the happiest people alive. I sighed. Throughout the entire journey, I imagined uncountable scenarios of how the day's events would unfold.

As London was an hour behind, it was as though we'd arrived fifteen minutes after we left Paris. Through the queue for passport control, I had many thoughts swirling around in my head, keeping my nerves on edge. For each loud thump of my heart, a new question was born in my mind. "What if she doesn't come? What if she can't make it? What if she changes her mind?"

Although our pace was quick, the journey out of the terminal seemed to take forever. Outside the arrivals section, we joined the long queue for black taxis. It felt as though a year had passed before it got our turn. In the back of the taxi, Nico reached for my hand and squeezed it. I had been looking out of the window. The sights were beautiful, but I couldn't enjoy them as I was busy assuring myself that I was truly in a cab in London, heading towards Piccadilly. Too nervous for thoughts, I was in no mood to compare and contrast London and Paris.

"Starbucks is over there on your right," the driver said, pointing after he stopped at Green Park Station in between strings of big red buses.

It had taken us more time to get there from the moment we stepped out of the plane than it took to fly from Paris to London. After Nico paid the driver, we stepped out of the taxi into a drizzle and walked towards the coffee shop. That grey morning, Piccadilly smelt of gas fumes and damp pavements. The cold wind blew against my face and every intake of breath hurt my nostrils. My hands were also freezing, but I didn't want to wear my gloves. I liked the assurance Nico passed on to me each time he squeezed my hand as I held on tightly to his grip. We had said little to each other since we stepped out of the plane, but had held hands more than we'd ever done since we met. When he pushed open the door of Starbucks, my heart stopped beating for long seconds even though I knew my long-lost baby sister wasn't there yet. She'd said she wouldn't arrive before 11:00 am.

As we walked into the welcoming warmth of the shop, my eyes darted around quickly, over every face that I could see, hoping she'd arrived early to surprise me. I was glad when we got a table by the window. The former occupants, two young identical-looking women, got up to leave just as we arrived. Although I wasn't hungry, the aroma of brewing coffee made my tummy growl. While Nico went and stood in the long line to get our order, I watched passers-by in the street, waiting to see Anna appear. I tried to stay calm, but my anxiety had triggered a consuming restlessness within me.

Nico returned with coffee for himself, and a big cup of hot chocolate for me. No vacant table stayed empty for a long time. People came and left, and empty tables were immediately occupied again. We sipped our drinks quietly as we both looked out of the window. From around 10:30 am, the clock adopted a snail's pace and every minute seemed like eternity. The traffic on the four-lane street at this time was almost stationary. Each time a red double-decker bus passed by, my heart stopped beating in expectation of Anna's appearance. I wondered what to do first when I saw her. I wondered if I should shake her hand or hug her. I wondered if I should hug her briefly, or if I could hold her long enough to know her new smell. How long would be alright? How long would be weird?

"Everything will be alright," Nico said, slipping his hand into mine.

I nodded and smiled at him, grateful for his presence.

"Your hands are icy cold," he said and then he began to rub my hands between his to warm me up.

Just then I saw her through the window, walking towards the coffee shop.

"She's here," I said to Nico in a trembling voice.

He turned around to follow the direction of my eyes. She pushed the door and stepped into the coffee shop. My heart was beating so fast, I thought it would shatter my ribs. I got up and waved at her. She was wearing a black winter coat and black boots. Her green sweater was the same colour as her gloves. Her smile was the same as Mama's. Everything about her reminded me of our dead mother. I couldn't believe that I was seeing little Tutu, now Anna who always said to me, *kawee me*, and always cried when I put her down afterwards. She looked slimmer, darker and shorter than she did in her pictures. She was so beautiful.

As soon as she came up to us, I stepped forward and threw my hands around her in a tight hug. At that moment, I felt the missing part of me return; the one that had taken flight with her when she was taken away all those years back. It returned and clicked into place as we melted the lost years back into each other in our emotion-laden embrace.

For minutes, we didn't untangle, and we didn't say a word. All the words I'd planned to say were no longer useful. My heart felt brand new. It was as though I had never been broken.

*** THE END ***

Acknowledgements

Thanks to God
Thanks to me.
Thanks to my husband, Alain Deforge.
Thanks to everyone who believed in me:
My siblings: Modupe, Seun, and Femi
My Spiritual Father and mentor, Rev. Pastor Fred
My editor, Deborah Oluniran Adeniyi
My cover designer, Joshua Effiong
Angel Patricks Amegbe and Chinwe Mercier
Ibrahim Babatunde Ibrahim and Aminat Adesanya
Maryann Ifeanacho and Chukwuemeka Famous
John Kelly, Daniel Fowowe, Bisi Ojora, and Oyindamola Ijewere
Martial Rougier, Michael Newman, Jessica Craig, and Carla Mercier
Thanks to POA and the Ignite Prayer Family.

Thanks to Chimamanda Ngozi Adichie, Binyavanga Wainaina, and my workshop classmates.

Thanks to all the writers and book reviewers who supported and gave me a helping hand.

About the Author

Ayo Deforge is a Nigerian writer who resides in the South of France.

An alumna of Chimamanda Adichie's inaugural creative writing workshop *(2007)* and the Faber Academy's writing course *(2022)*.

She has worked as a freelance poet for the Nigerian Daily Independent Newspaper and NGEX.com.

Her writing has appeared in Litro Magazine, Brittle Paper, Ayo Magazine, Kalahari Review, and Lucy Writers Platform *(an online writing forum established by Lucy Cavendish College, University of Cambridge)*.

She served as a reader for the inaugural Oxbelly Writers Retreat and teaches Read Like A Writer classes.

TEARLESS is her debut novel.

For more information and for a schedule of events, visit **www.ayodeforge.com**

To contact Ayo Deforge by email: **ayo.deforge@hotmail.fr**

To follow her on Facebook, Twitter and Instagram: **@ayodeforge**

Printed in Great Britain
by Amazon